D0380904

Love Finds You

in

Treasure

ISLAND

Florida

Love Finds You in Treasure ISLAND Florida

BY DEBBY MAYNE

summerside
PRESS

Love Finds You in Treasure Island, Florida
© 2009 by Debby Mayne

ISBN 978-1-934770-80-1

All rights reserved. No part of this publication may be
reproduced in any form, except for brief quotations in printed
reviews, without written permission of the publisher.

Scripture taken from the New King James Version®.
Copyright © 1982 by Thomas Nelson, Inc. Used by permission.
All rights reserved.

The town depicted in this book is a real place, but all characters
are fictional. Any resemblances to actual people or events are
purely coincidental.

Cover and Interior Design by Müllerhaus Publishing Group
www.mullerhaus.net

Published by Summerside Press, Inc., 11024 Quebec Circle,
Bloomington, Minnesota 55438 | **www.summersidepress.com**

Fall in love with Summerside.

Printed in the USA.

Acknowledgments
....

Thanks to Jeff Jensen with the city of Treasure Island, Florida,
for all the great information about this tropical paradise.

Thanks to Phyllis Kelly for her mouthwatering description
of the delectable menu offerings at Captain Kosmakos.

Dedication

....

This book is dedicated to my daughters Alison and Lauren,
my agent Tamela, and my friends Sandie, Paige, and Beth—
all women I respect, admire, and appreciate.

LOCATED ON THE GULF OF MEXICO, Treasure
Island is a delightful blend of old and new Florida. The
quaint beach town, originally called Coney Island, received
its current name from developers in the early 1900s who
"discovered" wooden chests that they claimed were filled
with treasure. The enticement brought an onslaught of
visitors, and the name stuck. This barrier island is a year-
round home to approximately 7,000 people and a vacation
spot for international and domestic travelers seeking sand,
sun, and a wonderful laid-back ambiance. During the
day, fun-seekers can choose between golf, fishing, biking
boating, parasailing, and other water sports. Then it's time
to amble down to the water's edge to watch the spectacular,
multi-hued sunsets of Florida's west coast.

Chapter One
....

"Why are all the best men taken?"

"Huh?" Amanda Burns glanced up at her mother, who stood on the other side of the counter in her bicycle shop.

The former hippie chick shrugged and tossed her long, gray-sprinkled auburn hair over her shoulder. "I can't find a decent man anymore. They're either married or otherwise involved with someone." She did an about-face and headed for the door. "Oh well, it's no big deal."

"See you tomorrow?" Amanda said.

Her mother stopped just as she reached the door. "I almost forgot—that's what I came in here to tell you. I'm leaving on a cruise in the morning, and I won't be back for a while."

Amanda frowned. "Who're you going with?"

"Some friends. You don't know them." She pushed the door all the way open and brushed past her other daughter, Lacy.

"Have fun on your cruise, Mom," Lacy called out.

"Trust me, I will!"

Amanda narrowed her gaze at her sister. "How did you know Mom was going on a cruise?"

"She told me last night."

Amanda didn't bother asking any more questions. She figured it would be easier to let things unfold naturally rather than press her fragile sister for answers.

Lacy growled as she took their mother's place in front of the counter. "I need your help."

"With what?" Amanda asked, setting down her pen and giving her sister all her attention. "What happened this time?"

"One of the kids in my class is making me seriously reconsider teaching, and I don't know what to do."

"He's in kindergarten. You're his teacher. Can't you make him behave?"

"No!" Lacy's voice screeched. "And he's making my life miserable. Timmy hurts the other kids, and he won't do anything I tell him to."

"What do you want from me?"

Lacy tilted her head and pouted as she whined, "I want you to tell me what to do."

"You really need to get a grip on things," Amanda warned. "What will you do if I'm not here when stuff like this happens?"

"But you're always here."

Amanda swallowed hard. Lacy was right. Every single day except Sunday, she was right here at her store, the Treasure Island Bike and Skate Shop, waiting on customers and watching them live full and meaningful lives, while all she did was remember the past. She reached out and gently placed her hand on Lacy's shoulder. "See if you can figure this one out on your own, sweetie. I'm sure you can come up with a plan to outsmart a little five-year-old boy."

Lacy yanked away and frowned as she glanced down at the shop's appointment book Amanda had left on the counter. Her pout gradually faded, and a smile spread across her lips. "Jerry Simpson? That cute guy I met last year is coming in today? No wonder you're acting all weird. I saw how you looked at him." Lacy fluttered her eyelashes and giggled. "Your eyes sparkled."

Amanda quickly turned away as her face heated up. "I have no idea what you're talking about." She took a deep breath, slowly let it out, then spun around to look Lacy in the eyes, hoping that some of her blush had faded. "Stop changing the subject. I hate when you do that."

"Well, I hate how you always have to boss me around and make me feel like a child. I'm a grown woman." Lacy sniffed and added, "I'll be twenty-six soon."

"You asked—" Amanda stopped herself mid-sentence. This was one argument she'd never win, so what was the point in continuing? "Look, Lacy, I have a ton of stuff to do today. Why don't you have a talk with little Timmy and let him know how important it is for him to behave?"

Lacy shrugged and grabbed a handful of peppermints from the bowl on the counter. "I don't think he'll listen, but I guess I can try." She headed for the door then paused. "You might want to put on some lipstick before Jerry gets here. You're starting to look a little peaked." She glanced over her shoulder, wiggled her eyebrows, then left Amanda standing there speechless.

As soon as the door shut behind Lacy, Amanda shook her head. What did she expect from her twenty-five-year-old sister, who made her decision to teach kindergarten after watching a sappy movie featuring a classroom full of precocious children and a ripped bodybuilder pretending to be a teacher? There were times when the fourteen-year difference between the girls really showed.

* * * * *

"Are we there yet?"

"Oh, hush, Harold. You know good and well we're more than an hour away. Why don't you close your eyes and take a nap? When you wake up, we'll be there."

Jerry allowed himself a quick glance over at his mother in the passenger seat and snickered. "I remember you telling us kids that all the time."

"Yeah, and some things never change." She turned to face her husband of fifty years. "I brought a snack if you're hungry."

"Don't want a snack, Rosemary. I'm just sick of riding in the car."

Jerry listened to his parents bicker while he took the turn toward the bridge leading them to Treasure Island. The first time he'd visited the area was during one of their family vacations about twenty-five years ago. He'd fallen in love with it and vowed to return every chance he had.

The closer they got to the bridge, the more casual everything around them looked—from the touristy beach souvenir shops to the endless number of come-as-you-are seafood restaurants. The familiarity of the setting brought a peacefulness that washed over him and bathed him in the feeling that all was right in his world.

Without closing his eyes, Jerry thanked the Lord for this special time with his parents, who'd sacrificed so he, his sister, and his brother could have everything they needed and much of what they wanted. He had to fight back the niggling of frustration over how his siblings had turned their backs after they'd grown up, when the relationship had changed and their parents began to need someone to look after them. So be it if the Lord had chosen to give Jerry the full responsibility. He could handle it.

"Son, why are you gripping the steering wheel so tightly? Are you upset about something?"

The gentle concern in his mother's soothing voice caused his chest to constrict. He intentionally released some of the pressure on the wheel. "No, I was just concentrating on the drive." He paused then added, "I wish y'all wouldn't argue so much."

"You worry entirely too much about your father and me. We'll be just fine."

Jerry bit the insides of his cheeks to keep from reminding her of her recent Parkinson's diagnosis and the fact that she was already having a hard time with his father, whose Alzheimer's kept her constantly on her toes. He had had no choice but to step up and care for them like they'd always done for him.

"Better stop daydreaming, boy," his dad bellowed from the backseat. "You just missed your turn. I don't want to get there too late to go treasure hunting."

His mother clicked her tongue. "How many times do I have to tell you that there's no treasure?"

"Then why did they name the place Treasure Island?"

Jerry almost found comfort in the same old argument he'd heard for years. His father was convinced that somewhere on Treasure Island there was a hidden treasure. All he had to do was find it and he'd be happy for the rest of his life.

They'd only gone two streets past the turnoff, so it didn't take Jerry long to correct his mistake. As he pulled off the main road and found his way back, weaving through the side streets, he took in the scenery that accosted his senses. He'd almost forgotten how close the sky seemed in Florida and how the swaying palm trees brushed all his cares away. The slight breeze with the lush, beachy flora brought him back to a much happier time—a time when he had nothing to worry about and he thought the future was his for the taking. Atlanta was a big city, so he never had to leave to find good jobs that eventually led to his own business. However, that was where his rainbow ended.

Jerry had imagined himself happily married with at least one child and an enviable career by this point in his life. Yet he was already forty-five, and he'd only gotten one of those right—the career. His import-export business was thriving, and he had the freedom most people would give anything for. As long as he had his laptop, he could be anywhere and still make a great income.

"What are you thinking about, son?" his mother asked.

He shrugged as he mentally brought himself to the present. "Just how happy I am to be here with you and Dad."

"If you can find anyone to believe that, I've got some swampland for sale."

He wasn't in the mood for explanations, so he changed the subject. "After we get you and Dad settled in the condo, I'll run over to the bike shop and pick up the tandem bicycle. Y'all had so much fun with that thing last year and the year before."

She nodded as she gazed out the window. "Yes, I enjoyed it, but not nearly as much as hearing you talk about that sweet young woman. What's her name again?" She glanced at Jerry then shook her head. "I just remember how you and the shop owner got along so well."

Jerry instantly tensed. His mother had been working on him to find someone, and he didn't want to go there.

"You're not getting any younger, sweetheart," she said softly. "I know you're worried about your father and me, but if you find a nice young lady who loves you as much as I love your father, that'll make us very happy."

* * * * *

Amanda had soft jazz playing on her stereo while she punched numbers into her spreadsheet. This time of year was quiet, and she enjoyed a chance to catch up from the busy tourist season. With the exception of visits from her sister, a few locals, and an occasional tourist, she pretty much had the place to herself all day—at least for the next couple of weeks.

When the bells on the door jingled, she glanced up, expecting to see someone she knew. And she did. A tall, slender-waisted, broad-shouldered, salt-and-pepper-haired man with an impish smile. What was Jerry doing here so early?

He hesitated by the door as he grinned. Lacy's last comment about the lipstick gave her pause, and she had to force herself not to lick her lips.

"Hey." She wondered if he noticed her squeaky voice.

"Hi there." Jerry raised his eyebrows and hesitantly moved toward her. "I know I'm early, but I was hoping you'd have the bicycle ready."

She came around from behind the counter and gestured toward the room with the rentals. "Yep. It's ready to go."

Amanda sensed an awkwardness, watching Jerry. Or was it coming from her? Funny how a few words from her sister could do something like this to her. Sure, she'd noticed how good-looking Jerry was, but this was the beach. Plenty of men looked good.

"I'd like to hang onto it for the whole month I'm here. I know I didn't mention that when I called." He glanced around the room as if looking for something then turned back to face her. "That's okay, right? I mean, you don't have a lot of people wanting to rent tandem bikes, do you?"

She smiled. "We do, but not now, so you should be fine. I have another one in the back room."

He handed her his credit card, and she welcomed the chance to scurry behind the counter to put some distance between them. As she minimized her spreadsheet and pulled up the retail program, he took hold of the handlebars and moved the bicycle toward the door.

The transaction took all of a minute and a half, and then he was gone. She felt as though her breath had been knocked out of her as she watched him hoist the bike onto the rack on the back of his SUV. Good thing she was alone. It gave her a chance to process what had just happened—and to wonder again why this guy kept renting a bicycle built for two. She'd asked him once if it was for him and his wife, and he said no but didn't offer anything else. She had more questions, but she didn't want to pry. Oh well, it didn't really matter. He was just another customer as far as she was concerned—a tourist at that. Besides, she didn't have much success with men, so she was better off keeping to herself.

Ever since Eric had left her at the altar, she'd managed to maintain her vow to stay single. No way would she allow her life to be consumed with a fairy-tale romance when it would inevitably end in heartache. She now knew that even if they had gotten married, the road would have been rocky.

Some people were meant to be married. Part of a duo. Paired in a happily-ever-after sort of way. But not Amanda. She'd watched her mother's revolving door with men coming and going at warp speed. None of them had lasted long enough for Amanda to call them "Dad." Her mother was downright dramatic about it, too.

Lacy's birth a couple of months after the last man left should have been a happy time for the Burns family, but it wasn't. Diane Burns had wigged out. Treasure Island, Florida, was a small town, so word traveled quickly that the Burns girls needed help. The folks from the church down the street sent people over with food and money that kept the family fed and in the tiny weathered cottage. Amanda couldn't wait to get out of there when she turned eighteen. After a semester in college that she couldn't afford, she shared a tiny apartment a few blocks from the beach with a couple of other girls, worked hard, and saved the money she earned from tips as a waitress until she had enough to open a bicycle rental stand by a popular hotel. Business was so successful, she eventually managed to rent a shop in a great location.

When Amanda turned thirty and met Eric, he seemed like a great guy—and a way to lead a normal life. However, the closer the wedding got, the more antsy Eric became. Amanda assumed it was pre-wedding jitters; she was no quitter.

If the wedding had gone through, Amanda now realized that she would have had a very difficult time giving up control and letting Eric make decisions; she'd been acting as head of the house since she was tall enough to see the top of the stove. No doubt she and Eric would have been at each other's throats constantly and their lives would be a miserable mess.

Yessirree, she was glad it hadn't happened. The way things turned out, now at the age of thirty-nine, she was free to enjoy life as she saw fit. She didn't want to cater to any man only to be dumped when he got sick of her. Like her mother.

A couple of customers came and went. Amanda wanted to finish organizing her spreadsheet before school let out. Lacy always liked to stop by on her way home and give her a play-by-play of her busy day with five-year-olds.

Even with her back turned to the front door, Amanda knew the second Lacy arrived. "Did Jerry come yet?"

"Um, yes, not too long after I opened."

"Well?" Lacy helped herself to a mint then pulled herself up onto a barstool at the counter. "How'd it go?"

"He just rented the standard tandem."

Lacy narrowed her eyes and tilted her head. "What did he say?"

"Just that he was here early and he hoped the bicycle was ready."

"That's all he said?" Lacy snickered. "You're holdin' back."

Amanda tightened her jaw and shook her head. "That's all I can remember. So tell me, how was Timmy today?"

Lacy growled and then went on a five-minute tirade about how the little boy wouldn't do a thing he was supposed to. "I just don't get it. All the other kids come back from time-out like little angels."

"I wonder why Timmy doesn't."

"I don't know what's wrong with that child. He misbehaves, I send him to time-out, and he's supposed to learn his lesson. Sometimes I think he likes to be punished."

"Exactly what did he do today that was so bad?" Amanda really didn't want to discuss Timmy—or anything else at Lacy's school, for that matter—but she was willing to do whatever it took to avoid talking about Jerry.

"For starters, he won't listen when I'm talking."

"I know I'm not a child expert, but isn't that normal for five-year-olds?"

Lacy shrugged. "Maybe, but I can usually get their attention with Jocko or one of the VeggieTales songs."

"So the monkey and vegetables didn't do it for him, huh?"

Lacy shook her head and clicked her tongue. "All he cared about was what Taylor had in her lunch box."

Amanda snickered. "Must've been yummy."

"That's beside the point. I simply can't have him disrupting the whole class like that all the time. The other kids won't be able to learn what they need to for first grade."

This time Amanda had to cough to keep from laughing out loud. Since when had kindergarten become prep school? "You're kidding, right?"

"Stop making fun of me. It's serious." She glared at Amanda, her chin jutting in annoyance.

Okay, so maybe it wasn't funny. Amanda tried hard to put herself in her sister's place and think of what she'd do if she had to deal with an unruly kid all day.

"You really should talk to his parents and see if they can help," Amanda finally said.

"I hate talking to the parents," Lacy said as she hopped off the chair. "They always seem to think I'm not a good teacher if I can't control their little brats. Besides, Timmy doesn't live with both of his parents, just his dad." She paused. "I guess you're right. I'll have to talk to him."

"Why don't you see if Mr. Oliver will do it for you?" Amanda suggested.

"Come on, Amanda. I can't run to the principal with this kind of thing. I'll deal with it."

Amanda had heard this kind of drama in Lacy a thousand times.

"Sometimes I just get tired of having to do everything myself," Lacy finished.

"Why don't we discuss this later?" Amanda paused for a couple of seconds before adding, "Maybe we can come up with a solution."

After Lacy left, Amanda felt a strong maternal tug. She'd encouraged her sister to go to college so she could have a career as well as more time to grow up before facing the real world she'd been so sheltered from. Since Lacy hadn't known what to major in and she'd enjoyed being a Sunday school teacher assistant, Amanda had suggested elementary education. By this time, their mother had been in and out of psych hospitals so much, she wasn't much help.

Diane Burns loved her daughters. There was never any doubt about that. She was just ill-equipped to deal with her own life let alone her daughters, who'd had to raise themselves. She seemed to be an emotional vacuum, without anger, pain, or love. The alcohol and antidepressant drugs kept her numb to normal life. And she'd always been like that.

Although Amanda didn't understand her mother's condition at the time, by the time Lacy came along, she'd figured out that it was her job to protect Lacy and teach her the important stuff. What she knew, she passed on to her little sister. What she didn't know, she faked. That was one reason she had crazy expectations when it came to finding someone to love. Lacy had never liked Eric, so when he proposed, Lacy had argued. Amanda should have listened to her sister's gut-felt advice.

"Eric isn't very nice to you," Lacy had told her as they shopped for Amanda's wedding gown.

"He's nice enough."

Lacy had grimaced and shaken her head. "That's not what you need, Amanda. You need—"

"Stop." Amanda held up her hand to shush her sister. "I know what I need. Eric loves me. He's just not good at showing his feelings."

Lacy did her sighing thing and rolled her eyes. "Okay, okay, but don't say I didn't warn you." She turned back to the dress rack. "So why don't you like the ones with beads and lace?"

Amanda picked out a very simple but elegant gown—or so she thought—and brought it to show the bridal party. Lacy said it was boring, and a couple of the other bridesmaids—girls she knew from church—agreed with her.

"I'm just not into froufrou," she explained. "That's more Lacy's style."

No one argued. They just exchanged knowing glances and, on the big day, took their places in the small room at the back of the church to wait for the music to begin. The music that never played. A half hour after the wedding was supposed to start, Eric's mother came back to the bridal dressing room in tears. "Amanda, honey, I'm so sorry. I'm afraid Eric isn't coming."

Her heart pounding, Amanda glanced up at the clock then turned back to her fiancé's mother. "I'm sure he'll be here. He's probably just detained."

"No," the woman said, before swallowing hard. "I just checked my messages on my cell, and he definitely won't be here. He went to Alabama, and he's not coming back."

That was nine years ago, and Amanda had kept her promise to herself to never allow another man into her life. Lacy had been right about Eric.

Everyone was amazed at how well she'd held up. "I don't think I could show my face if someone did that to me," Judy, the church organist, said. "But you're a much stronger woman than I'll ever be."

Stronger? Maybe. But perplexed was probably a better word. She didn't have any idea how men were supposed to behave.

Yeah, avoiding anything to do with romance was definitely the best thing for Amanda. Let other people who were more equipped to deal with it fall in love.

After she finished working on her spreadsheet, she went to the back room where bicycles were lined up in rows, waiting for adjustment, oiling, or some other service. Most of it Amanda could do. The more complicated repairs had to be done by a handyman who came over from Largo whenever he had some free time.

"Anyone here?"

Amanda spun around and quickly moved toward the front of the shop. She hadn't heard the person come in. "Sorry, I was just…" Her voice faltered when she saw Jerry standing in her shop, hands in his pockets, looking at her. She cleared her throat and forced a smile. "What can I help you with?"

He glanced around the room then zoomed in on her helmet display on the wall and pointed. "I need one of those."

"You need another helmet? You've got two, right?"

He hesitated then walked toward the wall and inspected the helmets. "How about that one?"

"That's one of our best, but it's not cheap."

"I don't want cheap," he replied, still not looking directly at her. "I'll take it."

* * * * *

Helmet in hand, Jerry headed down the street toward the condo where his parents were napping, the awkward moment back at the bicycle shop still playing in his head. He wanted to give himself a good swift kick in the backside for not being more prepared.

He didn't need a helmet. He had two, which was all he needed for a tandem bicycle. No, he wanted to see Amanda, with the soft halo of blond hair framing her heart-shaped face and big blue eyes. If he'd seen her on the street, he would have pegged her for something…well, something more glamorous. He was stunned to learn that she was an athlete. Her soft, feminine appearance belied her skill on wheels.

Ever since Jerry first met Amanda a couple of years ago, he'd sensed something off-limits about her. He hated to admit it, even to himself, but that intrigued him. She was nice, but there was always that distance she kept.

As he made his way up the street past small but well-cared-for houses with weathered doors and porches, he felt the sense of tranquillity that he felt only when he came here. The Florida Gulf Coast promised warmth, relaxation, and charm. It was all that and more for Jerry.

He turned toward the condo and quickened his step. Hopefully this would be an uneventful vacation and his parents would get along now that they were here. The trip had been rough so far. His dad knew he had Alzheimer's, and that only frustrated him more. His mother didn't cut him much slack. When Jerry called her on it, she reminded him that he didn't have to live with it day in and day out. Hopefully she'd have some time to herself during this vacation.

His dad was standing at the door, watching him come up the sidewalk, and held the door open. "About time you got back. Where ya been?"

Jerry lifted the helmet as he made his way past his dad. "I figured we needed another one of these."

"Don't know what for. I've been riding a bike all my life, and I've never needed one yet."

"I want you to wear a helmet, Dad." He placed the helmet on the kitchen counter. "Where's Mom?"

His father shrugged. "I can't keep up with that woman these days. When she sets her mind to going somewhere, she just puts on her walking shoes and takes off."

Jerry smiled. "So she went for a walk, huh?"

"I reckon so." He lifted his hands in surrender and hung his head. "I just don't get it."

"This is a better view than we had last year." Jerry pointed toward the back of the condo.

Silence filled the space between them as they wandered toward the great room that overlooked the Gulf of Mexico. The peacefulness of this setting couldn't be duplicated anywhere else.

His dad nodded and blew out a snort. "So, ya think the Falcons are gonna win next season?"

So that was how it was going to be. The best way to avoid anything serious was to turn to sports. Jerry bobbed his head. "They might."

"I wanna see them play the Tampa Bay Buccaneers in the Super Bowl." Jerry grinned. "I don't think that's likely."

"You're probably right." His dad clicked his tongue. "I never much liked what happened to the Super Bowl when they started getting all those stupid commercials and rock 'n' roll halftimes."

"Mom said that's the only reason she watches the Super Bowl," Jerry reminded him.

"Yeah, well, maybe she's better off going shopping instead."

Jerry figured it was best not to respond. His mother was right. The man was obviously spoiling for a fight.

The sound of the front door opening and closing caught both men's attention. Jerry's dad's head shot up. "Rosemary! Is that you?"

"Who else would it be, Harold?" she hollered back.

"Where have you been?"

"I don't have to tell you every single place I go." She blew out a breath of frustration as she dropped her sweater on the back of the sofa and walked over to the large window. "This place is lovely, Jerry. Every time I come, I think about how nice it would be to live here."

"We can't live here," her husband said with a grunt.

She folded her arms, rocked back on her heels, and leveled him with a glare. "And why not?"

"This is where we go on vacation. If we moved here, where would we go when we wanna get away?"

Jerry held his breath until his mother rolled her eyes and tossed him a teasing look. "I guess we could go to Atlanta."

"That doesn't sound like much fun," Harold said, the scowl on his face growing deeper.

"I'm just kidding. If we lived here, we wouldn't have to go anywhere, because we'd always be on vacation."

"Doesn't work that way. Ya gotta go somewhere."

Jerry finally stood and held up his hands to stop the two people he loved most from sniping at each other. "Let's just enjoy the moment, okay? I don't know what's gotten into you two, but this is supposed to be relaxing." He glanced back and forth at them. "And so far, it's been anything but."

His dad opened his mouth, but one piercing glare from Jerry stopped him. Harold clamped his jaw shut and hung his head. Jerry's mother tilted her head and gave him an apologetic smile. "Sorry, son. I guess we've gotten into a bad habit of fussing at each other over silly little things."

Harold frowned. "Who're you calling silly?"

Jerry held up his hands to shush them. "Why don't you two go for a short ride on the bicycle while I figure out what to do for dinner tonight?"

His mother's eyebrows shot up. "You're cooking?"

Jerry grinned back at her and nodded. "Yep. I took a cooking class so we could enjoy some meals here and you wouldn't have to lift a finger."

"I thought we'd go to Grouper's Seafood Grill," Jerry's dad quipped.

Rosemary shoved a fist onto her hip. "Last time we went there you said there was too much racket."

Jerry's dad made a face. "That was last time. I'm in the mood for a little fun tonight." He did a little twist that made Jerry smile.

"Okay, so what'll it be, folks? Eat here or out? I'm cool with whatever you two want to do."

"In," Rosemary said, beating her husband to the draw. "Since you went to all that trouble to learn how to cook, I think it's only right for us to enjoy it." She turned to scowl at her husband.

"Dad?"

His father grumbled a few seconds before finally nodding. "Whatever the two of you want. It's never been my decision anyway. Don't know why we should start now."

Before going into the well-appointed galley-style kitchen to start dinner, he helped his parents into their new helmets. His dad reached up and tugged at the strap beneath his chin. Jerry tilted his head forward, issued a stern look, and lifted his eyebrows. When his dad let go of the strap, Jerry relaxed.

"Don't be gone too long," he said. "Mom, if you don't recognize a street, don't go down it. I don't want you to get lost on our first day here."

"We're not children," his father snapped.

"Oh, get over yourself, Harold. He's just showing us he cares." With that, Rosemary adjusted her helmet strap and took the lead. "Let's go have some fun, Harold. Think you can remember what that means?"

"I know how to have fun," he grumbled.

"Then stop acting like a ninny and show it."

Jerry shook his head as his parents slammed the door shut behind them. In spite of all the griping and snappiness, he had no doubt his parents loved each other with all their hearts. It had to be frustrating to go from being active, productive people to dealing with the confines of aging.

Lord, please show me how to bring some joy into my parents' lives. All I want is for them to be happy...no, make that content.

* * * * *

Amanda dropped some pens into the holder by the cash register and removed her night-deposit pouch. Lacy had called and asked her to pick up some sandwiches on the way home.

She'd phoned in her order so it would be ready when she arrived. The instant she walked out the door, she spotted an elderly couple on one of her bicycles—the tandem bike. The one Jerry had picked up that morning.

Chapter Two

....

Amanda stood on the sidewalk for a few seconds as the elderly couple rounded the corner, the woman on the front obviously controlling their course while the man on the back pedaled as though his life depended on it.

From where she stood, they appeared to be an attractive couple, but they weren't the ones who'd rented the bike. She'd never even seen them before. Jerry hadn't mentioned anyone else. She hesitated, thinking about getting their attention and saying something—but what? *Who are you, and why are you on this bicycle?* No, that wouldn't be right. After all, she didn't have any rules about not letting other people use the equipment.

She turned and quickly walked toward the sub shop, where she knew her order would be waiting. Before going inside, she cast another glance over her shoulder at the elderly couple.

After they rounded the corner, out of sight, she turned and shoved open the door to the sub shop. The guy at the counter grinned. "How's the bicycle business?"

"Good," she said. "Enjoying a little breather after a crazy tourist season."

He laughed. "I know what you mean. I had to get help this year, and you know how hard that is."

"Oh yeah."

He finished wrapping her sandwiches and shoved them into a plastic bag before placing it on the counter. "Here ya go, Amanda. Want chips with that?"

"Sure." After paying, she dropped the bags of chips into the sack and headed for the exit. Soon she was right back out on the sidewalk, heading for home, which was a block and a half away.

As she stepped off the curb to cross the street, she heard the ringing of a bicycle bell behind her. "Hey, bicycle lady!"

The sound of a man's raspy voice caught her attention, so she spun around—just in time to see her tandem bicycle heading straight for her. The woman on the front grinned as she applied the brakes to slow down.

Spurred by curiosity, she took a step toward them. "Did you call me?"

Both the man and the woman extended their legs and planted their feet on the road. The woman loosened her chin strap, removed the helmet, and exposed a thick mane of solid white, wavy hair. "Yes, that was my husband. Sorry he sounded so rude."

"I didn't mean—"

"My wife doesn't like me very much anymore," the man interrupted Amanda. "She's always correcting me like I'm a child."

The woman shot her husband a glance. "I do not."

The man chuckled. "See? There ya go again. So what did you want to talk to the bicycle lady about? We just about broke our necks trying to catch up with her."

Amanda smiled, in spite of the man's tone of annoyance. "Is everything okay with the bicycle?"

"Yes, it's wonderful," the woman said as she leaned forward and extended her right hand. "I just wanted to introduce myself. My name's Rosemary Simpson, and this is my husband, Harold."

That explained it. *These must be Jerry's parents,* she thought. "I'm Amanda Burns. It's nice to meet you." Amanda shook Mrs. Simpson's hand.

"Our son never lets us go with him when he picks up the bicycle," Mr. Simpson said, "but we've seen you through the window when we passed by your shop. Jerry said you're the owner." He grinned and belted out a belly laugh. "You're even prettier up close."

Amanda had no idea what to say to that, so she shifted the sub sack to the other hand. Now that they had their helmets off and they were only a feet away, she saw the resemblance between them and Jerry.

"If you ever need anything, let me know, okay?" Amanda finally said. "In the meantime, I'd better get dinner home."

"You married?" Mr. Simpson said.

"Stop it, Harold," his wife scolded. "That is none of your business."

"Oh, that's okay." Amanda glanced back and forth between the couple. She finally settled her gaze on Mr. Simpson. "No, I'm not married." The heat of embarrassment crept up her cheeks.

"Jerry isn't married either," Mr. Simpson blurted. "He's our only unmarried child. He hasn't found the right girl yet." He paused and narrowed his eyes for a moment. "I think it's about time he settled down. He's forty-five years old and not getting any younger."

His wife jabbed him in the ribs. "I'm sure she doesn't care."

He scowled back at her and refocused on Amanda. "So you're eating alone?"

She had to hand it to him for his persistence. "Um...no."

"For heaven's sake," his wife said as she plopped her helmet back on her head and hooked the strap. "Let's go and let this sweet girl get back to her business. We're probably making her late for a date."

Mr. Simpson snorted. "So do you have a date?"

"No," Amanda replied. "I don't have a date. I'm bringing food home for my sister and me."

"You live with your sister?" A quick smile spread across Mrs. Simpson's face.

"Well, it's more like my sister lives with me, until she can find a place closer to the school where she teaches." *Too much information, but oh well.*

"Come on, Harold," Mrs. Simpson said, as she helped her husband with his helmet. "Let's leave this young lady alone so she can get home and eat. Besides, Jerry's expecting us back for dinner soon." She turned back to Amanda. "He's cooking tonight. Isn't that great? Our son knows how to cook."

"Back when we first met, my wife here did all the cooking," Mr. Simpson said. "But times are changing. Maybe you can come over sometime and Jerry can cook for you."

Mrs. Simpson shook her head. "Please forgive my husband." She gave him a look of displeasure. "But like I was saying, Jerry took a cooking class so we wouldn't have to eat out all the time."

Amanda couldn't help but giggle. "That's wonderful."

"I like eating out," Mr. Simpson said.

"Come on, Harold; let's go."

Mr. and Mrs. Simpson grinned and waved as they took off down the street, while Amanda stood and stared after them. What a nice couple. The man was a little crotchety and the woman was on the bossy side, but she found them rather charming.

Amanda started to turn toward home when she noticed a thin black wallet lying on the ground a few feet away. She picked it up and hesitated for a moment before opening it. Even though it was obviously lost and the only way to find the rightful owner was to look inside, she still felt like a voyeur.

Smack dab in front, in a window compartment, was a picture. She turned it so she could see the faces of what appeared to be a family of five with a younger version of the elderly couple she'd just met sitting in the midst of two young boys and a girl. The ground seemed to shift beneath her a little as she thumbed through more pictures showing a progression of time until present-day. When she got to what looked like a current picture of Jerry Simpson's smiling face, she experienced a quickness of breath. This was clearly Mrs. Simpson's wallet, and she needed to return it—after dinner.

As she closed the distance between herself and her small house facing the side street, she realized that knowing that Jerry had brought his parents on vacation made her like him even more. Well, she didn't exactly know him well enough to like him *that* much, but he'd always been very polite…and of course, very good-looking. And the way he looked at her was…well, heart-stopping. She scurried home and was met at the door by her sister, who snatched the bag from her.

"Who were those people on the bike?" Lacy said, as she rummaged through the sack and pulled out her sandwich and chips. "Mm, my favorite—cheese-flavored Sun Chips."

"Jerry Simpson's parents. Apparently he's been renting the tandem bicycle for them."

Lacy lifted an eyebrow. "I wonder if he's married."

"He's not." Amanda found a plate and put her sandwich on it as she thought of a different, more comfortable subject. She didn't want to mention the wallet, since she planned to return it without making a fuss. "So, did you figure out what to do about Timmy?"

"You don't wanna hear about that now," Lacy replied.

"Sure I do. I told you we'd figure out something together." *Anything to change the subject.* Amanda took a bite of her sandwich and pointed to the spot on the table adjacent to where she was sitting. After she swallowed, she used her most authoritative glare and nodded toward the chair. "You know it's not good for your digestion to eat over the sink."

"Okay, okay." Lacy pulled a plate from the cupboard and joined her sister.

Amanda bowed her head and hoped Lacy would take the hint and do the same. She'd tried to talk to her little sister about faith issues, but

Lacy usually accused her of preaching. As it was, Lacy at least went to church occasionally. She'd threatened to stop going altogether if Amanda pressured her.

When Amanda opened her eyes after the blessing, she couldn't tell if Lacy had just sat there and waited or if she had also bowed her head. Lacy had both hands in her lap, so Amanda could only hope—and continue praying.

"Okay, so tell me about school," Amanda prompted.

Lacy contorted her mouth. "All the kids were great today, except Timmy. I don't think there's anything I can do. That boy still causes more trouble than the rest of the class combined."

"What, exactly, did he do today?" At least that would keep the subject off Jerry. "There has to be more than the lunch incident."

"Well..." Lacy pursed her lips and frowned for a couple of seconds. "He didn't listen to a thing I said all day. When I told them to put everything away, he didn't budge."

"Was he disruptive?"

Lacy lifted her hands. "He's always disruptive. When I tell the kids to sit down, he runs around and makes stupid noises. When I tell them it's time to go outside, he puts his head down and says he doesn't feel like it."

"A kid who doesn't want to go outside?" Amanda said with a chuckle. "I'd be worried." Then she paused for a moment. "Do you think he might be sick or something?"

Lacy's cheek bulged with food as she shook her head. "He's not sick."

"But you said he didn't want to go outside, and he sounds like such an active child. I thought maybe..."

"Oh, he always wants to go outside. Just not when I tell him to. He does that to make my life difficult. When I tell them it's time to go back in, he wastes another fifteen minutes of my time by ignoring me."

"Did you ever find out why he doesn't have both parents at home?"

Lacy shrugged. "Not yet, but what should that matter? Most of the kids in my class only have one parent."

Amanda knew that it did matter, but Lacy wouldn't understand since Amanda had made it her job to protect her. "That's really sad."

"Not really." Lacy stood and leaned on the chair. "It's a reality they have to face. Very few kids have the old-fashioned kind of family with a working dad, a stay-at-home mom, and a house with a yard." She bobbed her head. "We only had one parent, remember?"

Unfortunately, that was true, but it still didn't make it right. Amanda found herself angry at Timmy's parents for whatever they were doing to disrupt him and cause him to come across as a problem child. She bit her lip to keep from commenting any further, because Lacy never understood family problems. She'd never had to deal with the problems as long as her big sister was there. Amanda had thought she was doing the right thing at the time, but now she knew better. She regretted protecting Lacy from life's dirty details.

"I guess I'll probably send a note home to Timmy's father and ask him to come in." She lifted a shoulder in a half-shrug. "He's probably too busy, but I'll give it a shot. Timmy's said his father works all the time and doesn't have much time for him."

"Who takes care of Timmy when his dad's not there?"

"Some teenager who lives down the street from them."

That put a whole new light on things. "No wonder he's acting out."

Lacy dropped the sandwich wrappers in the garbage and put her glass into the sink. "I think I'll go to my room and work on the cutouts for the bulletin board. See ya in the morning."

After Lacy left her alone in the kitchen, Amanda remained in her chair, staring out the window overlooking the street. The setting sun cast an orange glow on the horizon, which warmed the room with amber reflections on the wall and ceiling. She remembered how much her mother enjoyed walking down to the beach and watching the sunset on the Gulf each evening. Treasure Island had the most amazing sunsets. Her mother loved sitting outside and just staring at the western horizon until the last fleck of sun had disappeared into the water. Sometimes when Amanda visited her, they sat in silence and watched the sunset; yet other times, her mother talked about how different things would have been for them if the only man she'd ever loved had stuck around.

The irony of the situation wasn't lost on Amanda. The barrier island off Florida's West Coast was a favorite among vacationers who loved the serenity and charm. People came here to get away from the stress of life. However, this same charm and beauty served as a constant reminder that Amanda had taken over an adult role before she was ready.

Once the painful memories started flooding her mind, Amanda got up, cleared the table, and grabbed the wallet. She needed to stop by the shop to get the Simpsons' current address, since the information inside the wallet had Mrs. Simpson's permanent address in Atlanta.

* * * * *

Jerry couldn't help but notice the surreptitious glances between his parents during dinner. At first, he tried to ignore them, but that became increasingly impossible when his mother started giggling. He should have been happy they were getting along for a change, but they weren't acting right.

"Okay, you two. What's up?"

His dad grinned and winked at his mother then turned to face Jerry. "What do you mean, what's up?" He let out a brief snicker before he caught himself.

Jerry turned to his mother. "Are we going to play this answer-a-question-with-a-question game, or are you going to make this easier on all of us and tell me what's so funny?"

She tried to hide her grin, but Jerry saw right through that. "Nothing's funny. We just had a really nice time riding that wonderful bicycle-built-for-two."

If it weren't for the fact that his dad couldn't control himself, Jerry might have believed his mother. He wanted to. But if they wanted to share a secret, that was fine. He wanted to believe it was something special between a husband and wife, but he was pretty sure they had something up their sleeves.

After dinner, he stood to clear the table. His mother got up to help, but he held out his hand to stop her. "Why don't you and Dad go for a walk and enjoy some fresh air?" He paused and glanced at his dad. "Maybe you'll find that treasure you've been looking for."

She opened her mouth to argue, but his dad reached for her hand and tugged her toward the door. Jerry's chest constricted as he was reminded of a happier, more carefree time in his life—back when his parents were still deeply in love and not at each other's throats all the time. Before his father started showing signs of Alzheimer's.

As soon as he heard the door close, Jerry didn't waste any time before clearing the table and cleaning the kitchen. He wanted to relax and enjoy a little quiet time before his parents returned. He knew there would be a time—hopefully not for a while, but soon enough—when peaceful moments would be few and far between. His father's doctor had told him that Alzheimer's gradually took people's independence, and life would get more difficult toward the end.

The end. What a concept. Even though he was a faithful Christ-follower, the very thought of losing his parents was like a swift kick to the gut. He couldn't imagine life without them, although he knew it would eventually happen.

His eyes misted over as he remembered his childhood and how hard his parents had worked for him, his brother, and his sister. He knew his parents had sacrificed for their kids, but they never let on that they missed out on anything they wanted. They celebrated the kids' accomplishments and were there during the rocky times.

Jerry felt like he owed his parents everything. Too bad his sister and brother didn't share some of his concern. In fact, he hadn't seen either of them since the last time they wanted something. When Jerry had talked to his brother about how their dad's condition had begun to deteriorate, his brother made a few sympathetic noises but got off the phone as quickly as possible. Jerry's sister, on the other hand, said she'd try to come home, but she had so much going on in her life with her job and her husband's business commitments that it might be impossible.

As he rinsed the soap off the last of the pots and pans, Jerry thought about his own life and how differently things had turned out. He'd always assumed he'd find a nice girl, marry her, settle down, and have kids. Of course they'd attend church together. That was a given. He'd grown up in the church, so he couldn't imagine not going—unlike his sister and brother.

His deep-set anger brewed and bubbled to the surface. His jaws ached from clenching his teeth. He finally put the last of the pans in the cupboard, and he shoved the door so hard, the noise reverberated throughout the kitchen.

"Who are you so mad at, son?"

He spun around to face his mother, who stood behind him with her arms folded, while she glared up at him. "How long have you been here?"

"Long enough to see you slam the cupboard door." She shook her head. "We just got back, but I can tell you're miserable. Are you sure this little vacation isn't putting a strain on you?"

"Positive." Jerry forced a smile as he gently guided his mother into the living room, where his father had already made himself comfortable in the rocker/recliner in front of the TV. "You know I've always been heavy-handed."

She hesitated for a split second. "Did anyone call while we were out?"

Jerry frowned. "No, why? Are you expecting a call?"

She took a step back and quickly averted her line of vision. "No, of course not."

Jerry squinted his eyes and stared at her. She was definitely acting suspicious. As if on cue, the sound of someone knocking on the front door sent Jerry's mom scurrying.

He stood still as he listened to his mother greeting whoever was at the door. "Please come in," she said, her voice dripping syrup. "Oh, thank you so much! You found it! I was so worried I might have lost it for good."

Now his curiosity was piqued. He had to find out what was going on. The instant he stepped into the hallway between the foyer and the living room, he knew there was no doubt his mother was up to something, because there stood Amanda, the bicycle shop owner, right outside the condo on the doorstep. She cast a confused glance his way. All he could do was shrug.

"Please come in," his mother urged.

"No, that's okay. I—I just wanted to get this to you." Amanda offered a shaky smile to Jerry before she looked at his mom. "I figured you might need it."

When she took a step back to leave, Jerry's mother reached out and grabbed her by the arm. "I have something for you."

Jerry felt his lips twitch over the humor of the situation. He'd seen his mother in action before. This wasn't her first foray into matchmaking, since she'd done it with his brother and sister.

He wasn't about to fall for it, but he certainly didn't want to embarrass Amanda. "Hey, Amanda," he said. "I see you've experienced my parents."

His mother shot him a glance of annoyance before turning back to Amanda. "Don't mind my son. He can be such a pill sometimes. But he's really a very sweet boy with the most loving heart you'll ever know."

"How was dinner?" Amanda asked.

"You remembered!" His mom rubbed her abdomen. "Jerry is a wonderful cook. I don't think I've ever tasted anything so good. After tasting that, I bet he can cook anything."

Hoo, boy, she was turning it on thick.

Amanda's eyes widened, and she offered a forced smile. "I'm sure."

"Hey, gorgeous!"

The booming voice from behind Jerry commanded all the attention. Everyone turned to face his dad.

"What brings you to our neck of the woods…um, I mean *beach*?"

They'd had so much practice they made it seem natural, and no one would have suspected they'd tag-teamed prospective children-in-law before. Jerry tried not to laugh, but a chuckle escaped his lips.

"Don't just stand there laughing, son. Ask her if she wants some lemonade."

"Dad, I don't think—"

"I know you don't think," his dad whispered. "That's what you have your mother and me for. Go invite the pretty girl in." He gave Jerry a soft but powerful shove that would have sent him sprawling if he hadn't already widened his stance.

Amanda fidgeted and shifted her weight from one foot to the other. She clearly didn't know what to do—or how to handle his expert parents. His heart went out to her.

He grinned down at her and winked. "Would you like some lemonade?"

"Uh…" Amanda glanced from him to his parents, who stood on both sides of her, locking her in. "Sure?"

Her tentative answer tugged at his heartstrings. Jerry had liked Amanda before, and now he appreciated what a good sport she was. He made a mental note to stop by her shop later in the week to apologize and see if there was any way he could make it up to her.

"I don't know how I dropped my wallet," his mother explained, as she gestured toward the sofa. "I'm always so careful about things like that. You never know what might happen." Her cheeks were flaming red, and she avoided his gaze. "There are all kinds of dishonest people out there. I'm glad such a sweet, honest, caring person like you found it."

Jerry heard his mother going on and on about the wallet, and he knew good and well it was a ploy. In fact, he was fairly certain the black wallet Amanda had handed over wasn't even current. He remembered his mother pulling out a red one when she insisted on paying for the gas on the drive down.

When he got to the living room with the lemonade, he saw that his parents had occupied the only two freestanding chairs in the room, leaving the one spot right next to Amanda on the sofa. He handed her the glass, got a coaster and placed it on the table next to her—and chose to remain standing.

His mother frowned at him then turned and grinned at their guest. "So, Amanda, how long have you been in business?"

"About five years."

"Why a bicycle shop?" Jerry's dad asked.

Amanda hesitated for a split second—long enough to let Jerry know she was uncomfortable. "I thought it might be a nice thing to offer tourists, since there are so many places to ride."

"Hey, Mom and Dad, speaking of Amanda's shop, I'm sure she has better things to do than sit around here and play Twenty Questions."

His mother looked hurt as she turned to Amanda. "Oh, dear, I'm so sorry if we're keeping you from something…more important."

Amanda looked stricken. "Oh, no, that's fine." When she turned to Jerry, his heart melted. He resisted the urge to physically reach out and comfort her.

They chatted for a few more minutes—long enough for his parents to give him familiar looks, letting him know he hadn't been imagining things and they really were interviewing a prospective daughter-in-law. Finally, during a brief lull in conversation, Amanda stood and said she needed to get back home.

"Do come again," his mother said as she walked Amanda to the door. "Jerry enjoys cooking, so perhaps you can have dinner with us some evening." She tilted her head to the side and offered him a look that defied him to argue. "Right, son?"

Jerry stifled a chuckle. His mother was on her sales game, big-time. "Yes, yes, of course."

He felt like part of an entourage as they followed Amanda to the door. Suddenly his mother turned to him and said, "Why don't your father and I wait here while you walk Amanda to her car?"

"That's—" Amanda began but clamped her mouth shut when Jerry nodded.

"I'll be glad to. Why don't you and Dad go on back inside?"

"But—"

"Really, Mom, I'll be just fine. If I'm not back in…"—he glanced at his watch then looked up—"…fifteen minutes, then send a search party out looking for me."

His dad let out a deep laugh, while his mom looked on, her mouth open and her expression one of horror. He quickly shut the door behind them.

As soon as he and Amanda were alone and out of earshot, he spoke. "Look, I'm really sorry about my parents. They mean well."

Amanda looked up at him, her eyes wide, and a slight gust of wind blew a tendril of hair across her face. Jerry instinctively reached out, gently lifted her hair, and carefully tucked it behind her ear.

"I…uh," she began as she took a step back. She seemed to be struggling with her words, but he wasn't sure what to do. Finally, she said, "Your parents are very nice people. I understand."

"Then you won't hold them against me?" he teased.

She made a face. "No, of course not!"

"About something my mother said…" He glanced away for a bolt of courage and then focused on her face. "Would you like to come over for dinner sometime?"

"You don't have to do this. I'm sure your mother was just trying to be nice."

"Really. I mean it." And he did. In fact, the prospect of seeing her again soon appealed to him more than ever.

"Well, maybe…sometime."

He wasn't about to let her get away without pinning down a time. "How about tomorrow?"

"I, uh, have plans tomorrow."

"Then how about the day after tomorrow?"

As she tilted her head and looked at him, he had no idea what she was thinking. Then a slow smile spread across her lips, and she nodded. His heart sang!

"I'll call you," he said, before helping her into her car and closing the door.

Jerry remained standing there as Amanda pulled out of the condo parking lot; then he shielded his eyes to watch her drive down the street until she disappeared from sight. *Thank You, Lord.* He practically floated back to the condo.

* * * * *

All the way back to her place, Amanda thought about the things she should have said. Jerry's parents were very sweet but over-the-top pushy. She was glad they hadn't asked what she did before she owned the shop, because she hadn't felt like explaining. Based on prior experience, once people learned one thing about her, it led to another. Her life was a thread she didn't care to unravel.

Lacy greeted Amanda at the door when she got back to the house. "Where were you?" She pulled her head back and offered a questioning look. "Why do you have a weird look on your face?"

Amanda still didn't feel like explaining anything—even to her sister. "I had to run out for a few minutes. I thought you had some bulletin board work to do."

Lacy shook her head. "I forgot to bring home some of the stuff I needed. I'll have to go in early in the morning."

"Then why don't we both go ahead and turn in? I have to get to the shop early and get the books ready for the accountant."

Later that night, as Amanda lay in bed staring up at the ceiling after struggling for almost an hour to find sleep, she thought about her encounter with Jerry. His parents' conniving efforts were rather charming, although overwhelming at the same time. Then her thoughts turned to their son.

She wondered if Jerry was aware of how he'd affected her when he touched her hair. The way he pulled his hand back left her with the impression that he'd acted instinctively. She didn't want to like it…but she did. A lot.

Her mind spun back to the issue of Mrs. Simpson's wallet. After spending almost an hour with the three of them, she was fairly certain it was a setup. It should have bothered her, but it didn't. In fact, she was flattered. That took some planning on Mrs. Simpson's part, and she had a feeling Mr. Simpson had had plenty of input, based on their exchanged glances.

Jerry had said he'd call, but was it to get his parents off his back? She hoped not, but she couldn't be sure. She liked him, and there was nothing wrong with being friends, right?

Thoughts whirled and swirled through her mind until she fell into a fitful sleep. By the time the sun rose, she'd tossed all her pillows off the bed and the sheets looked like they'd been through the wringer.

"Ew, you look rough," Lacy said as she trudged into the kitchen. "You need coffee."

"Thanks," Amanda snapped. "I appreciate the kind words."

"You wouldn't want me to lie, would you?"

"No, of course not." But there were some things better left unsaid.

"I dread going to school today." She sipped her coffee then set her mug on the counter. "Timmy makes me want to retire early."

One thing Amanda could count on was that it was all about Lacy, and at times like this, she was glad. "It won't get any better until you deal with Timmy. The sooner you talk to his dad, the better off you'll be."

Lacy picked her mug back up and blew into the cup. "I know, I know. I just hate doing it."

"That's why you need to do it today. Get it over with."

After she made a few faces, Lacy downed the rest of her heavily creamed-and-sugared coffee. "I might call you later."

"That's fine," Amanda said. "You know where I'll be."

After Lacy left for the elementary school in St. Petersburg, Amanda got ready to go to her shop. Like her sister, she dreaded going to work, but not for the same reason. She still didn't have Jerry and his parents figured out. She wanted to climb back into bed and pull the covers up over her head so she wouldn't have to worry about Jerry's motive in asking her over for dinner.

Amanda took a quick shower, shook out her hair, and pulled on some bike shorts and her favorite T-shirt. She didn't feel like messing with makeup just yet, so she tossed some lipstick and mascara into her shoulder bag and left for the shop.

The second she rounded the corner, she saw him standing by the front door. Her heart picked up an extra beat, and she swallowed hard. Why hadn't she at least smeared on a little of that lipstick?

Chapter Three

....

"Hey," Jerry said, as she pulled out the key and shoved it into the lock. "I wasn't sure what time the place got busy, so I figured I'd get here first thing." He paused until she pushed open the door. "I hope you don't mind."

"Of course I don't mind." She heard the sharpness in her own voice and tried to soften it. "Really."

He looked around as though he'd never seen the place before. "This is quite a nice business you have here."

"Thank you." She paused and cast a glance his way then quickly scurried behind the counter. His nearness unnerved her. But he was here, wasn't he? That must mean *something*.

"I guess you're probably wondering why I'm here." He leaned on the counter while she prepared the register. "Mom thought I gave you the wrong idea last night."

She must have imagined his attraction to her. Amanda's heart fell with a thud, which annoyed her to no end. "What kind of idea did your mom think I had?"

Jerry shrugged. "She thought I came across like I didn't really want to see you again." He thrust his hands in his pockets and rocked back on his heels. "And she said I should take you someplace nice rather than the condo with her and Dad hanging around."

"But I thought the whole point was…" She glanced down. "Never mind."

"Yeah, I know. She acted like it was all about my cooking, but I figure it was all part of her ploy." He chuckled. "Apparently *their* ploy. My dad keeps reminding me that I'm not getting any younger. He acts

51

like forty-five is over the hill." Another laugh escaped his lips. "I'm rambling. Sorry."

She stilled for a couple of seconds, until she forced herself to speak. "That's—"

"Don't feel like you have to say anything. I just wanted to stop by and let you know that I'm really looking forward to doing something with you. And I think Mom might be right. Why don't we go someplace fabulous and get to know each other better?"

Amanda opened her mouth to reply, but her breath caught in her throat. She was so confused now, she didn't know how to respond.

"I'd love to be friends," he added.

She forced a smile but still didn't trust her voice to remain steady. She reached up and pushed her hair off her forehead.

A look of concern instantly covered Jerry's face. "If you don't want to, that's okay. I understand. After all, once my mother gets started, she doesn't let up."

Amanda quickly recovered. "Oh, it's not that. It's just that…" How could she say what she felt—that ever since Eric jilted her, she'd been gun-shy when it came to relationships? She didn't want to set herself up for another heartbreak, and with her track record, she'd given up on trusting men.

"Would you like to go to a nice restaurant somewhere in Treasure Island or St. Pete Beach?"

Even though there were plenty of nice restaurants, Amanda didn't feel like going down that path again anytime soon. Sitting across the table from a man with just the two of them enjoying an intimate conversation over dinner would be dangerous. She slowly shook her head.

He held up his hands. "I give up. What's going on? Do you want to go out with me or not?"

Their gazes locked as she felt the heat rise to her cheeks. "I think it would be nice to do something together, but not a fancy restaurant, okay?"

His hands came down and slapped his sides in obvious frustration. "So what would you like to do?"

"Well…" She thought for a moment. "The Sun, Sand, and Swing Festival starts tomorrow. We can go there."

Jerry chuckled. "The Sun, Sand, and Swing Festival? I've seen plenty of sun and sand here, but where's the swing?"

Relief flooded Amanda, and she laughed. "Music. Every kind of live band you can think of. On the beach. Lots of fun." Lots of noise, kids, and insanity—everything she needed to keep her from focusing on him.

He rubbed his chin for a moment then nodded. "Music is good. Yeah, I'd like that."

Her heart thudded at the thought of doing anything with him. "Then let's go to the festival."

"I think you'll enjoy it." She glanced at the screen on her computer then turned back to face him. "I have to work tomorrow morning and early afternoon, but I have a teenager coming in when she gets out of school."

"Sounds good. Why don't you give me your address so I'll know where to pick you up?"

She wasn't ready for that yet. "We can just leave from here."

Jerry's smile faded just a little before he caught himself and grinned even wider. "Is three o'clock okay?"

* * * * *

He'd been right about one thing. Amanda obviously didn't want to hang out with his parents, and he couldn't blame her. He wished he could talk to them about it and show them how intrusive their behavior was. But what was the point? If they hadn't seen it in the lives of their other two children, he doubted they'd see it with him, so he didn't bother addressing the issue. At least he wouldn't abandon them like his sister and brother had.

He shifted his thoughts to how much he wanted Amanda to trust him. He liked her, even beyond the physical chemistry, which was powerful from the moment he'd touched her hair last night, and he at least wanted her respect and trust. It bothered him that she might think he was in on some scheme with his parents.

Trust is something to be earned, and it doesn't come easily. Those words were spoken by his father years ago during a discussion about relationships, business, and life in general. It certainly held true now. For some reason, probably due to his parents' obvious matchmaking plot, Amanda didn't trust him enough to give him her home address. At least he had time and she wasn't completely giving him the brush-off.

He tried to put it out of his mind, but that was all he could think about for the rest of the day. Thankfully he only had a few simple business details to take care of for work. He spent the time necessary to make sure the business flowed smoothly before shutting off the laptop and focusing on what to wear the next day.

As Jerry stood in front of his closet, he felt at a loss. What did a guy wear to a music festival on the beach when he wanted to make a great impression on someone he cared about? Someone who appeared to like him but didn't quite trust him?

Since his wardrobe consisted mostly of khaki and navy chinos, there wasn't much of a choice. "Why don't you run out and pick up something new?" his mother asked from his bedroom doorway.

He shrugged and pulled out his favorite pair of khakis and a burgundy golf shirt. "I'll be fine with this."

"Bo–ring," she crooned with a smile.

Was it boring? he wondered. Or, more importantly, was *he* boring?

"Since I've never attended a beach festival, I have no idea what to wear. This is probably safe."

Jerry felt his mother's gaze as she tinkered with his confidence, so he turned to face her. She remained in the same position, arms folded, head tilted to one side.

"You think I'm too safe, don't you?" he asked.

"Sometimes," she admitted. "But that's part of your charm."

"So what do you think I should wear?" His arms dangled at his sides as he looked from his wardrobe to his mother.

She grinned back at him. "Never mind what I said earlier. I don't think it really matters what you wear to this festival. I'm sure Amanda is just happy to be going with you."

"Are you sure?"

She nodded. "Positive. I hope she was okay with the change in plans."

He didn't tell her what he was pretty sure Amanda was thinking—that anything would be better than coming to the condo for dinner and having to suffer through an interrogation. "I hope so," he said softly. "She acted like she really wanted to go to this festival."

"Well, it certainly sounds like fun to me. Your father and I used to do all sorts of things like that when we were younger." The sadness in her voice was evident. Ever since his dad had started wandering off and getting lost, they weren't able to do much that involved large crowds. And now that his mom had Parkinson's, she was at the mercy of an increasing amount of physical limitation.

A surge of guilt washed over Jerry. Why was he so worried about what Amanda thought? These were his parents, who'd been with him through everything. They'd never acted ashamed no matter what he did. He loved these people unconditionally.

Forgive me, Father, for the terrible thoughts and lack of respect for Mom and Dad. They're special people, and I wouldn't want to hurt them for anything.

He felt a little better, but there was still a tiny grain of remorse.

Mom and Dad had never been embarrassed about him, even when he was on his worst behavior.

Guilty feelings aside, it was too late to do anything about that now. But next time—assuming there would be a next time—he'd work on his attitude and display his parents with pride.

* * * * *

Early the next morning, Amanda downed the last of her coffee before grabbing her gear and starting for work. Lacy intercepted her before she got to the door.

"I won't be home for dinner tonight," Lacy said, grinning from ear to ear.

"Neither will I."

Lacy's smile faded as she pulled back and squinted her eyes. "So where are you going?"

Amanda had spoken too quickly. "Sun, Sand, and Swing Festival."

"By yourself?"

"What do you think?" Amanda popped her helmet on her head and snapped the strap under her chin. "I'm going with a friend."

A slow smile tipped the edges of Lacy's lips, and she batted her eyes. "It wouldn't just happen to be Jerry Simpson, would it?"

"Okay, yes, I'm going with Jerry. So how about you? Where will you be?"

Lacy grinned. "I'm going to the festival, too, and I bet you'll never guess who I'm going with."

Rather than play one of Lacy's favorite games, Amanda opened the door, stepped halfway out, then turned to face her sister. "So who are you going with?"

"You'll see," Lacy said with a giggle.

"Fine, don't tell me." She started to pull the door closed but paused when Lacy reached out and flung it open again.

"Are you coming home to change before you leave?"

"No," Amanda said slowly. "Why should I?"

Lacy grimaced and shook her head as she pointed to Amanda's clothes. "You're going like that?"

Amanda glanced down at her bike shorts, sports top, and Windbreaker. "What's wrong with this? I wear it almost every day, and you haven't said anything about it before."

"But you don't normally have a date after work."

"This isn't exactly a date," Amanda tried to explain. "He's just looking for something to do, and I said we could go to the festival."

"Trust me, Amanda, this is a date." Lacy reached out and gently pulled Amanda back into the house. "It's fine if you want to wear that for work, but you need to change into something a little more flattering afterward. C'mon, I'll find you something that'll knock his socks off."

Rather than waste time arguing with her sister, fashion icon and basic shallow thinker, Amanda allowed Lacy to rummage through both of their closets until she came up with trousers from Amanda's wardrobe and a cute little tunic from her own.

"I'm glad I bought this in a size smaller," Lacy said as she shoved the tunic into a tote. "I thought I was going to lose a little weight, but since it didn't happen, at least you can get some use out of it." She grabbed a necklace from the wicker table and dropped it into the side pocket. "Put this on, too."

"Thanks." Amanda took the tote and headed out the door before her sister thought of something else she might need. As it was, she had a little difficulty maneuvering everything while steering her bicycle toward the shop.

Between customers, Amanda thought about the clothes in the bag and wondered if she really needed to worry so much about what to wear. If Jerry really liked her, would it matter if she put on that cute little top of Lacy's?

The day seemed to drag, but a half hour after the high school let out, Tiffany arrived to take over. Amanda handed her the reservation book then headed for the back room where she'd stashed the tote from her sister.

When she heard the bell on the door, she stilled and listened for Jerry's familiar voice. Her heart pounded when she was sure it was him.

"Just a minute," Tiffany said. "I'll see if she's ready to go."

Amanda hadn't changed yet, so when Tiffany stopped at the door of the back room and eyeballed her before speaking, she made a decision. She wasn't changing clothes. This wasn't a date, and she'd decided it would be easier and more fun to ride bikes to the beach.

"Tell Jerry I'll be right out," she said. "Oh, and does he have biking clothes?"

Tiffany slowly shook her head no. "He's a little overdressed for riding a bike."

"That's fine." Amber glanced around the room until her eyes settled on some returns she'd kept on hand for emergencies. "He can wear that. Why don't you send him back here?"

"Okey-dokey." Tiffany disappeared as Amanda searched until she found everything Jerry would need.

"You wanted me for something?" Jerry asked.

Amanda crooked her finger and motioned for him to join her. "You're a little too dressed up for riding bikes, so I found something for you to change into. I hope you don't mind."

His lips formed a straight line as his forehead crinkled. "We're riding bikes?"

She nodded. "I thought that would be fun."

After a brief pause, he looked at the clothes. "I'm game." A goofy expression spread over his face as he raked a gesture over his outfit. "You don't approve of what my mother picked out?"

She laughed. "You look nice, Jerry, but next time, you might want to remember where you are. This is Treasure Island. The beach. We like to go casual around here."

"Good thing I keep sneakers and workout socks in my SUV."

"Perfect!"

Jerry picked up the bike shorts and T-shirt then glanced around. "Where should I change?"

"The restroom is over there in the corner. Just hang your stuff on the hook."

As Jerry went into the restroom and closed the door behind him, Amanda thought about what a great sport he was. Not every man would be so agreeable.

She went out to the front of the store to chat with Tiffany while she waited. "He's cute," Tiffany said softly, "for an older guy."

Amanda smiled. "Yeah, he's okay."

She started to add that they were just friends when she heard the sound of Jerry clearing his throat behind her. She spun around in time to see him doing a model pose in his shorts and logo tee.

Tiffany came around from behind the desk and gave him a slow once-over. "You look just like a professional biker," she said.

Jerry grinned and winked at the teenager then turned to Amanda. "Better now?"

"Much better," she said. "We need to get going. I have a couple of bikes ready and waiting. I need to go drop something off with a friend at John's Pass. Hope you don't mind."

"Fine with me," he said. "You lead the way."

Amanda heard a long, dreamy *ahh* from Tiffany as they left the store. She made a mental note to squelch any romantic notions the girl had before it got around that she was dating a man. Rumors, particularly among the Treasure Island high school crowd in St. Petersburg, traveled fast and knew no limits.

They took off, starting on the road then bumping up onto sidewalks where the traffic was heavy. Amanda had to stop and wait for him a couple of times as he maneuvered between cars.

"This is interesting," Jerry said as they pedaled along. "The traffic keeps getting worse."

She nodded. "If you think this is bad, you should have seen it a couple months ago."

They were approaching a bridge that was slightly trickier to maneuver. She was glad there was no westerly wind, or they'd have had to deal with the salt spray. Most of the time she didn't care if she got the frizzies, but for once, her hair was behaving.

After they crossed the bridge, Jerry veered to the side, stopped, and pulled off his helmet. He straddled his bike as he lifted his hand and shielded his eyes from the sun. "This place blows me away."

She maneuvered her bike closer to his. "You like it?"

"It's breathtaking."

"If you like this, maybe we can go on a longer ride sometime."

As he turned to face her, his expression changed. He slowly nodded. "Yes, I'd like that."

Her heart hammered, and her lips quivered. She hoped he didn't see how he was affecting her. After this was all over, she'd make a list of reasons it wouldn't be good to fall for this guy—the first one being that he was a tourist and nothing would ever pull her away from her sister and the business she'd worked so hard to build. The second one being the fact that she stunk at relationships.

After positioning her foot on the pedal, she motioned for him to step it up. "Let's keep moving. I don't want to miss more than we already have."

* * * * *

Jerry felt a sliver of hope. Amanda was fun. She'd definitely liven up his vacation. He'd have to keep it on just-friends terms; otherwise he could see himself falling for her, which would be a disaster. He didn't need any distractions to keep him away from taking care of his parents when they needed him most.

They took turns with the lead for most of the trip, but after they crossed the bridge, Jerry followed her the rest of the way to John's Pass, where she delivered some fliers at a friend's surf shop. Then they hopped back on their bikes and headed across the bridge to Treasure Island. She obviously knew exactly where she was going, and she was focused. He liked that about her.

"I was hoping we could catch at least part of one of my favorite bands," she hollered as they drew closer to the activities.

"What band is that?"

"It's an old-time swing band."

"Sounds interesting."

They parked their bikes in a rack and locked them together. If he'd had any doubt about how to dress, he shouldn't have worried. People wore anything from golf clothes to swimsuits—and everything in between. No one looked out of place—not even the businessmen who appeared to be networking. The beach was packed, and the crowd spilled out from the sidewalks to the road.

"Look." Amanda pointed to something behind him, so he turned to see what it was.

An elderly gentleman sat in front of an easel and was painting the crowd before him. Even though movement was fluid, he managed to capture the essence of what was around him.

"This is really great," Jerry said.

"I know," Amanda said. "There's always something fun going on here. When I was younger they had pirate festivals, but that ended a few years ago."

Jerry squinted an eye, flexed a muscle, and said, "Arrgh...."

Amanda chuckled. "Very good."

He dropped the pose and grinned. "Did I scare you?"

"Can't you see me shaking?" Her broad smile was warmer than the sunshine reflecting off the white sandy beach.

They watched the artist for a few minutes then headed toward a makeshift stage, to where Amanda pointed. "I think we made it here in time."

It didn't take long for Jerry to get in the spirit of things. On the way to the stage, he ducked into a small shop, bought a T-shirt with the Sun, Sand, and Swing logo, and slipped it on over his bike clothes. He held up a tiny plastic treasure chest. "For my dad," he said. "He's always on a treasure hunt." Amanda's smile flooded him with warmth.

"Hey, Amanda!"

Amanda whispered, "That's my sister, Lacy. Remember her?"

Jerry nodded, although he only vaguely remembered another slightly taller girl with lighter blond hair. "Did you know she was coming?"

"Yeah." Amanda turned her attention on the woman who quickly approached. "So where's your date?"

Lacy offered a coquettish shrug. "I'm supposed to meet him here in about an hour. I was just so excited, I got here early."

"Would you like to hang out with us until he gets here?" Jerry offered.

She looked over at Amanda, smiled, then glanced back at him and shook her head. "No, I don't think so. Some of the other teachers are here, so I'll just go talk to them. See ya at home tonight." She started to walk away, until Amanda called after her.

"Lacy!"

She turned around to face Amanda. "What?"

"You never did say who you were meeting here."

Lacy cast a quick glance in Jerry's direction, shifted her weight from one foot to the other, then shrugged and flipped her hand from the wrist. "It doesn't really matter. I'll tell you later."

Jerry quickly turned to Amanda to see her response. He watched a flicker of pain then a look of resignation.

"Fine," she said then briefly hesitated. "Don't stay out too late."

Lacy looked like she was about to argue, but she didn't. Instead, she looked down then back at Amanda. "I won't."

After Lacy turned and walked toward the restaurant on the corner, Jerry frowned. "Did her behavior seem strange to you?"

"Not really." Amanda shook her head. "Lacy has always been like that."

"Did you want to stick with her and meet her date?"

"I don't think she wants us to. I'll deal with her later." The set of her jaw was firm, and she seemed less carefree than just a few minutes earlier.

Jerry got the impression that Amanda was more like a mother to Lacy than a sister. He wanted to ask questions, but it wasn't any of his business.

They spent the rest of the afternoon and early evening listening to music, watching the dancers, and browsing through the art in the booths throughout the festival. Jerry stopped off at some of the vendors and got some snacks to keep up their energy. He couldn't remember having this much fun in a very long time, in spite of the fact that Amanda kept looking around, most likely for her sister.

Finally, shortly after the sun barely hovered over the water, Amanda turned to him. "I guess we'd better start heading back before it gets dark."

Jerry agreed. He wasn't about to let his disappointment show that the day was quickly coming to an end. After all, she was right. Not only did they need to get back before dark, he didn't want to leave his parents alone too long. He'd reminded his mother to call his cell phone if there was an emergency. But he also knew she wanted him to find a nice girl, and Amanda just happened to be the only prospect in sight. He'd have to talk to his mother later and set her straight on what was really important to him.

The ride back was quiet, with the exception of the times when Amanda pointed out things they'd missed on their way to the festival. They were back at her bicycle shop in fifteen minutes.

"I had a great time," he told Amanda as they approached the front door. "Where do you want me to put this bike?"

"Inside. I'll hold the door while you wheel it in."

She didn't even look him in the eyes as she spoke. She reminded him that his things were still in the restroom.

"I'll launder the shorts and shirt and bring them back tomorrow," he told her.

"No rush. In fact, you can keep them if you want. I have plenty more just like them."

He stood at the door until she finally glanced up at him. "Thank you for everything, Amanda."

Her cheeks turned pink as she blinked and forced a smile. "My pleasure."

There was no doubt in his mind that she wanted to be alone now. So he left.

* * * * *

The next day, Amanda arrived at the store exhausted. She'd tried to wait up for Lacy, but midnight came and went with no sign of her. She finally left a note for her sister and then crawled into bed, hoping for a good night's sleep. But it didn't happen.

For more than an hour she tossed and turned as she rehashed the day with Jerry. She'd had a great time, but nothing out of the ordinary had happened between them. In fact, it was one of the most eventless festivals she'd ever attended. However, she felt as though she'd been turned inside out.

Being in the bicycle business had exposed her to plenty of attractive, single men, so she knew that his physical good looks had nothing to do with how she felt about Jerry. He was kind and gentle, but so were most of her steady customers. There was some sort of chemistry with him that she couldn't define.

She'd been with him most of the day, and she still didn't know if he was a Christian. He didn't curse, and she didn't see him act in a non-Christian manner. However, there were plenty of people with good morals who weren't believers. The couple of times she'd thought about bringing it up didn't seem appropriate, so she kept her questions to herself. Besides, what did it matter since he was only there on vacation?

She got up and went to work with a lack of sleep and an unsettling feeling that something had changed between her and Jerry. Every time the door opened, she jumped. By noon, she felt like she'd been beaten and dragged through the shell-encrusted parking lot.

"What happened to you? Was Jerry mean? You look awful," Lacy said as she entered the store midmorning.

"No, Jerry wasn't mean. And thanks a lot. What time did you get in last night?"

Lacy narrowed her eyes in defiance, but she didn't say anything. Amanda decided to keep trying to get through to her.

"What are you doing here? Don't you have school?"

Lacy shrugged as she glanced at her fingernails to avoid Amanda's scrutiny. Amanda saw the tiny smirk of defiance that lifted the corners of Lacy's mouth. "I took a sick day and called a sub."

"You don't look sick to me."

Lacy scowled and folded her arms, reminding Amanda of when Lacy first hit puberty. "Don't talk to me like that, Amanda. I'm sick of it. You're always telling me what to do."

Amanda started to argue that someone needed to tell her what to do then thought better of it. She shook her head. "Sorry about that." She minimized the window on the computer then stepped around from behind the counter. "Did you need something?"

"Why would you think I need something?" Lacy pouted and scrunched her forehead, further enhancing the prepubescent look.

"I dunno," Amanda replied, "maybe because you came by in the middle of the day when you're supposed to be sick?"

"I just wanted to tell you that I thought you and Jerry make a cute couple."

Amanda sputtered before she was able to talk. "Um, first of all, we're not a couple. He's simply a customer who wanted something to do. I thought it would be fun to go to the festival. His mother invited me to have dinner in their condo, and, well, I just thought that might be a little too uncomfortable." *Whoa.* Too much explaining was always a sign of guilt.

"So you're in tight with his parents?" Lacy asked.

Amanda glared at her sister. "We're all friends. That's all."

Lacy's pout turned to a sly grin. "If you want to believe that, fine. But I saw how he looked at you."

"Don't imagine something that doesn't exist," Amanda warned.

Lacy did a double take at something outside, so she turned to see what her sister was looking at.

Chapter Four

....

The second their gazes met, Jerry felt a thud in his chest. He'd been standing outside the shop for a few seconds, trying to decide whether to go inside or act like he was on his way to somewhere else. He didn't have a reason to be there—other than to gawk at Amanda. But that didn't seem like enough.

A smile slowly spread across Amanda's lips, and she waved. Now that he'd been caught, he couldn't very well keep going.

His mind raced for a reason to be there as he pushed open the door and walked in. "I had a great time yesterday," he said.

"Yeah, me, too." Amanda's face reddened as her sister snickered.

The last thing he wanted to do was embarrass her in front of her sister, so he blurted the first thing that came to mind. "I just wanted to stop by and ask if there were any good churches around here."

Amanda's sister frowned then turned to Amanda. "I'd better get going. See ya tonight."

After she left, Amanda cleared her throat, blinked a couple of times, then looked him squarely in the eyes. "There are several churches," she said. "It all depends on what you're looking for." Was that a tone of defensiveness in her voice?

"I want the pure gospel of Christ," he replied as he squared his shoulders.

She pursed her lips then looked him in the eyes. "We have several in the area." Her attention went to the door, so he turned around in time to see Lacy looking back at Amanda.

He wasn't sure what was going on, but he hoped he hadn't caused a problem between the sisters. "Did I come at a bad time?"

"No, not at all." Amanda offered a smile as she focused all her attention on him. "Now about church. Do you like contemporary or traditional?"

His parents had moved to a more contemporary service when he and his siblings became teenagers, and they seemed to enjoy it. "Contemporary would be nice."

She drummed her fingers on the counter for a moment, as though she wasn't sure what to do. He was about to let her off the hook and tell her never mind when she looked up. "I go to Treasure Island Community Church. A lot of tourists are there every week, so you might like it."

His heart sang just knowing she went to church. "Just tell me when and where, and we'll be there."

"Let me write it all down for you," she replied. "We have two services because it's kind of small and the regular membership is growing. We're looking for a bigger place, but that's not easy in a place like Treasure Island."

"At least you're growing." He'd been through church growth in Atlanta, so he knew what a challenge it could be.

"The place is bursting at the seams, so we need to do something soon."

He felt his body relax just knowing he was in the presence of another believer. "That's a good problem to have."

She nodded. "Would you prefer the early service at nine, or would eleven be better?"

Jerry's parents hated to sleep in. "The early one."

"That's the one I like to go to, too. We have an adult Bible study between services, if you're interested in that."

Jerry wasn't sure if his parents would be up to it, so he shrugged. "I'll have to see what the folks want to do, but I know they'll want to at least go to the church services."

Her face brightened as they talked about church and the Christian songs they liked. He hadn't planned the conversation, but he was glad he'd had to come up with a reason for being there. Knowing she was a believer intensified his feelings for her. That might not be a good thing, but he figured he could handle it since he'd only be in the area for a short while.

"What do most people wear?" he asked. "That's the first thing my mom will want to know."

"It's casual," she replied, "just like everything else around here. Pretty much anything goes. I generally wear lightweight cotton pants and a comfortable top with sandals. But some people still like to dress up."

"My mom likes to wear skirts."

Amanda nodded. "Believe it or not, until just a few years ago, so did I for a long time. I couldn't bring myself to wear pants to church, but it didn't bother me that other people did."

"My mom said the same thing."

After they discussed church, the subject naturally changed to the festival they'd attended. Then it progressed to other things. Conversation came natural between them.

It didn't matter what they talked about; Jerry found himself deeply interested in everything she said, and nothing else mattered. When he heard the cough behind him, he jumped. He hadn't heard anyone come in.

He spun around to see Amanda's sister. It seemed like he'd only been there a few minutes.

"What's wrong, Lacy?" Amanda asked, her forehead crinkling with concern.

"I just got a call from the school. My sub walked out, and they wanted to know if I'm feeling good enough to come in."

* * * * *

Lacy's timing couldn't have been worse. Now that Amanda knew Jerry was a Christian, she wanted to talk about church, their faith, and everything else that came to mind. For the first time ever, Amanda felt that she could completely be herself around a guy. Guilt instantly rushed through her. Lacy needed her.

"Who's with your class?"

Lacy cleared her throat. "Suzanne."

Suzanne was the school's administrative assistant and Amanda's best friend since childhood. When Lacy needed her first teaching job after college, Suzanne had been the one who vouched for her with the principal.

As much as she hated discussing family issues in front of someone else, she didn't see that she had a choice. "Why don't you just go on to school then?"

Lacy offered an exaggerated frown. "I don't feel like facing them today."

Amanda was painfully aware of Jerry's interest in their conversation. She turned to him to explain. "There's a problem child in her class."

"Must be pretty bad to make you feel this way," he said directly to Lacy. "Is there anything I can do?"

Lacy snickered. "I wish. Even his dad is beside himself with worry about him."

"So you finally talked to his father?"

"Yeah, in fact, he's the one I met at the festival."

No wonder Lacy had acted so strange. "Was Timmy with him?"

"No," Lacy said as she gave Amanda a look like she should have known better. "Why would he bring Timmy along on a date?"

A date? Amanda forced herself to act like she knew it all along, so she shrugged. "Maybe because Timmy would enjoy going to a festival. There were a lot of kids there."

Jerry shifted his weight and leaned against the counter. "Are his parents divorced?"

"His mother died when he was three," Lacy explained. "Ever since then, Brad's been a single dad without much help. It hasn't been easy for him."

"I can imagine," Jerry said softly as his gaze met Amanda's. He looked back at Lacy. "I bet it's been hard on both of them."

"Especially Brad. Can you imagine having to deal with a bratty little boy every single day for the rest of your life?"

"Maybe not the rest of his life," Jerry said with a wry grin. "Just the next fifteen years or so."

"Might as well be the rest of his life." Lacy scrunched her face. "Brad is such a sweet guy, but he's at his wit's end about Timmy."

"Has he thought about spending more time with his son?" Amanda interjected. "Sometimes that's all it takes."

"More time?" Lacy grunted. "That would be miserable."

Amanda glanced over at Jerry, who exchanged a knowing look. He nodded then turned back to Lacy.

"Maybe the five of us can do something sometime," he offered.

Lacy's forehead crinkled. "The five of us?"

"Yeah, you, Brad, Timmy, Amanda, and me."

Lacy shook her head. "I don't know about that. Timmy's a handful."

"I don't mind," Jerry said. "Or maybe the four of us can go out—without Timmy."

A slight smile formed on Lacy's lips. "A double date? That would be, like, so fun!"

"I think so, too," Jerry said.

Lacy glanced at her watch and let out a long-suffering sigh. "As much as I hate to do this, I guess I need to go to school." She headed for the door then stopped and turned. "Why don't you figure out where we can go on our double date, and I'll call Brad?" Then she left.

Amanda shook her head and let out a little laugh. "Amazing."

Jerry grinned back at her. "Your sister is very cute, but I'm surprised she's a teacher."

"Yeah, well, she needed to do something with her life, and she always enjoyed children…maybe because she's still sort of a child herself."

"Don't be too hard on her," Jerry said. "There might be a few things she still needs to learn, but I bet the kids love her."

Amanda appreciated his ability to see something beyond her sister's whiny demeanor. Lacy really did have a good heart, but she didn't know how to direct it. And yes, from what she'd heard from Suzanne, the kids did love her. Obviously so did some of the parents.

"So…" Jerry kicked his toe on the floor and looked around the store. "What do you think about the four of us going out sometime? I hope I didn't put you on the spot or anything."

"No." She spoke a little too fast. "What I mean is, I don't feel like you put me on the spot. I just hope you don't feel like you have to do this."

"Trust me," he said slowly as he held her gaze, "I want to do it."

Her heartbeat quickened, so she reached beneath her counter and pretended to work so he wouldn't see how flustered she was. She'd just pulled out a pad of invoices when she spotted someone coming in the door. It was Jerry's mother.

"Hi, Amanda," she said quickly before turning to Jerry. "I thought I might find you here, son. Your father wants you to help him with something back at the condo."

Jerry's face drained of all color as he backed toward the door. "Is he okay? I shouldn't have been gone so long."

His mother flipped her hand from the wrist. "Oh, he's fine. He just wants a little attention from his son, that's all."

Amanda watched their interaction with interest. Something else was going on, but she wouldn't even try to guess what it was. She had a feeling there were quite a few unresolved issues in that family.

"You run on back to the condo," his mother added. "I think I'll just take a look around here."

Jerry's forehead crinkled, and he glanced back and forth between Amanda and his mother before settling his gaze back on Amanda. "Is that okay?"

"Yes, of course," Amanda replied as she forced a smile. Now there was no doubt something was going on.

The second he left, Jerry's mother plopped up on the barstool and folded her hands on the counter. "So, Amanda, how do you like living in Treasure Island year-round?"

Maybe she just needed a little female companionship. Amanda smiled. "It's all I know. I've lived here all my life."

"Have you ever been to Atlanta?"

Amanda nodded. "Yes, but it's been a long time. Do you enjoy living there?"

The older woman shrugged. "I used to love it, but it's gotten so big and congested, I don't know anymore."

"I know what you mean. Treasure Island hasn't grown in size for obvious reasons, but there are so many more people here than when I was younger. I'm afraid the traffic is a little crazy."

"But it's still beautiful."

"Yes," Amanda agreed. She wished she could think of something else to say, because this conversation was starting to feel awkward.

Mrs. Simpson studied her for a moment then hopped down off the stool. "Reckon I better be getting back, or the boys will think I'm up to something."

No doubt. Amanda smiled. "Thank you for stopping by, Mrs. Simpson."

"Oh, please don't call me that. It makes me feel so old. I'm Rosemary, and my husband is Harold."

"Okay…Rosemary. I guess I'll see you at church on Sunday."

Rosemary had her hand on the door but paused and turned to Amanda. "Church?"

"Yes. Jerry stopped by to find out about churches, so I told him about mine."

"So you're a Christian girl?" Rosemary smiled and let go of the door. "That's really nice."

To keep the conversation from going in a whole new direction—one that would make her squirm even more—Amanda quickly thought of something else. "I told him the services are at nine and eleven with a Bible study in between. We generally have refreshments, too." She walked to the door and held it for Rosemary. "It'll be nice to see you there. Oh, and don't worry about dressing up. Everything here is casual."

"Oh…okay," Rosemary said as she stepped outside. "See you Sunday."

Suddenly, Amanda found herself alone and slightly confused. What was Rosemary's real reason for stopping by the shop? Did her husband really need Jerry, or did she want some time alone with Amanda?

* * * * *

"That woman!" Jerry watched as his dad's face contorted from frustration as he paced back and forth in the condo. "She needs to learn to mind her business."

"Dad, don't be so hard on her. She just said you needed me."

"It could have waited."

Yes, Jerry agreed. It could have waited. His parents had gone out to the beach with a couple of plastic bags, and now his dad wanted some help in sorting through the stuff they found and taking what wasn't any good to the Dumpster.

"That's okay. Want to go through it now?"

His dad shook his head as he stood. "Might as well, since you hoofed it all the way back here. Let's go out on the balcony."

Jerry went to the front door, lifted both bags, and carried them through the condo to the balcony where his dad waited. "How do you want to do this?"

"I'll look at it first, and if I don't know what it is, you can take a look at it."

"What do you think you'll find?" Jerry asked.

His dad snorted. "If I've told you once, I've told you a hundred times—this place isn't called Treasure Island for nothing. There's treasure out there somewhere, and I aim to find it."

Jerry wasn't sure how much of this was his dad looking for something to do and how much was the Alzheimer's talking. His parents had always been a little eccentric, but this was a little weird. His mother had told him that his dad had wanted to buy a metal detector, but she'd stopped him.

"Have you ever stopped to think that someone might have already found the treasure—that is, if there really was some?"

His dad held up what looked like an old battery case then dropped it into the wastebasket he'd put between them. "I think it's still out there. If someone had found it, don't you think we'd know about it?"

"Maybe whoever it was kept it to himself."

"Nah, something like that would be on the front page of the newspaper."

Jerry gave up. He took each item his father handed him and looked it over. Almost everything was garbage, but there were a few items of interest—like a faded photo of a family and a small coin pouch with a few pennies and nickels.

Each time his dad held something up for inspection, Jerry studied his expression. He was pretty sure his dad wasn't strictly thinking about the items in the bag.

"So…," his dad began, "…you like this girl?"

Jerry should have seen it coming. He paused for a moment to edit himself. "Are you talking about Amanda?"

His dad dropped the trinket he'd been looking at back into the bag, tilted his head forward, and gave him a look that brought him back to his teenage years. "Who else would I be talking about, son? For someone so educated, I'm surprised you have to ask."

Jerry squirmed for a few seconds before nodding. "She's a nice girl."

"That's not what I'm asking."

Jerry knew exactly what he was asking. "We're friends. Period."

His dad shook his head and snorted. "I thought I taught you better than that. I hope you don't think you'll be happy sitting around watching your mother and me grow old. That would be miserable."

A momentary silence fell between them. Both Jerry and his dad picked up some more junk from the bag and pretended to look it over. Finally Jerry decided it was time to move on to something else.

"Well, did you find what you were looking for, Dad?"

"Nope. That treasure is still out there somewhere, and I aim to find it."

Jerry stood up and paused to look down at his father, who sat slump-shouldered in the patio chair and staring out at the Gulf of Mexico. It was a lovely view, but he didn't think his dad even noticed.

"Maybe you and Mom can go out again tomorrow," Jerry said. The fresh air was good for them.

"Your mother hates looking for treasure. She griped nonstop."

"Then why don't you compromise and do something she likes?"

"She doesn't like to do anything fun."

"Okay, Dad, I'm going back inside. I'd like to have a little dinner and then we can come back out here and watch the sun set."

* * * * *

As Amanda cleaned the shop before going home, she spotted something on the floor next to the bicycle rack near the door. It was an address book. She picked it up and flipped through it.

Rosemary was at it again. Amanda chuckled to herself as she thought about how unimaginative Jerry's mother was with her ploy to matchmake. She'd already used the item-left-behind tactic—and now she was using it again.

This time Amanda wouldn't fall for it. She'd bring it to church on Sunday and give it to Rosemary then.

It still made her smile, thinking about what lengths Rosemary was willing to go to for her son. Her own mother had been so wrapped up in herself, it wouldn't have crossed her mind to find a man for Amanda. Not that Amanda needed a man….

After she finished sweeping, Amanda locked up, hopped on her bicycle, and headed home. She'd just bumped off the curb when a car horn blasted behind her. She stopped and waited for the car to make the turn before proceeding. Treasure Island used to be so peaceful, and now the traffic was getting so bad that riding a bicycle was becoming a dangerous sport. Still, she loved riding with the sun beating down on her back and the gentle breeze caressing her face.

She pulled into her yard and secured her bicycle at the pole by the side door leading to the kitchen. When she walked into the house, she encountered Lacy standing at the stove, stirring something in a pot. That was something she didn't see often.

"What's for supper?" she asked as she stepped up to glance in the pot.

Lacy turned, her face contorted in a frown. "I'm trying to make stew, but it's all lumpy."

Amanda saw clumps of flour floating on top of the thick brown liquid. "Why don't you spoon some of those out? It looks pretty good underneath. What kind of stew is it?"

"Hamburger, potato, carrot, and bean stew."

"Interesting." She'd never had hamburger stew before. "Where'd you get the recipe?"

"I made it up."

That explained why she'd never heard of it. At least Lacy was getting creative and making an effort. "Why the sudden interest in cooking?"

"Brad misses home-cooked meals."

Amanda pursed her lips and nodded. "Makes sense." She leaned over and looked in the pot again. "I like all the ingredients, so I bet it's pretty good."

Lacy looked up at her, and a smile slowly crept over her face. "I hope so. I told Brad I'd come over and cook for him and Timmy sometime."

Amanda took care not to act too surprised. She put her gear on the side counter by the door and sat down at the kitchen table. "So how's it going with Timmy?"

Lacy shrugged as she turned back to stir her stew. "What do I do with these lumps?"

"Want me to help you?"

"No." The sharpness in Lacy's voice startled Amanda.

Amanda held up her hands in surrender. "Okay, I was just offering my assistance. Put the lumps in a bowl."

"Then what?"

It took every ounce of self-restraint to remain sitting. Amanda had always done everything for her sister, so she knew she needed to accept Lacy's desire to do it herself.

"After you get all the lumps out, you can toss them."

Lacy looked at her quizzically. "Isn't that wasteful?"

What would be wasteful was having to toss the entire contents of the pot. "No, cooks do it all the time."

"Oh." Lacy opened a cupboard, pulled out a bowl, and held it up for inspection. "This one okay?"

"It's fine." Amanda doubted that the small cereal bowl would hold all the lumps she'd seen floating, let alone the ones beneath the surface, but she wasn't about to interfere any more than she needed to.

"So what's going on with you and Jerry?" Lacy asked.

Startled by this out-of-the-blue question, Amanda hesitated for a few seconds before answering. "Nothing is going on. Why?"

Again Lacy shrugged, as she continued lifting golf-ball-sized lumps from the stew. Amanda wondered if there would be anything left without the lumps.

"I think it's time you let down your guard. It's been awhile since Eric…well, you know."

Amanda didn't want to even think about Eric, let alone talk about him. In fact, when she allowed thoughts of Eric to linger in her mind, she became physically ill. "I don't think it's any of your concern."

Lacy turned and glared at her with squinty eyes. "You can't keep hiding from men forever, Amanda. Jerry seems like a sweet guy, and it's obvious that he likes you a lot."

"Yes, and it's also obvious that he's on vacation, and after it's over, he'll go back to Atlanta. Then what?"

"People move all the time."

Amanda snickered. "Yeah, like I'm going to shut down the bicycle business I've worked so hard to build, and he's going to abandon his elderly parents who obviously need his help."

"If you really love each other, you'll figure out a way."

Who said anything about love? Lacy could stay in her fantasy world if it made her happy, but she didn't need to intrude on Amanda's reality.

"Don't worry about it, Lacy," Amanda said as firmly as she could without sounding bossy. "You stick to your love life, and I'll worry about mine."

Lacy grinned. "Your love life, huh?"

Amanda rolled her eyes then glared at her sister. "Stop it, okay? Don't make something out of nothing."

Lacy's eyes widened then she slowly nodded. "Okay, okay, just sayin'…"

A half hour later, Lacy sat down at the table with Amanda, bowls of still-lumpy stew between them. Amanda bowed her head and softly said a blessing for the meal. When she lifted her head, Lacy was staring at her.

"Tell me what you think."

Amanda nodded as she lifted her spoon and scooped some of the meat and gravy. One taste was all it took to let her know that Lacy needed more instruction in the kitchen.

"Well?"

Amanda pointed to Lacy's bowl. "Try it yourself and tell me what you think."

Tears instantly glistened in Lacy's eyes. "I don't want to. It looks gross."

"It tastes a little better than it looks," Amanda said. "But maybe next time, you can cook something a little easier."

Lacy looked down at her bowl and made a face. "Is it that bad?"

Amanda fished out a carrot and ate it as she thought of something that wouldn't destroy Lacy's spirit. "The veggies aren't bad." She forced a smile.

Lacy looked crestfallen. "I'm hopeless in the kitchen."

"No, you're not," Amanda said. "You're just inexperienced. You never had to cook before, so why would you expect to be an expert at it? It's my fault you don't know how, and I'm going to do something about that starting tomorrow."

Lacy rolled her eyes. "It's totally not your fault. You're my sister, not my mother." She lifted a green bean then dropped it back into her bowl. "It's not your job to teach me how to cook."

Biologically that was true, but in every other sense of the relationship, Amanda had acted as Lacy's mother since she was very small. "Okay, it's not my job, but I want to do it. It'll be fun."

Lacy thought about it then nodded. "So what do you want me to cook first?"

"How about meatloaf?" Amanda figured that would be hard to mess up.

She watched Lacy mull over the idea. "Okay, but I want you to let me do it all. You can be there, but I don't want you touching it."

Amanda lifted her hands. "I'll be totally hands-off. Why don't I make you a shopping list so you can get everything you need, and when I get home, we can get started right away?"

Lacy frowned. "I wanted to go to the mall tomorrow. Can you stop off on your way home and get the stuff?"

So much for being hands-off. "Sure, I can do that." She stood and carried her bowl to the sink. "Let's get these dishes done so we can walk down to the beach and watch the sunset."

Lacy tilted her head to one side and gave Amanda a look she knew very well. "I hope you don't mind, but I promised Brad I'd meet him for ice cream…" She glanced at the clock. "In about fifteen minutes."

Maybe Lacy was hopeless. "Okay, go ahead then. I'll clean up."

Amanda seethed as her sister headed back to her room to primp before running off to meet Brad. She wondered if Timmy would be with him or if he'd be stuck with the teenage sitter.

Lacy popped into the kitchen on her way out. "In case you're wondering, Timmy is acting a little better in the classroom. I told Brad what you said, that it might be a good idea to give him a little more of his time, and it seems to be working."

"That's good."

"No, really," Lacy said as she hovered at the door. "I really do think he wants to do the right thing. It's just that he has never known what that was."

Amanda saw her sister's sincerity. "I'm happy for both of them."

Lacy waved her fingers. "I won't be too late. I have to get up early tomorrow." The door slammed behind her, leaving Amanda alone to finish cleaning the kitchen.

Her anger now diffused, Amanda's thoughts drifted to other things… like Jerry and his folks. She didn't expect a future with Jerry, but she had to admit that she enjoyed hanging out with him. His parents' matchmaking attempts were a little annoying, but they were cute.

Lacy was only gone a couple of hours, but when she walked in, she had a dreamy look on her face. Amanda liked seeing her sister happy, so she went to bed feeling good. The next morning, Lacy was gone by the time Amanda got to the kitchen. She'd left a note on the counter letting her know they'd have to put off her meatloaf cooking lesson for a few days because she had plans for dinner. That was fine with Amanda. The rest of the week was uneventful, with the exception of seeing Rosemary and Harold riding past her shop on their rented bicycle-built-for-two. They always slowed way down and sometimes stopped as Rosemary pretended to adjust something with her shoe or pants. Amanda knew they hoped for a chance encounter with her, and she made sure it didn't happen. It didn't seem right, since Jerry wasn't there.

On Sunday morning, Amanda awoke with a hint of expectation and a healthy dose of self-restraint from rushing to the church. She hated to admit, even to herself, how much she looked forward to seeing Jerry after not even a glimpse of him for days.

She forced herself to slow down during a light breakfast of oatmeal and orange juice. Lacy had decided to sleep in, something she did more often than not on Sunday mornings, to Amanda's dismay. It was much more difficult getting Lacy to church these days, now that she had so many other things on her plate. Amanda prayed for her sister daily, and she knew she needed to leave all the saving up to the Lord.

Standing in front of her closet, Amanda surveyed the possibilities of what to wear. Since she wore athletic clothes to work all week, she only had a few nicer things suitable for church. *Hmm. Maybe the sale is still going on at the mall.* She made a mental note to make a trip to her sister's favorite department store.

She finally settled on a pair of lightweight navy slacks and a sleeveless white cotton button-front blouse with a tie neckline. On her way out the door, she stepped into a pair of closed-toe flats. Yeah, she looked drab, but until now, she never really cared—at least not since Eric.

After pulling into the church parking lot, Amanda's skin tingled with excitement over the mere thought of seeing Jerry. She forced herself to hold back as she said a prayer for peace and the ability to keep her emotions in check. The last thing she needed was to get all worked up over a guy who wouldn't be here more than a few weeks.

Finally, she sucked in a breath and got out. The sun had already heated up the blacktop, so she hurried toward the air-conditioned church situated in a strip center on the edge of Treasure Island. Since all the other businesses in the building were closed on Sunday mornings, she knew the church would be packed, based on the number of cars in the parking lot.

The first thing she did once she got inside was scan the crowd. No sign of Jerry or his parents. Suzanne had turned around and was waving for her to join her. She grinned at her friend and made her way to the second row from the front.

"Looking for someone?" Suzanne asked. "I heard you invited that handsome guy who brought his parents down on vacation."

"Lacy has a big mouth."

Suzanne smiled and turned to face the front, where the band had already begun playing one of her favorite worship songs. The services lasted a full hour and then the pastor invited all visitors to hang around for coffee and pastries. Since she'd forced herself to keep looking straight ahead, Amanda wondered if Jerry was somewhere behind her.

As soon as they were dismissed, she darted over toward the room they used to greet visitors, but there was no sign of Jerry. Disappointment washed over her.

She'd left her Sunday school workbook in the car, and since she still had about twenty minutes before it started, she ran out to get it.

"Amanda, sweetie, we've been looking all over for you." Rosemary's strong, raspy voice caught her attention. She turned around and spotted Jerry standing between both of his parents—all of them dressed a little nicer than anyone else in the church. Her heart flipped as she waved back and headed toward them.

"I was close to the front," Amanda said.

Rosemary rolled her eyes. "These two took forever getting ready, so we slipped in a little late and had to sit in the very back along the wall. I could barely hear the preacher, but it sounded like a nice message."

"Yeah, I like what he said about finding heavenly treasures here on earth," Harold added.

Rosemary gave him one of her trademark looks. "You would."

Amanda forced herself to overcome the fluttering sensation that had accosted her. "We're about to start Sunday school. You're welcome to join us."

Jerry glanced at his parents then looked at her. "Maybe next week. We need to get back to the condo."

Harold looked tired. He was a little more hunched over than normal, so Amanda nodded. "I understand." Even Rosemary appeared wiped out. Her heart went out to the Simpson family.

Rosemary clicked her tongue as one side of her mouth quirked. "I've got an idea. Jerry, why don't you take us to the condo and come back?"

Jerry looked lost for a second before he recovered and turned to Amanda. "How long do I have?"

She glanced at her watch. "Fifteen minutes, but it's okay if you walk

in a little late. We generally do a round of introductions before the
Bible study actually begins."

"Okay, let's go, folks," Jerry said as he ushered his parents away. He
turned back to Amanda. "Save me a seat, okay?"

She nodded and smiled as she went to her car for the workbook.
Suddenly, her heart felt lighter than it had in days.

Chapter Five

....

Amanda told Suzanne she was waiting for Jerry and then took a seat near the door. She didn't think Jerry could possibly make it back on time, but the group was larger than usual, and it took awhile for Pastor Zach to get everyone's attention.

"Hey, thanks for saving my seat," Jerry said as he slipped into the chair next to her. "My parents have been pushing themselves pretty hard lately, so I needed to get them back to rest."

"I understand," Amanda said, as she opened her workbook to the page where she'd filled in the blanks for the weekly Bible lesson. She showed him the verse they were studying, so he opened his Bible to follow along.

After introducing himself, Pastor Zachary Holister had everyone say their names and where they were from. Then he asked everyone to bow their heads for an opening prayer.

As she sat there while Pastor Zach prayed, she was aware of the effect Jerry's presence had on her nerves. It had been a very long time since she'd been in church with a man. When the prayer ended and she opened her eyes, she turned to Jerry. He sat staring straight ahead at the pastor, who'd taken his place on a stool at the front of the room.

The Bible study lasted about forty-five minutes. As Pastor Zach wrapped it up, he invited anyone with questions to go to the front of the room, and then he was swarmed.

Jerry turned to Amanda and gave her a thumbs-up. "He's a gifted preacher."

Amanda nodded. "We're fortunate to have someone who can relate to so many people."

He shifted from one foot to the other. "I'd like to chat with him, but I don't want to leave my parents alone too much longer."

"They're probably fine," Amanda said. "They just looked exhausted, but I bet that's from doing so much. I know how I am when I go on vacation. I want to get it all in before I come back home."

He cleared his throat and looked around before settling his gaze back on her. "I wish that's all it was. There's something I failed to mention. Not only is my dad in the early stages of Alzheimer's, but my mother just found out she has Parkinson's. They're in an independent-living retirement facility in Atlanta, but it's just a matter of time before they either have to go into assisted living or move in with me."

Amanda's heart lurched. "Oh, I didn't realize that."

"I know." Jerry gestured toward the door. "Let's walk out together… that is, unless you want to hang around for something."

"No, I'll walk with you." They headed out in silence, and when it was time to part ways in the parking lot, she turned to face him. "Is there anything I can do? I mean, if you need someone to help out or something…"

He slowly broke into a grin and shook his head. "I appreciate it, but I think we'll be fine. They're still able to do things without me, but they tire easily and Mom is so worried all the time. That's part of the problem. In case you haven't noticed, they're on edge with each other."

Amanda opened her mouth but closed it before she stuck her foot in it. From what she could tell, Jerry was at least as worried and as on edge as his parents were. Calling that to Jerry's attention wouldn't bode well at the moment.

"Thanks for inviting us to your church." Jerry took a step back.

"I'm glad you all came." Suddenly, Amanda remembered his mother's address book. She pulled it out of her handbag and handed it to Jerry. "Do you mind giving this to your mom?"

Jerry chuckled as he took it from her. "She doesn't give up."

"I can see that." The brief brush of his hand against hers sent a tingle up her arm.

He hesitated for a moment before lifting his hand in a wave. "See ya."

Amanda turned and headed toward her car, but she heard her name. Suzanne was flailing her arms. "I wondered where you went after the Bible study!"

"What's up?" Amanda asked.

Suzanne looked like she was ready to pop with excitement. "Jerry is very cute! So what's next with you two?"

Amanda shook her head. "He's a nice guy, and I'm trying to make sure they have a good vacation."

"Why is he with his parents?"

After Amanda explained what Jerry just told her, Suzanne's eyes widened and she nodded her approval. "Don't let this one get away, Amanda. Any guy who cares enough about his parents to take them on vacation is a great catch."

"I'm not looking to catch anything."

"That's your problem. You're letting one lousy experience with a guy who was a complete idiot get away with messing up your whole life."

"That's not true." Amanda looked down and kicked the asphalt with the toe of her shoe. "My life is just fine without a man, and I don't want to change anything."

"I've got news for you, girl. Your life is going to change, no matter what you do or don't do. The Lord has brought this wonderful man into your life, so don't let him slip away."

Amanda snickered. Leave it to her friend to find a spiritual angle. "I'll keep that in mind."

"Seriously. He's a Christian, he's nice, he loves his family, and he obviously likes you. What's wrong with giving him a chance and seeing where this thing can go?"

"I don't know, Suzanne. I just don't think I'm ready."

"You'll never be ready unless you open up a little." Suzanne reached out and placed her hand on Amanda's shoulder. "I'm not saying you have to fall in love with him and make plans for the future. All I want is for you to open up to the possibility of a relationship."

"I'll think about it." Amanda hugged her friend. "Thanks for caring. I need to run. Why don't you stop by the shop one afternoon this week, and we can hang out for a little while?"

"Okay, fine. I know when you're closing me off. But you know I won't give up, right?"

Amanda nodded. "Yeah, you can be pretty persistent."

"Only because I know what's good for you."

"At least someone does." Amanda unlocked her car door and got in. "See you soon, okay?"

"Oh yeah, you can count on it." The sound of Suzanne's laughter faded as Amanda closed her car door.

All the way home, she thought about Jerry's parents. She knew they had some physical limitations, but she didn't realize how serious they were. From what she knew, neither Alzheimer's nor Parkinson's could be reversed. She wondered about the brother and sister Jerry had told her about. Were they as active in Rosemary and Harold's lives as Jerry was?

When she got home, she found Lacy still in her nightgown, sitting at the kitchen table sipping coffee and flipping through a fashion magazine. She glanced up. "So how was church?"

"You might want to go sometime and see for yourself."

"My, aren't we snippy today?" Lacy stood up, crossed the kitchen, and poured more coffee.

Amanda instantly felt bad. Sarcastic comments weren't good for a gentle witness, and they definitely wouldn't make her sister want to go to church. "Sorry."

"That's okay. I figure something must have happened between you and Jerry, or you'd be a lot happier."

Okay, that did it. "Why does everyone think my moods can be made or broken by Jerry? He's a nice guy, but I have a perfectly fine life without a man in it."

Lacy held up her hands and leaned away from Amanda. "Whoa, you're really in a snit today. Sorry I said a word. Let me know when I can talk to you without having my head bitten off."

"I'm sorry." Amanda looked down at the magazine. "So what's the latest in fashion?"

Lacy turned the magazine around so Amanda could see the picture. "Look at these Louboutins. Aren't they the cutest?"

"How can anyone walk in those?" The heels had to be at least four inches high.

"Lots of girls wear them." Lacy gave her a pleading look. "I want some."

"Where would you wear them? Certainly not to work." The mental image of Lacy teaching kindergarten in stilts made her giggle.

"Of course not, silly." Lacy ran her fingertips lovingly across the page, as if she could actually feel the shoes. "These are special-occasion shoes."

"There's no occasion special enough for me to ever wear something that I'd never be able to stand up in," Amanda admitted.

"What if Jerry asks you out to someplace really nice?"

Amanda sat down at the table and started fidgeting with the placemat. She felt Lacy watching her, but she wasn't sure what to say. Both Lacy and Suzanne had acted like she and Jerry should be an item, so she must have given off some sort of signal that indicated that. Now she needed to undo whatever she'd done to give them the impression that there was even a chance. She flipped the edge of the placemat back and forth a couple of times, creating a rhythmic *thump-thump*.

After a few seconds, Lacy reached out and grabbed Amanda's fidgety hand. "Stop doing that. It annoys me."

If Amanda told Lacy all the things she did that were annoying, they'd be here all day. Instead, she stood up. "I think I'll change clothes and go for a bike ride."

"That's your answer to everything, isn't it?" Lacy said. "Have a bad day, ride your bike. Too many customers, ride your bike. Not enough customers, ride your bike. Argue with me, ride your bike. You need to give yourself some time to deal with your issues and not just take off on your bicycle every time something happens that you don't like."

Amanda stopped in her tracks and planted her fists on her hips. "And how do you suggest I do this?"

Lacy shrugged. "I don't know. Maybe just be still for a while."

As much as Amanda hated to admit it, her sister was right. When she wasn't busy, her mind raced, and that was depressing. So she rode her bike to let the Gulf breeze lift her problems and take them away.

"I can't just sit around here all day. What do you suggest I do?"

Lacy stood up, grinning. "Let's go shopping. You need some new things."

"Like what?" Amanda couldn't keep her voice from squeaking.

"Like some new clothes and makeup. You've been stuck in a rut, and you could certainly update your look."

Amanda had no doubt Lacy wanted to make her over for the relationship she was supposedly having with Jerry. No matter how many times Amanda denied there was anything between them but friendship, Lacy stuck to her fairy-tale dreams. Oh, what did it matter? Her wardrobe was rather boring. Maybe a couple of new tops and a brighter shade of lipstick would serve two purposes: It would get Lacy off her back, and it would add some choices for what to wear to church.

"Okay, but don't even try to talk me into any of those killer high heels."

Lacy giggled. "Don't worry. If I see them, they're mine anyway."

An hour later, they were on their way to the mall in St. Petersburg—something that always brought a smile to Lacy's face and a lilt to her voice. "The sales are still going on, but they might be picked over."

"That's fine," Amanda said. "I'm not all that picky—at least not about what I wear."

Lacy widened her eyes and offered an exaggerated nod. "I know, and that's part of the problem."

Amanda felt her jaw tighten. If she talked to Lacy like Lacy talked to her, they'd be in an all-out sister war.

* * * * *

Jerry had looked in all of the rooms and still his parents were nowhere in sight. Their queen-size bed showed signs that someone had lain down on top of the comforter; it was still rumpled. It had only been an hour and a half since he'd dropped them off—not nearly enough time to get the rest they said they needed.

At least his mother was gone, too, so they were probably together. He would have been more worried if his dad had gone out by himself since even at the early stage, the Alzheimer's took away his sense of direction.

He'd hoped to treat his parents to lunch out, but since he had no idea where they were or when they'd be back, he decided to fix something at the condo. As he put the finishing touches on club sandwiches, he heard the door open and slam shut. Then his mother's voice echoed through the condo.

"Harold, you can be such a pill sometimes."

Jerry cringed. Before his parents were diagnosed with Alzheimer's and Parkinson's, they rarely argued. Now the tension was so tight, he felt like he was walking on eggshells most of the time.

"Mom, Dad, I have lunch ready," he called out, trying his best to sound cheerful.

His dad was the first to appear in the kitchen doorway. "What did you fix?"

"Sandwiches." Jerry gestured toward the table where he'd put their heaping plates.

"That's not lunch," his dad grumbled. "It's a snack."

His mother stabbed her finger toward the chair. "Just sit down, Harold. When your son goes to this much trouble, you don't need to act out."

"He's your son, too."

Jerry cleared his throat. "When I came back and didn't see anyone here, I was worried."

His dad pointed to his mom. "Your mother got some lamebrained notion that we could go watch turtles mate." He snorted. "That sounds about as exciting as watching paint dry."

"That's not exactly true, Harold, and you know it." She turned to Jerry. "One of the ladies downstairs told me that this is turtle nesting season. I just wanted to see if I could find some of their nests."

"Did you see any?" Jerry asked.

Once again, his dad spoke up. "All we saw was a bunch of half-naked bodies covered in grease and sand."

"Stop complaining, Harold." Jerry could hear the weariness in his mother's voice.

"Oh, I'm not complaining." He lifted a section of his sandwich and inspected it. "What all did you put in here? No onions, I hope. They give me heartburn."

"No onions," Jerry assured him. "Just a little honey maple turkey, some turkey bacon, lettuce, tomatoes, and cheese."

"Turkey bacon, huh?" His dad made a throaty noise. "That's not real bacon. What's wrong with pork?"

"Nothing's wrong with pork bacon if you don't care about your cholesterol," his mother said.

"No one ever worried about cholesterol until some health nuts started telling everyone it was bad for us."

Jerry held his hands up to silence his parents. "Okay, you two. That's enough. You never let us kids get away with arguing at the table, and I'm not going to let y'all do it. Let's say our blessing and enjoy our food. If you want to argue later, fine. But not now."

"Did you hear the boy?" Jerry's dad grinned with pride. "He actually paid attention all those years."

"So tell me more about the nesting turtles," Jerry asked his mother.

"According to our neighbor, loggerheads make nests on the beach around this time every year."

"Sounds interesting," Jerry said. "I wonder if we'll see them."

Jerry noticed his dad intently eating his sandwich and pretending not to listen. His mother shot a glance in her husband's direction then turned back to face Jerry.

"I certainly hope so. It would be a shame to miss something so special…so natural to this place."

After lunch, both of his parents headed off to their room for naps. Jerry took his time cleaning the kitchen and trying to think of something his parents might enjoy later. Maybe Amanda would know of something.

* * * * *

When Amanda's cell phone rang, she was tempted not to answer. One of the two people who ever called her was with her, and the other—her mother—was on a cruise with some friends.

"I hate it when people just let their phones ring," Lacy said. "At least look and see who it is."

Amanda pulled it out and saw a different area code, so she punched the TALK button and said, "Hello?"

The sound of Jerry's voice gave her an instant tingle. She rubbed the goose bumps on her arm and glanced over to see if Lacy noticed. The smile on her sister's lips let her know nothing had gotten past her sister's eagle eyes.

"I'm looking for something to do with my folks this afternoon. Any ideas?"

"Um…" She glanced over to Lacy, who watched with a smirk. "Can I call you back in a few minutes?"

"Sure, take your time."

"It'll only be a few minutes," she said. "Want me to call this number?"

"That's fine."

As soon as she flipped her phone shut, she glared right back at Lacy. "Why are you looking at me that way?"

Lacy tilted her head back and laughed. "You should see the goofy look on your face when you talk to Jerry."

"How do you know it's Jerry?" She cleared her throat to get rid of the squeak in her voice.

Lacy was still grinning. "C'mon, Amanda. I can tell."

Time to change the subject. "Okay, so I need to call him back with something for him and his parents to do this afternoon."

Lacy lifted a finger to her chin as she thought about it. She really was a sweet person—just a little misguided about some things. "What do they like?"

"I'm thinking maybe a movie," Amanda said.

"They can do that anywhere. How about one of the day cruises?"

"It's probably too late for that," Amanda replied. "But that's a good idea for another day."

"There's always shopping."

Amanda smiled. "Yes, and I need to call him back so we can finish ours."

She pulled up Jerry's number and punched CALL. He answered before the end of the first ring. "What took you so long?" His chuckle let her know he was kidding.

"Why don't you take them to a movie today and maybe to one of the day cruises tomorrow?"

"Good idea," he said. "Any chance you might want to join us for a movie since your store is closed?"

"Sounds good, but I'm at the mall with my sister, and we probably won't be back for another hour or two."

"The folks are napping, so that sounds perfect." He paused before adding, "That is, if you'd like to join us."

"Okay," she blurted. "Want me to meet you somewhere?"

"We can pick you up at your place," he offered. "Or if you're not comfortable with us doing that…" His voice trailed off.

Since he'd put it that way, she didn't want to say no. However, it now seemed an awful lot like a date.

"That's fine." She gave him her address as Lacy stared at her, looking smug.

Once she got off the phone, Lacy smirked but didn't say a word. That drove Amanda even crazier than if she'd had to endure her sister's relentless taunting.

"Okay, so I'm going out with Jerry and his parents. Are you happy now?"

Lacy quirked an eyebrow. "The question is, are *you* happy?"

Amanda looked away. "Stop it. Let's get this shopping thing over with so we can get back home."

"For once, that sounds like an excellent idea," Lacy said. "As much as I enjoy shopping, your love life must come first."

"Wait a minute!" Amanda felt the heat rise to her face as she thrust her fist onto her hip. "No one said anything about a love life."

"Then don't get so worked up. I just made a comment."

Lacy was right. "Okay, we can let it drop then." Amanda had gotten way too worked up over a silly little comment.

"Besides, Brad and Timmy are stopping by a little later. They're taking me to dinner."

"Do you think that's such a good idea, with Timmy being one of your students?"

Lacy looked genuinely puzzled. "Why wouldn't it be?"

* * * * *

Jerry went out onto the balcony to read the Sunday paper. He heard the sliding glass door and turned to face his mother. "Did you get enough rest?"

"Yeah, until the bear's snoring woke me up."

"Mom, seriously, you and Dad need to stop this sniping at each other."

Her shoulders sagged as she stared out over the Gulf. "Yes, you're probably right. We've gotten into a bad habit, I'm afraid."

"Then just break it."

She looked at him and smiled. "It's not as easy as all that. We've been doing this for years—since you kids grew up and left."

"I've been around you enough to know it hasn't always been this bad. Last year when we came here on vacation, you actually seemed to enjoy each other."

"Anyone can behave for a couple of weeks," she said. "If you think back, your father and I barely spoke to each other during the whole vacation last year."

Now that he thought about it…

"We made a pact to not talk so you wouldn't worry. But this year, we didn't. I figured you needed to see how things really were."

Jerry was puzzled. "But why would you ever hide anything from me? I'm your son. I love both of you no matter what."

She leaned down and gave him a brief hug but quickly straightened up. "We love you, too, and that's why we tried to protect you from the ugly truth."

Worry coursed through him. "Is there something you're not telling me?"

She shook her head. "Nothing you haven't already seen on this trip. Your father is getting more and more difficult to live with, and we haven't gotten along in a long time. I'm not sure how much longer I can control him."

Jerry looked out over the water as he inhaled deeply and slowly blew out his breath before turning to face her. "Have you thought that maybe you shouldn't try to control him?"

"You've seen him. He wanders off, and he gets mad at the slightest thing."

Jerry nodded. "Yes, and you fuss at him all the time. Maybe you should try a different approach."

She folded her arms. "Like what?"

He shrugged. "Maybe smile a little more and let him know you love him."

With a flip of her hand, she backed into the condo. "He knows I love him. I wouldn't put up with his nonsense if I didn't."

After she closed the door, he lowered his head and prayed for his parents. Yes, things were getting increasingly difficult, but it wasn't just his dad. His mother's lack of tolerance didn't make the situation any easier to deal with. And maybe, just maybe, he was guilty of interfering a tad too much.

Jerry went back inside as his dad came out of the bedroom. "Dad, why don't you go comb your hair and go for a walk with me?"

"You don't like my hair?" He reached up and smoothed it. "You should see how some of the kids wear theirs."

His mom laughed. "You're not a kid. You just act like—"

She stopped as Jerry turned and gave her a warning look. She rolled her eyes and ducked back into the kitchen.

"Where do you wanna go?" his dad asked.

"Just around the block. I have plans for us in a little while, and I'd like to talk to you first."

After a brief pause, his dad nodded. "Go on outside. I'll be right there."

Jerry waited less than a minute before his dad joined him. "Okay, so what did I do wrong this time?"

"I never said you did anything wrong. It's just that...well, I've noticed how you and Mom bicker a lot."

His dad chuckled. "Is that what you call it? Seems to me more like nagging."

Jerry snorted. "Dad, seriously, this has me worried."

"That's your problem. You worry too much. Your mother and I are fine. We're annoyed at some things, but it's nothing you can do anything about." He took a few steps before adding, "None of us can do anything about it—not even the doctors."

"I'd like to see you at least try to get along."

The elderly man snickered. "Where's the fun in that?"

"Speaking of fun," Jerry said, "I've made plans for you, Mom, and me to go to the movies with Amanda this afternoon."

"Did you tell your mother yet?"

"No, not yet. I—"

His dad interrupted. "Why don't you run along with Amanda and leave us here?"

"No." The word escaped Jerry's mouth too quickly. He cleared his throat. "I'm here with you and Mom, and I want us to do stuff together. Besides, I think Amanda might enjoy it more if it doesn't seem like too much of a date."

"What's wrong with a date? Most girls like dates."

Jerry shrugged. "I'm not sure. She seems a little skittish about anything that resembles a date, and I don't want to frighten her."

"I never heard that one before, but if you think it'll help your cause with this girl, sure. It might be fun to see how my son operates." He grabbed his collar with both hands and pretended to smooth it. "Your old man was once a very smooth operator."

"Dad..." Jerry turned to warn his dad, but when he saw the smile quirking his father's lips, he stopped. "This should be fun."

By now, they'd circled the block, so they headed back to the condo. "Let me talk to your mother about our non-date with Amanda."

Jerry laughed. "Okay, I'll go get ready."

When he came back out to the living room, both his parents looked him up and down. "Are you wearing that?" his mother finally asked, pointing to his clothes.

He glanced down then looked back at her. "What's wrong with it?"

"Nothing, if you like boring."

"Leave the boy alone," his dad piped up. "You can't pick out his clothes forever."

Jerry shot him a warning look, making the elderly man chuckle. His mother pursed her lips and shook her head.

"What would you like for me to wear, Mom?"

She frowned and thought for a moment. "I guess what you have on is okay. But maybe we need to take a trip to a men's store soon. I can help you pick out some things that are more flattering."

"Ready?" Jerry asked and crooked his elbow in her direction.

"I s'pose," she said as she took Jerry's arm. "I'm not sure we're doing the right thing, tagging along like this."

He patted her hand. "Trust me, Mom, it's the right thing."

Amanda was waiting outside when they pulled up to her house. Jerry wasn't surprised.

She ran to the SUV, and he barely had time to get out, go around, and open the door for her. As soon as she got in and bucked her seat belt, she turned and grinned at his parents. "Enjoying your vacation?"

"Very much," his mother said in a too-formal tone.

His dad snickered. "I'm thinking about taking up surfing."

"Too bad the waves are too small for surfing," Amanda said, "or I'd join you."

He nudged his wife. "See, there's one girl who knows how to have fun."

Amanda tossed Jerry a confused look. He just shrugged.

* * * * *

The tension in the car was so thick, Amanda wasn't sure if she'd made the right decision. But here she was, and she was determined to make the most of it.

"Have you decided on a movie?"

He handed her the paper. "I thought you could pick. I don't know anything about any of them."

Amanda scanned the listings. "Do we want to see adventure, science fiction, or romantic comedy?"

"Romance sounds good to me," Harold quipped. "Anything else might be bad for my heart."

Chapter Six

....

Jerry cast a quick glance in his rearview mirror in time to catch his dad's twinkling eye. There was no doubt what he was up to.

"How about you, Amanda?" He stopped for a traffic light and turned to face her. "What do you prefer?"

Red had crept up her neck and covered her face. She was on to his dad, too. She shrugged. "I'm open to anything as long as it's not too gory or risqué."

Jerry wasn't sure if this was such a good idea—all four of them going to a movie. But it was too late to change that now.

"How about an animated movie?" he offered.

She smiled. "Yeah, that might be good. That is, if your parents are okay with it."

"Sure," his mother piped up, "I'm always up for a cartoon."

"Then animated it is," Jerry said.

Even though Amanda tried to pay her own way and his mother grabbed her wallet, Jerry insisted on paying for all four tickets. Once inside, his parents told him and Amanda to find seats and said they'd be right there.

His folks joined them with containers of popcorn and four soft drinks. "I hope you like cola," Jerry's mother said. "The line was long, and I didn't want to have to go back, so I got us all the same thing."

"Sure, that's fine," Amanda said. "But you didn't have to get me anything."

"I know," Rosemary said, "but we wanted to."

"A movie's no fun without popcorn and a drink," his dad said.

With three sets of eyes on her, Amanda smiled. "Thank you."

Jerry sat on one end with Amanda next to him then his mom and his dad beside her. While the two women chatted, he focused on the advertisements on the screen until the movie started. After it was over, Jerry stood up and stretched then instinctively reached for Amanda's hand. She blinked, offered a shaky smile, and took his hand in hers. His mother leaned over, winked, and gave him a thumbs-up.

Once they got outside, his dad announced that he was starving and wanted some pizza. Amanda said she knew of a wonderful pizza place on Treasure Island. "GiGi's has the best pizza in the area, and the employees are my customers."

"Then we'll go to GiGi's." His dad puffed up his chest. "Any customer of yours is a friend of mine."

As they waited for their order, Jerry reached for his mother's and Amanda's hands. "Let's go ahead and say our blessing before the food arrives."

* * * * *

Jerry was sweet and comfortable to be around. However, she felt some tension between him and his parents, and she couldn't put her finger on the cause. Harold kept the conversation going, even though Rosemary shot him warning glances. Amanda didn't know why, though, because the man was downright charming.

The waiter brought the pizza and placed it in the middle. "Smells delicious," Rosemary said.

"It's the best in the area," the waiter said. "Would you like anything else?"

Jerry shook his head. "We're fine." He helped his dad with a slice of pizza and offered to get his mother one. She grabbed the server from him and got not only her first slice, but also Amanda's.

"So, Amanda, how long have you lived on Treasure Island?" Rosemary asked.

"All my life."

"That's amazing. Not many people live somewhere all their lives."

Amanda nodded. "Especially in this area. I've seen some huge population growth."

"I can imagine." Rosemary took a sip of her tea and looked back and forth between Amanda and Jerry. "This is such a beautiful place; I can see why people want to move here. In fact, we've been thinking about it."

"No, we haven't," Harold blurted, holding his slice of pizza a couple of inches from his mouth. "Why are you making up stories, Rosemary?"

"You have pizza on your chin, Harold." Rosemary dipped her napkin in his glass of water and started to dab his face.

He swatted at her. "Stop that. I can wipe my own face."

Rosemary glared at him before turning back to Amanda. "This really is a lovely place."

Amanda nodded. "I agree. It's beautiful." She cast a nervous glance toward Jerry, who shook his head.

"Jerry, did your mother tell you she's become a turtle lover?" Harold barked. "Next thing ya know, she'll be out there hugging palm trees."

"At least I'm not on some stupid treasure hunt all the time," she snapped back. "Amanda, my husband seems to think there's buried treasure somewhere on this island."

His lip curled. "I never said it was buried. I just think—"

"Well, there's probably not any treasure around here anyway," she said, "buried or not."

"Then tell me something, Miss Know-It-All." Harold leaned forward, his eyes wide and his expression demanding. "If there's no treasure, why do they call it Treasure Island?"

Rosemary held out her hands. "How should I know?" She looked at Amanda. "Was there ever a treasure on Treasure Island?"

"Actually, back in the early 1900s, one of the first developers came up with a gimmick to get people interested in his land. He claimed he'd found treasure on the beach, and word spread."

"How interesting," Rosemary said as she tilted her head and smiled at her husband. "So there's no treasure here after all." She paused while Harold fidgeted. "Did you hear that, Harold? It was just a real-estate gimmick."

"Yeah, I heard, but that doesn't mean there's not any treasure now. I think there is." He pounded his fist on the table, causing the patrons at the next table to look.

"Dad," Jerry said softly as he patted his dad's shoulder. "Calm down, please."

Amanda's heart went out to Jerry's dad. He obviously wanted to believe there was treasure on the island, and suddenly she wanted it, too.

"So what else can you tell us about this island?" Rosemary urged.

"Well…" Amanda looked at Jerry, who offered an encouraging nod. "The first people here came from several walks of life, including fishermen and pirates."

"There ya go," Harold said. "That just proves it. Wherever you see a pirate, there'll be some treasure. Everyone knows that."

"Let her finish," Rosemary said. "Go on, Amanda, I want to hear more."

As they ate their pizza, Amanda told them everything she could think of about the history of Treasure Island. She was thankful for the conversation because it kept her from having to answer too many personal questions. By the time she finished the history lesson, the pizza was gone and the server had brought the check.

"Ready to head home?" Jerry asked.

On the way to Amanda's house, Rosemary started with the personal questions. "How long have you lived in that house?"

"Most of my adult life," Amanda replied. "I bought it as soon as I had enough for a down payment."

"I'm impressed," Rosemary said. "Do you plan to stay there?"

"Yes, I think so. It's small, but it's close to my shop, and I really don't need any more space—especially after my sister moves out."

Jerry reached over and touched her hand to get her attention. When she looked at him, he mouthed, "Sorry."

"Are your folks still around?" Harold asked.

"Harold!" Rosemary's voice was shrill.

"What?" he asked. "Weren't you wondering the same thing?"

"Let's not drive Amanda crazy with so many questions at once," Jerry said.

"That's okay." Amanda cleared her throat. "I'm not sure where my dad is, but my mother lives in a house not far from mine."

"That's nice," Rosemary said. "I'd like to meet her someday." She paused then started up again. "Your house looks very charming. What kind of car do you drive?"

"Mom." Jerry cast a warning glance in the rearview mirror toward his mother.

"Okay, okay, I was just asking. If Amanda doesn't want to answer my questions, all she has to do is say so."

"I think we need to give her a break from interrogation." Amanda appreciated the firmness of Jerry's voice.

They rode the rest of the way in silence. When Jerry pulled up to the curb in front of her house, she turned to thank everyone and let them know what a nice time she had.

"I'm thirsty," Harold said. "Got a glass of water for an old man?"

"We're five minutes from our condo, Harold. You can wait."

"I figured you wanted to see her place," he mumbled. "I was only trying to help."

"If you're thirsty—" Amanda began before Jerry gave her a look that stopped her.

"That's okay," Jerry said. He got out and walked around to hold the door for Amanda. His parents were sweethearts, but she was exhausted and needed some time to herself.

On the way to her door, Jerry apologized profusely for his parents' behavior. "I don't know what's gotten into them. Mom never used to be this bossy. A little manipulative, maybe, but she used to be quite a bit more subtle. And my dad, well…" Amanda detected the pain in his voice as it trailed off.

"Really, Jerry, I understand. Wait until you meet my mom." She suddenly caught herself. What was she saying? Why would he ever meet her mother?

He grinned. "I'm glad you understand."

They'd reached her door, so Amanda fumbled for her house key. As she turned toward Jerry, she saw his parents watching from the car. Surely he wouldn't try to kiss her.

"I had a wonderful time, Jerry. Your parents are very sweet, and they're just trying to deal with aging."

"Yes, and I'm afraid they're not dealing very well."

"Your mother likes to feel needed."

"I know. Too bad she doesn't have her grandchildren nearby. My sister and brother don't bring their families around much." His voice cracked, so Amanda knew this was a painful topic.

"Maybe she'll find a cause—something she can do to help others."

Jerry shrugged. "I don't know. If I suggest things, she's quick to let me know all the reasons she can't."

"It's hard taking care of parents." She quickly decided it would be okay to admit her own relationship with her mother. "My mom wears me out with some of her issues."

"You two gonna stand there all day?" his dad bellowed from the car.

Amanda smiled and waved at the elderly couple in the car. "I'd better go in."

Jerry reached for both of her hands and leaned over to kiss her on the cheek. She felt her face heat up as she turned away and shoved her key in the door. When the door closed behind her, she heard the sound of his car pulling away.

She'd barely been inside long enough to turn on the lights and kick off her shoes when she heard her sister's voice, letting her know they weren't alone. As much as she wanted to hide in her room, she was also curious about Brad, so she headed to the living room.

"Hey, there," Lacy said. "Have fun with Jerry and his parents?"

"Yes," Amanda replied as she turned to the very tall, very handsome man standing beside her sister. She extended her hand. "I'm Amanda Burns, Lacy's sister."

"Sorry," Lacy said. "This is Brad…" Her gaze lingered on him for a couple of seconds before she gestured toward the little boy sitting on the edge of the sofa, who was rolling a toy car over the palm of his hand. "And that's Timmy."

"Hi, Timmy." Amanda smiled, but he broke eye contact and went back to fidgeting with his car, so she turned to Brad. "So how was dinner?"

He looked annoyed as he pointed to his son. "Would've been good if we didn't have so many interruptions."

Amanda blinked. She didn't like what she was seeing. Brad never should have said that in front of his son. "He's just a little boy. I think interrupting is what they do best."

Brad raked his fingers through his close-cropped hair. "I've tried teaching him manners, but he doesn't listen very well."

Timmy jumped down off the sofa and zoomed his toy car over her coffee table. Amanda had no doubt he was reacting to his father's comments.

"No, Timmy!" Brad took a couple of strides toward his son, but Amanda held up her hand to stop him.

"Hey, Timmy, do you wanna see my bicycle collection?" she asked.

"He doesn't want to see that," Lacy whined.

"I do, too!" Timmy scowled at Lacy then turned and looked at Amanda. "Where is it?"

Amanda turned toward the sunroom and motioned for Lacy and Brad to stay put. Timmy was right beside her.

Before she opened the cabinet to show Timmy her display, Amanda squatted down next to him. "Do you know what an antique is?"

His eyes widened, and he shook his head no. "What's a 'tique?"

Amanda smiled. "An antique is something that's really old. Some of my bicycles are antiques."

"Why do you have old stuff?"

"Because it's valuable. It was owned by someone who really liked it, and now I have it because I really like looking at it. Sometimes really old things are breakable, though, so we have to be very careful with them."

"Can I see?" His eyes were wide as he turned to the cabinet.

She hesitated. Had she made a mistake? *Too late now,* she thought with a tinge of regret. "You can look, but don't touch them."

"Okay."

As Amanda slowly opened the cabinet, Timmy's eyes grew even wider. "See that one in the corner?"

He nodded.

"It was my grandfather's. He used to build bicycles for a company up north, and they gave him that for helping design a new model."

"Wow." He turned to her with a quizzical expression. "Do you ever play with them?"

"No," she said. "I'm afraid I'm too clumsy, and I might break them. I just like to have them to look at."

"But why?"

Good question, coming from a five-year-old. "Do you have anything you like to look at in your room?"

She smiled at his cuteness when he propped his chin on his finger and scrunched his face in thought. Suddenly his forehead crinkled, and he smiled. "Yeah! I have some BMX posters."

"So you like bicycles, too?"

He nodded. "I love bicycles. Daddy took my training wheels off and showed me how to ride a two-wheeler."

Brad just jumped a few notches in the parenting department. "That's great, Timmy! Maybe one of these days you can come see me at my store."

"You have a store?"

She nodded. "A bicycle store. I sell and rent bicycles and skates."

"Cool!"

Out of the corner of her eye, she noticed that they weren't alone anymore. She turned and motioned for Lacy and Brad to come in.

"Hey, Daddy, ya gotta see Amanda's cool bicycles!" Timmy crossed the room, took his dad by the hand, and led him over to the cabinet. "But you can't touch them because they're 'tiques. They're just to look at."

As Brad turned to her, Amanda saw the look of amazement behind his smile. "I'd love to see them."

Timmy told his dad all about how Amanda and Lacy's grandfather used to work for a bicycle company and how he got the miniature replica now displayed in Amanda's cabinet. Now that she had confidence that he understood the value, Amanda took a step back and let him look for a few more minutes.

Brad finally took her aside. "I don't remember the last time he was this calm," he admitted to Amanda. "What did you do?"

Amanda shrugged. "I just answered his questions and explained why I never touch this display."

Brad exchanged a glance with Lacy, who'd stepped up beside him. Timmy turned around.

"Daddy, I'm hungry."

"But you just ate," Brad replied.

Amanda sensed a temper tantrum, so she made a quick decision. "I have some oatmeal cookies in the kitchen. Want some?" She paused for a second then offered an apologetic look at Brad. "That is, if it's okay with your father."

"Yes, of course," Brad replied. "That is, if it's not too much trouble."

"No trouble at all."

As Amanda led Timmy to the kitchen, she overheard Brad speak to Lacy. "Do you think your sister would consider being a nanny?"

"Not a chance," Lacy replied. "She's always at her shop, and she doesn't have much time for anything or anyone else…not even me."

Ouch! That's harsh.

Timmy squirmed in the chair as Amanda got his cookies and milk ready. The second she placed the plate in front of him, he grabbed one and shoved it into his mouth. The boy needed some manners, but she didn't think he'd learn them from his dad, who seemed overwhelmed by being a single father.

She took a cookie for herself and sat down at the table across from him. "So how do you like school?"

He swallowed his cookie, took a sip of milk, and offered a milk-mustache smile. "I'm gonna be a first-grader soon."

"That's wonderful!"

Lacy and Brad appeared at the door together. "You'll be a first-grader if Miss Burns passes you," Brad said.

Lacy rolled her eyes and chuckled. "Yeah, like I'm not gonna pass a kindergartner."

Amanda cleared her throat to get their attention. When she was sure

Timmy wasn't looking, she drew her finger across her throat, letting them know they didn't need to be discussing this in front of Timmy. Lacy looked puzzled.

* * * * *

"I can't believe you didn't lay one on her." Harold sniffed. "You let a prime opportunity slip by."

"Harold! That's not the way to court a girl." Jerry's mother scowled, but his dad didn't back down.

"It worked with you," he said.

Jerry shook his head. "Too much information, folks. I don't think 'laying one on her' is such a good idea right now. We're still just friends, and I'm not sure if that'll ever change."

"Humph! Friendship is overrated."

Jerry cast a warning glance at his mother. It was obvious that his dad was spoiling for an argument, and Jerry wanted it to stop. Thankfully, his mother didn't respond.

"So what do you plan to do now?" his dad asked.

Jerry had to be honest. "I'm not sure." But now that the subject had surfaced, he needed to think about what was best for both him and Amanda.

He decided to back off for a few days and let Amanda have her space. But it was difficult because he really wanted to see her.

On Monday, while running errands for his mother, he took the long way home so he could drive by Amanda's shop and possibly catch a glimpse of her. The glare on the window prevented him from seeing inside, so he just kept going.

Tuesday, he took a walk along the beach to do some thinking—and his thoughts kept taking a turn back to Amanda. He hadn't planned for his feelings to be so strong for her; after all, this was vacation, and he wouldn't be on Treasure Island much longer. Too bad his parents kept forgetting and every chance they had, they mentioned her name.

By Wednesday, he couldn't take it anymore. He had to see Amanda, so he took off toward her shop. On his way there, he rehearsed what he'd say and how he'd ask her out for the evening. He charged through the door and stopped when he saw the teenage girl—what was her name again?

She glanced up at the sound of the bell on the door and grinned. "Looking for Amanda?"

"Uh…yes, is she here?"

The girl glanced up at the clock on the back wall. "She had to run to the bank and then over to her mother's place to water some plants and feed the cat. Want me to call her?"

"No, that's okay," he said, feeling dejected. "I'll just come back tomorrow."

"I think she'd like to know you're looking for her."

What did she mean by that? He shoved his hands into his pockets and rocked back on his heels as he thought it over. What did he have to lose? He exhaled. "Okay, I'll wait while you call her."

It took her all of three seconds to have Amanda on the phone. As soon as she mentioned that Jerry was in the shop, she lit up with a smile and held the phone out for him. "She wants to talk to you."

"I hope you don't think I'm stalking you," he said into the receiver.

She laughed. "Why would I think that? Tiffany just said you were looking for me. What's up?"

"I was wondering if you were doing anything tonight after work." There. He'd said it. Now that wasn't so bad, was it?

"Just a minute, okay?" He heard the muffled sound of her talking to someone as she placed her hand over the mouthpiece. She was back on the phone a few seconds later. "Whatcha got in mind?"

He hadn't settled on anything yet, so he threw the ball back in her court. "What do you normally do after work?"

Again she let out a laugh. "I normally just go home, eat supper, and watch a little TV. Once in a while I walk over to the beach and watch the sunset."

"Hey, that sounds like a plan," he said. "Why don't we find a spot on the beach and watch the sunset?"

Chapter Seven

. . . .

"Okay, that'll be fun." She paused for a moment. "It sets about an hour and a half after I get off work, so why don't we meet at the beach-access sign at seven?"

He wanted to tell her that he didn't mind picking her up at her place, but he thought better of it. He was just happy to have plans with her.

"Can you put Tiffany back on the phone?" she asked.

Tiffany. He'd almost forgotten the teenager's name again. Amanda did that to him—muddled his mind so much he would have forgotten his own name if people didn't keep saying it. He committed her name to memory. "Sure thing. See ya at seven." Then he handed the phone back to the girl who hadn't taken her eyes off him the whole time he'd talked to Amanda. "Thanks, Tiffany."

She grinned. "No problem."

On his way back to the condo, he stopped off at a market and picked up some flowers for his mother. Maybe that would ease some of the tension. It seemed like nothing either of his parents did could make the other one happy.

His parents were watching TV when he walked in. "Mom, I brought you something."

She smiled as she slowly rose from the chair. He'd noticed how much more difficult it was getting for her to do that, so he made a mental note to look into special-needs furniture. He'd seen a TV commercial featuring a chair with a motorized lift, and he wondered if she'd be open to it.

"Those are beautiful," she said as she took the flowers and carried them to the kitchen, shuffling a little more than usual. "I made salads for dinner. Yours is in the refrigerator, so you can eat it whenever you're ready."

He leaned over and gave her a kiss on the cheek before opening the fridge and pulling out the large salad on top. "Thanks, this is perfect. After I eat, I'm going for a walk and meeting Amanda on the beach."

His mom's hand stilled on the vase as she slowly turned to face him, a look of concern in her eyes. "Are you getting serious about this girl?"

"No, of course not. We just enjoy hanging out."

She relaxed and chuckled as she resumed arranging flowers. "Back when I was your age, if a girl and a boy *hung out* this much, they were as good as engaged."

"Is that what happened with you and Dad?"

"Your father couldn't stay away." She turned to him and rolled her eyes in a comical manner. "He was smitten the moment he first laid eyes on me."

Jerry actually knew that to be true. His dad had said he knew Rosemary would be his when they met.

He pulled his salad from the refrigerator and set it on the table. "Dad seems rather depressed lately."

"Yes, and I don't quite know what to do about it. He's getting increasingly difficult to manage." She put the vase of flowers on the kitchen table in front of Jerry's salad and spun around to face him. "It has nothing to do with control, either, Jerry. I think you've gotten a small taste of what I've been dealing with, but you haven't experienced him wandering off and getting lost yet. We're getting close to needing a different level of care, I'm afraid."

Jerry's gut clenched. The very thought of his parents becoming so dependent on others was more painful than he'd ever imagined. His beautiful mother, who'd been active all her life with gardening and running around tending to everyone who needed help, could barely get out of a chair. And the father who'd protected the family was becoming more confused and depressed. He felt helpless.

"Just remember, Jerry, it's all part of what happens in life. We brought you into this world and helped you become a confident, productive adult. Then we had several years of freedom before our age caught up with us."

He hesitated before pulling out the chair so he could eat. "I know, Mom, but it's hard watching this happen—especially with Dad."

"Yes, sweetheart, but we've accepted it. I know how miserable we must appear. Really, though, it's not that bad."

Jerry swallowed hard. "I want you to promise to tell me if there's anything I can do."

"There is," she said with a smile, "and you're doing it. Thank you for being here for us." Then she let out a snicker. "Oh, and one other thing."

"What's that?" Jerry would do anything for the people who'd been so good to him.

"If you feel something for Amanda, don't let her get away." She pulled a bowl of homemade salad dressing out of the refrigerator, set it in front of him on the counter, then pointed. "This is fresh. I made it an hour ago."

"Thanks."

"Did you hear what I said?"

Yes, he'd heard it, but he'd hoped he wouldn't have to respond. No way was his mom letting him off that easily.

"Jerry?" She leaned against the counter, folded her arms, and glared at him. "I'm serious about Amanda. Girls like her are rare. If you like her, you need to take action."

He ladled some of his mother's dressing on the salad and carried it to the table. "That would be difficult since we live in Atlanta and she's clearly tied to Treasure Island."

"But you said it yourself—you can do your work anywhere."

"I know, but you and Dad are in Atlanta, and I'd never leave y'all."

She grinned. "There's nothing that says we have to stay in Atlanta."

Jerry sat down before turning to his mother. "That's where your friends are, so I think that's a moot point. We're on vacation now, and we're leaving in a couple of weeks. I just want to have some fun while I'm here."

"Okay, son, but don't ignore something that's obviously meant to be." She poured herself a glass of iced tea and joined him at the table.

Perfect time to change the subject. "So what are you and Dad planning for the evening?"

She shrugged. "I don't know about your father, but one of the ladies on the second floor said that a group is heading down to the beach to see what they can do about helping the loggerhead turtles, and I was thinking about joining them. There's some concern that these turtles might be getting close to extinction if we don't do something about it."

Jerry was puzzled. "We?"

She looked away. "Well, somebody."

"Are you taking Dad?"

"If he'll go and keep his opinions to himself."

Jerry laughed. "That's not likely."

"Maybe I'll tell him we're hunting for treasure."

"That might work," Jerry agreed. "Or I can invite him to join Amanda and me."

She tilted her head forward and gave him one of her familiar "you've-got-to-be-kidding" looks. "You really know how to turn a girl's head, don't you, son?" She made a clicking sound with her tongue. "I don't know where we went wrong with you."

* * * * *

Could anything be more romantic? Amanda remembered sitting on the beach with Eric, talking about their future together as the sun melted into the Gulf.

Now that she thought about it, the deep, abiding love hadn't been there. The beach setting had been much more romantic than the relationship. Eric was handsome enough, and he had goals in life. The fact that he went to church regularly was important, as well. But besides that, what had been the bond between them? It obviously wasn't strong enough to hold them together. Then her thoughts drifted to the present.

Why would Jerry want to watch the sunset with her? She didn't want to risk giving him the wrong idea. And she certainly didn't want to risk her heart with someone after what had happened with Eric.

She gave herself a mental shakedown. That was Eric, and it was a long time ago—and she needed to quit dwelling on the past. Besides, watching the sunset hadn't even been Jerry's idea. She was the one who mentioned it.

"Earth to Amanda."

The sound of her mother's voice startled Amanda. "Sorry. I didn't realize you were back."

"Obviously." Her mother smiled. "So what's on your mind?"

Amanda tried to put Jerry out of her mind. "Not much. So tell me about your trip."

That was all it took to get her mother's mind off her and onto the cruise. She went on and on about the size of the ship, the number of activities from dawn to dusk, and the abundance of food.

"I must have gained at least ten pounds," she added, patting her tummy.

Amanda smiled and shook her head. "Well, I certainly can't tell. I think you look fabulous."

Her mother grinned back. Amanda knew just the right thing to say to make her mother happy.

"So how's Lacy doing? Poor girl was having a problem with some little troublemaker. Sometimes you can just tell when you have a juvenile delinquent in the making. After all the things Lacy's said about this little boy…what's his name? Tommy...or Timmy? I bet he's one of those kids who'll wind up in jail before he even graduates from high school." She shuddered.

"Um, Mom, I don't think he's all that bad."

"How would you know?" As Amanda's mom tilted her head, a strand of straight gray hair slid across her face. She pushed it behind her ear. "Have you met him?"

"As a matter of fact, yes, I have." Suddenly Amanda wished she hadn't admitted so much. She couldn't lie to her mother, but it wasn't her place to discuss her sister's relationship, and she wanted Lacy to tell their mother about Brad. She had to quickly think of a diversion. "I'm meeting someone at the beach in a little while."

Her mother tilted her head to the other side and started to smile. *Oops! Wrong diversion.* Before she jumped to conclusions, Amanda knew she had to nip this in the bud.

"It's someone who rented a bicycle for his parents. They're on vacation, and I think he just needs a little time away."

"So you met a guy, huh?" The woman's grin widened. "Any hope for a long-term relationship?"

"No, of course not." That came out too quickly. "What I mean is, they're on vacation, and they're going back in a couple of weeks."

"Okay, if you say so. I met your father when he was here on vacation. I know how those things go."

Amanda decided not to remind her mother that her father was no longer around—that they didn't bother with marriage and he'd left as soon as he knew her mother was pregnant. "I guess I better get back. Maybe you can stop by the shop sometime tomorrow."

"I just might do that."

On her way home, Amanda stopped off at the shop to make sure everything was okay. Tiffany told her she could close up so Amanda could have a little time to herself before meeting Jerry at the beach. Not that she needed to do anything special to get ready.

She was relieved that Lacy wasn't home. After circumventing questions from her mother, she didn't want the pressure of avoiding them from her sister, as well. She stepped into the bathroom and took a quick glance at herself in the mirror. No makeup, hair pulled back with a plastic band, and a faded blue T-shirt. Lacy would have something to say about that. Maybe she should make some effort…

An hour later, Amanda left her house wearing lipstick, mascara, and a light dusting of blush. And she felt a little silly thinking that it really mattered. But she did feel pretty.

With the heat and humidity of the Florida summer, it never really mattered what she started out with on her face—most of it would melt. Heat waves shimmered from the blacktop road in front of her house, so she stayed on the sidewalk, carefully dodging toys left outside by neighborhood children.

A few minutes later, she approached the Treasure Island beach access. She didn't see Jerry near the sign, so she wandered toward the footbridge to check out the beach. Beyond the massive stretch of sand, the sun glistened on the whitecaps, creating a diamond effect.

"Hey there. I thought I'd have to wait for you."

The sound of Jerry's voice behind her quickened her pulse. She took a deep breath, slowly blew it out, and turned to face him. With the sun behind her, she got a clear picture of his expression—one of pure joy. She swallowed hard at the thought that he might be as happy to see her as she was him.

They walked across the bridge together and stopped to remove their shoes when they got to the beach. The faint sound of someone strumming his guitar and singing a Jimmy Buffett song wafted through the air, lifted by the gentle Gulf breeze. A group of high school boys tossed a football nearby.

Amanda had just turned to say something to Jerry when suddenly he was airborne. A split second later, he caught the football in one hand and grabbed her by the waist with the other.

"Whoa, there, boys," he hollered out to the guys. "Watch where you're throwing that thing."

"Sorry, sir," the closest boy said. "You okay?"

Jerry tossed the ball to the kid. "Yeah, I'm fine. Just be careful, okay?"

The boy looked Jerry in the eyes with respect and nodded. "It won't happen again."

"Good," Jerry said. They watched the boys take off down the beach.

"I'm impressed," Amanda said as she caught her breath. "I could have been hurt."

He rubbed his shoulder. "Yeah, I know."

"It happened so fast. How did you do that?"

"I was the wide receiver on a high school football team with a wild-armed quarterback."

"You played football?" She would never have guessed.

"Yeah, all four years."

She chuckled. "I'm glad to know that high school football is good for something."

"I grew up thinking I'd play college ball and then get drafted into the NFL." He adjusted his shoulder and rubbed it again. "That obviously didn't happen."

"Are you okay?" She instinctively reached out and massaged his shoulder.

As he slowly turned to face her, she knew what was about to happen. Her palms instantly became damp, and her stomach did a flippy thing.

* * * * *

Jerry didn't mean to kiss her. It just happened. All he'd done was grab a wayward football—something he'd done many times. And it had never turned out like this—a pretty girl in his arms, her face tilted up toward his, a look of utter awe in her eyes.

He tried to quiet his thudding heart.

She licked her lips and blinked, which turned him inside out. "Thank you for catching that ball. I didn't even see it coming," she repeated.

What else would he have done? He lowered his eyelids to hide his feelings. "It was nothing. Really."

Still smiling down at her, he slowly released his grip on her. She inhaled and closed her eyes as she let out her breath.

Difficult as it was, Jerry turned to face the Gulf, where the sun barely hovered over the water. "Look. We're about to see what we came here for."

She shaded her eyes as she looked toward the water. "I've lived here all my life, and I never get tired of sunsets."

The colorful sky provided a breathtaking panorama, with blues, purples, and various shades of red and orange. The water reflected the sky, and the beach provided the bottom of the frame. Jerry squeezed his eyes shut and thanked the Lord for the glorious scene before them. When he opened his eyes again, he caught Amanda staring up at him.

"The Lord is good, isn't He?" she whispered.

He opened his mouth to speak, but nothing would come out. So he nodded and wrapped his arms around her once again. He was tired of fighting the attraction he'd felt from the day they rode bicycles to the festival.

Her shoulders tensed, but she soon relaxed and leaned into him. This felt so right, but there was that one obstacle he would have to face. He and his parents only had a short time left on Treasure Island. Then what? He shuddered as he tried to put that out of his mind.

"Amanda!"

He and Amanda both turned around and saw a woman coming toward them. He was fairly certain he'd never seen her before. She had a slender build, chiseled facial features, and a halo of frizz above her otherwise straight, gray-streaked, auburn hair.

"Hey, Mom." She quickly pulled away from his embrace, leaving him standing there with his arms dangling awkwardly by his sides.

The woman looked him up and down before turning to Amanda. "Is this your new boyfriend?"

"Um…Mom, I'd like for you to meet Jerry Simpson. This is my mother, Diane Burns."

Jerry extended his hand. "Nice to meet you, Mrs. Burns."

"Miss Burns," she corrected as she took his hand. "I've never been married."

"Oh." Jerry had no idea what to say now. If he commented, he risked embarrassing Amanda. So he just gulped and said, "Sorry, Miss Burns."

She flapped a hand and smiled. "Just call me Diane. Everyone else does."

"We were just enjoying the sunset," Jerry said, trying to divert the conversation. He sensed Amanda's discomfort, but at least now he understood a little more about her. "There's no amount of money that can buy something so beautiful."

Diane cackled. "You're kidding, right? Money can buy just about anything you want, including a condo on the beach where you can have this sunset every day of your life."

"Mom," Amanda said softly, her voice laced with an undertone of warning.

"Oh, Amanda," the older woman said with another flap of her hand, "you know what I'm saying."

Jerry felt like he'd been caught in the middle of something he wasn't prepared for. Although Amanda had mentioned that her mother had problems, she hadn't gone into enough detail to get the whole picture.

"I'm sure he knows what I mean," Diane said as she grinned at Jerry. "Don't you, sweetie?"

Her casual term of affection startled him. He glanced over at Amanda, who appeared to be steaming beneath a controlled exterior.

After gently reaching down for Amanda's hand, he decided to take charge of the situation. "It was very nice meeting you, Diane. Maybe I'll run into you again sometime in the future." He took a couple of steps away from the woman who clearly had Amanda in a dither. "I'd like to find a spot where we can watch the sun go down for the night."

"You can do that just about anywhere on this beach." Diane gestured widely.

"Good evening, Diane," he said, trying to be firm yet polite.

Without another word, he pulled Amanda toward him, hoping to leave a clear sign that they wanted to be alone. Fortunately, Diane took the hint and waved as they walked away.

Once they were out of hearing distance from her mother, Amanda offered Jerry an apologetic smile. "I'm really sorry about that. My mother can be so...so...I don't know..."

"Motherly?" he asked with a chuckle.

She grinned up at him. "Yeah, I guess you can say that. You probably want to know about my father, right?"

He had to admit he was curious, but he wasn't about to make Amanda any more uncomfortable than she already was. "Not unless you want to tell me."

He sensed her uncertainty about telling him, so he squeezed her hand to let her know he was there for her.

"Maybe some other time, okay? Right now I just want to enjoy the moment."

He agreed with a nod. "Sounds good to me."

They found a spot with dry sand and sat down to watch the sun as it melted into the water. The smell of the salty air mixed with the sweetness of the coconut oils that lingered from the sunbathers. The sounds of the waves lapping onto the shore blended with distant strains of music and children playing and added to the ambience Jerry knew he wouldn't find anywhere else.

"There is absolutely nothing like it," Jerry said. "No matter how many times I see this, I feel a newness in God's presence."

She leaned toward him and rested her head on his shoulder. This simple gesture surprised him, but it felt nice. He held as still as he could until she finally pulled away.

"Ready to go?" she asked.

"Not really." He winked at her. "But I can take a hint."

They stood up and walked hand in hand back to the beach access, where they stopped. "I had a wonderful time, Jerry. And thanks again for saving me from the crazy football."

He wanted to kiss her again, but the timing didn't seem right.

* * * * *

Nothing had been so difficult as leaving Jerry to go home. She could have stayed on the beach for hours, watching the horizon and enjoying the peacefulness that washed over her when she was with him. But that wouldn't be good for either of them. She needed to keep her emotions in check or risk being abandoned again. She took her time plodding home.

Fifteen minutes later, Amanda opened the door to her house. Lacy and Brad were on the couch watching TV.

"Where's Timmy?" Amanda asked.

"Mother stopped by to tell us she saw you and Jerry acting all cozy on the beach." Lacy paused. "I asked her to take Timmy out for ice cream."

If Brad hadn't been there, Amanda would have asked questions—lots of them.

"Timmy was impressed with your miniature bicycle collection," Brad said. "That's all he can talk about anymore. I never thought he'd be interested in collecting stuff."

Amanda suspected there were a lot of things Brad never thought Timmy would be interested in, when, in fact, he might be pleasantly surprised if he actually exposed his son to more than a tiny nibble of his time. But that was none of her business.

"It was fun showing it to him. Not everyone gets excited about old stuff like that."

Brad tilted his head. "I used to collect trains, until my family moved. Dad packed them all up, and I never saw them again. I wonder if they still have them."

"You might ask them about it," Amanda suggested. "I bet Timmy would get a kick out of them."

"Yeah, I bet he would."

Lacy rolled her eyes. "What good is all that stuff? It's just clutter."

"Some people might say the same thing about your shoe collection," Amanda quipped.

Lacy gasped. "I wear all my shoes. I don't just pull them out to look at them."

"True." Amanda didn't mean to insult her sister. It just came out that way. "I hope Mom doesn't forget how young Timmy is. It's been a long time since she's been in charge of a child." And she didn't do very well the first time around, Amanda remembered. When Lacy came along, Amanda was her main caregiver practically from the beginning. Not many fourteen-year-olds had the full responsibility of baby siblings while their mothers wigged out and simply took off, not telling anyone where they were going.

"So," Lacy said with a mocking voice, "tell me all about you and Jerry. Mother said you two were acting very romantic."

A lump instantly formed in Amanda's throat. She didn't want to talk about her feelings with Jerry because she hadn't had time to sort them out in her own mind.

Brad locked gazes with Amanda for a split second then turned to face Lacy. "That's their business, Lacy. I've been meaning to ask you if you'd like to go to the other coast with me next week, after school is out for summer break. It'll just be for the day. I have to make a couple of business calls in Daytona and St. Augustine, and it would be nice to have someone to talk to."

Lacy's eyes lit up. "Sounds like fun. Can you drop me off at the mall while you make your calls?"

"Of course," he said. Then he turned to Amanda. "Now all I have to do is find someone to help out with Timmy."

There was no doubt he was hoping Amanda would volunteer. But she wasn't sure if she should. After all, she had a business to run.

"Amanda wouldn't mind," Lacy piped up. "Would you?"

Now she couldn't avoid the subject. "Um…" The hopeful look on Lacy's face made her waver. Finally she offered a clipped nod. "Sure, I can watch him. It's just for the day, right?"

"Absolutely," Brad assured her. "I can drop him off with you when I pick up Lacy. That is, if you don't mind."

"That's fine." Exhaustion fell over Amanda, so she turned toward her room. "See you tomorrow, Lacy."

Simmering with a blend of anger and frustration, Amanda flipped on her bedroom lamp and closed her door. This had been an exhausting day—both physically and emotionally. Caught in the midst of her mother's return, Jerry's kiss, and being cornered by Lacy to watch Timmy, she felt like she couldn't breathe.

After a fitful night of restless tossing and turning, Amanda got up the next morning. Lacy was already in the kitchen sipping coffee.

"So," Amanda said as she poured herself a cup of the strong brew, "you ready for the last day of school?"

Lacy set her mug down on the table and looked up at Amanda. "You know, I can't believe I'm saying this, but I'm really going to miss those kids."

"Believe me, I understand."

"It's strange. All I could think about all year was that if I could make it through the school year, I got a couple of months off during the summer, so I counted the days until now. But I'm sort of sad."

"Do you have anything special planned?" Amanda asked as she remembered her own elementary school days.

Lacy slowly shook her head. "No, should I?"

"Well, let's see. You're sad about today being the last day, and I'm sure the kids feel attached to their very first teacher." Amanda paused and thought for a couple of seconds. "Why don't you stop off at Publix and pick up some cupcakes and punch?"

Lacy's face lit up. "We can have a good-bye party!"

"That's the idea."

Amanda left Lacy with that and headed to the shop. She'd barely gotten inside and turned on all the lights when she heard the bell on the door behind her.

Chapter Eight

....

Her mother stood by the door, looking around with a smirk on her face. "This is insane, Amanda."

"Huh?"

"I don't see a thing in here that looks the least bit girlish."

Amanda squinted. "What are you talking about, Mother?"

"All these…these bicycles and skates and skateboards. It's all guy stuff."

Amanda had heard it all before. Her mother was of the mind that anything sporty or athletic was reserved for boys, and girls needed to be…well, needy.

"What kind of man do you think you'll attract if you can do everything better than him?"

"Um…if I ever wanted to attract a guy, I would hope he'd be secure enough with himself to accept that I'm competent."

"That's ridiculous," her mother said. "Speaking of men, I like that boy…. What's his name…Jerry?"

"Yes, his name is Jerry." Amanda could only imagine what her mother thought was going on between them.

The woman pointed her finger and wagged it at her. "Just don't make the same mistake I made and let him take advantage of you—at least not until you have him hooked completely."

"Mother, I'm not trying to hook Jerry or any other man."

Her mother helped herself to a mint at the counter and propped herself up on the stool. Looked like she planned to stay awhile.

"I have a lot going on this week," Amanda said.

Her mother tilted her head and challenged her with a stare. "Like what?"

"I have several people coming by to pick up rentals, and the summer skateboarders are stopping by for safety clinics. We have the college kids today, high school kids tomorrow, and middle schoolers the next day."

"That's not a lot."

"It is when I'm the only person working here," Amanda said.

"Are you saying you need my help, or are you telling me to get lost?"

"No." Amanda placed her hand on her mother's shoulder. "I'd never tell you to get lost. You can stay if you want, but I might not be able to chat much."

"That's okay. I don't have anything else to do all day. I'll just sit here and watch."

"Fine."

Amanda went to the back room and got some folding chairs, in case Matthew needed them for the clinic. She'd been letting them meet in her shop for the past two summers, and even though it took some of her time and most of her sales-floor space, it paid off in the long run. Most of the people who attended the class bought merchandise from her immediately after the class, and they often returned later for more.

As she worked, her mother chatted about her upcoming trip to Miami. Amanda stopped and turned to her.

"How long will you be gone?"

Her mother shrugged. "Until we get bored."

Some things never changed. Her mother flitted and fluttered wherever the wind took her, leaving Amanda to do all the responsible things, including care for her mother's pets and plants. At least now she had a trust that Amanda's grandparents had the good sense to set up, and the money came in monthly increments. Amanda's mother was five years away from being able to add Social Security income, so in spite of her lack of discipline, she was pretty much set for life—as long as she didn't pile up too many credit card bills.

The turnout for the skateboard clinic was better than expected, so the store was packed mostly with overgrown boys and a few girls. She was so busy helping Matthew, she didn't realize that her mother had slipped out until it was over.

"Thanks, Amanda," Matthew said as he helped her put away the chairs. "I think we saved a few broken bones and concussions today."

She smiled. "I'm just glad you don't mind giving your time."

After they had the last chair put away, he ambled up to the counter and waited for her to go around to the cash register. She gave him a questioning look. "Did you need something?"

He lifted an eyebrow. "So who's that guy you've been hanging out with lately?"

"Have you been watching me?"

"Not really…well, sort of. Who's that guy you were sitting with in the Bible study at church?"

"His name's Jerry. He's here on vacation with his parents."

Matthew gave her a knowing grin. "So just how serious are you two?"

Amanda snorted. "Serious? He's a customer who happened to ask me where he and his parents could go to church."

"I didn't notice any parents. Just the two of you sitting really close."

What was up with everyone? Didn't they have anything else to do but worry about her love life?

"After church, he brought them home so they could rest, and then he came back to the Bible study."

"Right." He grabbed a mint and popped it into his mouth.

"Trust me, Matthew, we're barely acquaintances."

"Sure, Amanda." He pulled away from the counter and headed for the door. "See you tomorrow. I'll bring food."

After Matthew left, Amanda rubbed her temples and admonished herself. She didn't need to get so worked up just because people assumed she and Jerry were an item.

Business was steady since most of the colleges were out on break. The tourist season still ebbed and flowed, but there were still plenty of year-round customers lately, and she had lots of rentals scheduled. Life was good. So why did she feel so out of sorts?

When she got home, Lacy was sprawled out on the couch, with the remote control in one hand, a candy bar in the other, and some mindless soap opera blaring from the TV. She looked up at Amanda, offered a brief smile and wave, then turned her attention back to the TV.

"Well?" Amanda said as she kicked off her shoes. "How'd the party go?"

"It was fun for a little while, but the kids got all squirmy."

Amanda lifted her brows. "Isn't that what kindergartners do? Squirm?"

Lacy rolled her eyes. "Yeah. I am so glad school's out for a while. I need a break." She sat up and hit the MUTE button on the remote. "That reminds me. Brad asked if I could spend some time with him tomorrow. He's getting off work early and trying out his new boat."

"Are you going to?" A strange feeling washed over her, like she was somehow involved in her sister's decision.

"I'd like to, but, well, there's Timmy."

"What about Timmy?" Amanda asked.

"He'll want to go, unless we can find someplace else he'd rather be." Lacy had stood up and closed the gap between them.

"Got any ideas?" Amanda asked.

"He really likes you."

This didn't take much figuring out. "So you want me to keep an eye on him while you and Brad hang out on Brad's boat?"

Lacy's eyebrows shot up, and she clapped her hands together. "Would you?"

"Why don't you ask Mother?"

Lacy tilted her head and rolled her eyes. "Since when could we ever depend on her for something like this?"

Amanda's shoulders sagged. There was no way she could resist her sister's pleading looks. "I guess I don't mind watching him for a little while."

"You're the best sister ever!" Lacy grabbed her cell phone off the end table and headed toward her room. "I can't wait to tell Brad we can go."

The next morning, Amanda gathered some things she thought might entertain a five-year-old boy and stuffed them into a tote. When she got to work, she went through the same routine of getting out the chairs and setting up for Matthew's clinic.

He arrived a half hour before it was scheduled. "You don't have to do everything yourself, Amanda. I could have set up."

She shrugged. "I was here, and I didn't have anything else pressing."

Matthew offered a warm smile. "You've always been a nurturer, and that's nice. But sometimes you need to let others do things for themselves."

She'd known Matthew since high school, and they were like brother and sister when he wasn't touring with his skateboard group. Whenever she needed to vent, Matthew had always been there with a listening ear and sometimes a few wise words. When nothing else worked, he'd toss out a wisecrack and she'd slug him in the shoulder. No one else would even attempt to talk to her like that.

"Don't worry about it," she said. "You can put everything away after it's over."

Matthew set up some refreshments on the table in the back of the shop. A few minutes later, kids started arriving. By the time the clinic began, the room was even more packed than the day before when the college kids were there.

Amanda stayed behind the counter and answered the phone when it rang. Otherwise, there wasn't much she could do, since there wasn't much space left in her store. She kept an eye on the door, just in case a customer approached and needed something.

She'd just hung up when she glanced up and spotted Jerry and his parents at the door, looking in. His dad had his hands propped up, shielding his eyes. She tugged at her shirt to make sure it wasn't hiked up as she came around from behind the counter and went to the door to let them in.

"What's going on in there?" Harold asked. "Are those kids taking over the place? Want me to scare 'em away?"

"No," Amanda replied with a chuckle. "We have annual safety clinics for skateboarders. Did you need something?"

"We were on our way to St. Petersburg, and we decided to stop off and see what you were up to." Rosemary looked around her at the crowd in the store. "I think it's very sweet that you do this for your customers."

Jerry nodded. "It is nice. Sorry if we interrupted, though. We'll leave and let you get back to your clinic."

"No, that's okay. Matthew has everything under control."

Harold pointed inside. "Is that guy up at the front Matthew?"

"Yes," Amanda replied. "He's a professional skateboarder."

"That's silly and rather childish for a grown man, don't you think?"

Jerry reached out and touched Harold's arm. "Dad."

Amanda laughed. "That's okay. I understand. Matthew and I have been friends for years. Everyone wondered what he'd do with his life since he was such a slacker back in high school. All he ever did then was skateboard." She looked over her shoulder and saw Matthew looking at her, his gaze narrowed. Then she spun back around to face Harold. "At least he's able to make a living doing something he enjoys."

"Is he your boyfriend?" Harold asked.

Amanda laughed at the mere thought. "No."

"Has he ever been your boyfriend?"

Jerry touched his Harold's arm. "C'mon, Dad, that's not any of our business."

"No, he's never been my boyfriend. We've just always been very good friends."

Harold slowly shook his head. "That's how it often starts."

"Stop it, Harold!" Rosemary offered an apologetic glance at Amanda. "I'm sorry my husband is acting this way."

"Amanda!"

The piercing sound of a child's voice caught everyone's attention. The instant Amanda turned around, Timmy was practically on top of her. She giggled as she lifted him off his feet and gave him a big hug before putting him back down.

He looked up at her, his eyes wide. "Daddy says you're gonna babysit me today. I told him I'm not a baby."

"Of course you're not a baby," Amanda agreed as she turned to Brad then looked back at Timmy. "You're a big boy. You're going to help me work." She reached down and took his hand as she looked over at her sister and Brad. She thought Lacy had said they'd leave in the afternoon, and it wasn't even noon yet.

"See, Daddy? I'm her helper."

Brad looked helpless as he took a step back. "Are you sure you're okay with this?"

Even though it was more than an hour before she expected them, Amanda nodded. "Sure, I'm fine."

"We won't be gone too long. In fact, we'll probably be back before you close the shop."

"Take your time," Amanda said.

* * * * *

Jerry had no doubt that Amanda was being taken advantage of as he watched the whole interaction. And it bugged him to think that her own sister would do this to her. Timmy was obviously a spirited little boy who would try the patience of anyone—let alone someone trying to run a business.

He glanced over at his dad, who'd clearly noticed the same thing. Something was brewing in his dad's mind—he could tell by the look on his face.

His dad leaned over to get on Timmy's level. "So, you like to work?"

Timmy shyly nodded as he tightened his grip on Amanda's hand. "Daddy sometimes lets me help him work. I get to write on paper and work on files."

"What else do you like to do?" his dad asked.

"I like to play soccer and kickball and army." Timmy pointed at his shoes. "Look what Daddy got me." He turned his foot to the side to show off the wheels on the bottom.

Jerry's dad squatted. "Whatcha got there?"

"Wheelie shoes, and I can go really fast!"

"Those are some cool shoes." Harold slowly stood from his squat. "I might get me some of those."

Timmy frowned and shook his head. "I don't think they make them in big-people sizes…." He put his index finger on his chin and thought for a moment. "But maybe we can tell the people at the store, and they'll start making them."

"Good idea." Harold looked up and winked at the adults, who stood there amazed at how well he and the little boy were hitting it off. "So tell me, Timmy, have you ever been on a treasure hunt?"

Jerry slowly looked over toward Amanda, who appeared amused, before addressing his father. "Dad, this treasure hunt thing is getting—"

His dad held up his hand. "Wait a minute, son. I'm not talking to you. I'm talking to the boy." He looked back at Timmy. "Do you think you'd like to look for treasure with an old man?"

Timmy's eyes lit up as he turned to Amanda. "Can I look for treasure with an old man, Amanda?"

"I don't know," Amanda said. "I'll need to call your dad."

Jerry knew he'd been defeated when she looked back at him. He hesitated only for a second then nodded. "Mind if I go along?"

"Let me see if it's okay first. Be right back." Amanda quickly turned away from them, leaving Timmy with Jerry and his parents.

Jerry kept an eye on her as she went inside, edged around the people as inconspicuously as she could, and grabbed her phone. Then she stepped outside, away from where anyone could hear, and made a call. She was on the phone about ten seconds before she rejoined the group.

They all looked at her expectantly. "Well?"

Amanda looked relieved. "Sure, Timmy, but you need to behave and do what you're told."

"He's a good boy, aren't you, Timmy?" Jerry's dad looked down at the child.

"Uh-huh." Timmy beamed up at Jerry's dad. "Where are we hunting for treasure?"

"How should I know? We have a lot of ground to cover, so let's get going."

Jerry's throat tightened at the touching sight of his dad taking the little boy's hand and walking away from the shop. When he turned toward Amanda, he could tell she felt it, too.

She blinked. "Don't keep him too long, okay?"

"Trust me," Jerry said. "We'll be back very soon."

His mother decided to head back to the condo, while Jerry tagged along with his dad and Timmy. It had been a long time since he'd seen his dad so animated and…well, happy. He had to admit, Timmy was very cute and funny—even when he referred to Jerry's dad as "Old Man," which made his dad howl with laughter. But it didn't sound good, so Jerry intervened.

"Let's think of a different nickname, okay?" Jerry suggested.

His dad's smile changed to a scowl. "What's wrong with what he's calling me? I think it's cute."

"How about Gramps?" Jerry offered.

Timmy looked up at his dad. "Want me to call you Gramps?"

Jerry's dad shrugged, made a face at Jerry, then looked down at Timmy and grinned. "Sure, why not." He hung back for a moment then snickered. "In fact, I kind of like it. Gramps. Yeah, that's a good name for me."

Jerry suspected his dad had had a moment of reflection about how his own grandkids rarely came around. Timmy was like a substitute grandchild, and he figured his dad was probably the closest thing Timmy had to a grandparent. From what he could tell, this was a win-win relationship.

For the next hour, Jerry listened to Timmy and "Gramps" talk about all the possible places pirates could have buried their treasure. It could be in the sand or behind the Windjammer Hotel. Or it could even be in one of the many stores lining both sides of the main road.

"It might take us all summer to find it," Gramps said.

Jerry cleared his throat. "We're only going to be here a couple more weeks, Dad."

Timmy looked at Gramps with obvious disappointment. "You're leaving? How will I find the treasure if you're not here?"

"We'll figure out something." Gramps tossed Jerry a look of extreme disapproval, making Jerry slink back a few paces. He felt like a heel, but he didn't want his dad making promises he couldn't keep to this little boy. Based on what he'd seen, Timmy had had more than his share of disappointment in life. Like Amanda.

After a couple of blocks of treasure hunting, Timmy looked up at Gramps. "I'm hungry."

"Then let's eat. Whaddya want?"

"Um, Dad, what if Amanda has plans for Timmy's lunch?"

His dad gestured with a flick of the wrist. "Call her and tell her we're taking Timmy to lunch."

He pulled out his cell phone and found Amanda's number in his directory. She answered on the second ring and said it was fine for them to grab a bite to eat and then continue looking for treasure. "To be honest, I didn't even expect Timmy until after lunch anyway, so I wasn't sure what to do." She paused then added, "You saved me. Thanks."

"My pleasure," he replied then snapped his phone shut, hoping she didn't detect the sarcasm that had slipped out.

They stopped off for hamburgers and fries. Jerry rarely ate fast food, but he would have been willing to bet it was standard fare for the little boy.

After lunch, they walked around a little more, and his dad ducked into a store to look for a treasure chest similar to what Jerry had picked up during the festival. Apparently they were mass-produced, because it didn't take more than five minutes to find one. He handed it to Timmy. "I think that's a replica of what we're looking for."

"Wow!" Timmy rubbed his tiny fingers over it then slipped it into his pocket. "This is cool!"

They finally made a circle and came back to Amanda's store. As he pushed the door open, the sight at the counter gave him a stomachache.

Amanda and that guy…what's his name—Matthew? Whatever it was, they were standing very close, their heads together, looking at something in what appeared to be a magazine or catalog. He felt as if the earth had shifted beneath him, but that was ridiculous. She could put her head next to any guy she wanted. When she heard the door, she quickly glanced up and waved.

"Hey, Jerry." She leaned to the side and looked behind him. "Where's Timmy?"

"He's coming." Jerry couldn't keep the gruffness out of his voice. At the moment, he wanted to strangle Matthew.

Matthew stepped back from the counter and turned to face him, a smile plastered on that too-tan face. "Hey, man, it's cool that you and your folks took care of Timmy. Amanda's been telling me all about him. Poor kid."

"Yeah, poor kid." At the moment, Jerry was too busy feeling sorry for himself and wanting to punch Matthew, but he didn't want Amanda to know. Jealousy was never attractive—and it was something he'd never dealt with before. What an odd feeling.

Matthew took the opportunity to close the catalog and head for the back room to get his stuff. Jerry edged up to the counter to wait for his dad and Timmy, who were lollygagging outside but within view. He tried hard to act casual, like it didn't matter that she was very chummy with a pretty boy.

"So, how'd it go?" Amanda asked. "Find any treasure?"

"My dad bought him a treasure chest like the one I got him." He knew he still sounded surly, but he couldn't let his feelings keep him from talking to her.

She tilted her head and studied him then blinked as she looked right past him. "Call me with the item numbers, Matthew. I'll get whatever you think we need."

Matthew waved as he sauntered out of the store. "See ya, Amanda. Hope to see you around again soon, Jerry."

"Likewise." Jerry waved then turned back to Amanda, who had a very odd expression on her face.

* * * * *

Jerry was acting weird and not at all like himself. Amanda wasn't sure but he didn't seem to like Matthew, and there wasn't any reason she could see. They'd barely met, and Matthew had been polite. In fact, she'd never seen Matthew on such good behavior. Guys could be so weird.

"Did Timmy give you any trouble?" Amanda asked, hoping to break the icy chill in the room.

"None whatsoever. He and my dad got along great."

"Well, that's good," she said. "I'm glad Timmy has a grandfather type in his life."

"Yeah, in fact, he now calls my dad Gramps."

Amanda laughed. "That's cute!"

She watched as he visibly relaxed and glanced outside. "Today was good for him. For the first time in ages, he actually seemed happy. Ever since my dad was diagnosed with Alzheimer's, he's been angry."

"I can imagine," she said. "I probably would be, too."

"Mom managed to keep him from snapping until she found out she had Parkinson's. Now it's all I can do to keep them from barking at each other every second they're awake."

"Getting old is rough." Amanda thought about her own mother. "My mom is a bit younger than your parents, but she's not dealing with aging well, either."

Timmy and Harold still hadn't come inside. They stood outside the shop, chatting away, clearly engrossed in a conversation they both enjoyed.

"Might as well make yourself comfortable." Amanda gestured toward the stool. "Looks like they're not ready to say good-bye."

Jerry did as he was told. "It's the strangest thing. Who would've thought that a little boy would be what my dad needed?"

She watched the elderly man pat Timmy on the shoulder, as if consoling him for something. Then she turned back to Jerry. "Looks like it works both ways. I'm really glad they met."

"Yeah, it's too bad we only have a couple of weeks left here."

Amanda instantly felt a sensation of dread as it washed over her. She loved being around Jerry, in spite of the promise she'd made to herself not to fall for another guy. And in a more respectful way, he was doing the same thing that both her father and Eric had done. He was leaving. No surprise. It wasn't as though she didn't know before letting herself get this way.

Finally Timmy and Harold finished their conversation and came into the store. Timmy held out the little plastic brown toy treasure chest.

"Looky what Gramps got me!"

Amanda took it, turned it over in her hand, winked at Harold, then smiled at Timmy. "How nice! Did you find any other treasure?"

Timmy made a face and shook his head. "Not yet, but Gramps said he'll take me out hunting again."

"That sounds like a lot of fun!"

Harold patted Timmy on the back. "I guess I gotta go home and take my nap, champ. When you get as old as me, you gotta do stuff like that."

Timmy rolled his eyes and nodded conspiratorially. "Yeah, me, too. My daddy says when I don't get a nap, I'm a real bear."

Harold held his hands up like claws and growled. Timmy jumped then burst into laughter before he mimicked Harold. Amanda looked at Jerry, who stood by the door shaking his head.

"C'mon, Dad, we need to get back so Mom doesn't worry about us."

"Bye, Gramps!" Timmy waved until Harold turned and followed Jerry out the door.

Once they were gone, Timmy's shoulders lifted then sagged. "I like Gramps. He's funny."

"What did you two talk about?"

He quickly shrugged. "Just stuff."

"Stuff?"

"Yeah, you know, like treasures and pirates and bicycles and God and stuff like that."

"And God?" Amanda questioned.

Timmy nodded. "I told him Daddy was mad at God 'cuz Mommy died. But I like to go to church—'specially Sunday school."

"I'm sorry, Timmy."

Suddenly, Timmy lit up. "Gramps said he'd take me, if it's all right with Daddy."

Amanda smiled. She was glad Timmy had a nice time, but it was getting close to time to go home, and she hadn't heard a word from her sister.

"What time did your dad say they were coming back?"

"I don't know," Timmy replied as he wiped his eyes with the back of his hand. He looked sleepy.

"I'll call my sister." Amanda lifted the phone and punched in Lacy's cell phone number. No answer. She should have expected that. "Why don't you go in the back room and sit in the beanbag? I have some bicycle magazines you can look at."

"Okay." He hung his head as he did as he was told. In no time, she didn't hear a peep from the back room, so she ducked her head into the room to see if he was okay and found him fast asleep in the middle of her overstuffed, twenty-year-old, neon-green beanbag chair.

The next hour passed with still no word from Lacy and Brad. Finally, fifteen minutes after closing time, she gently tapped Timmy on the shoulder. He made a sound, but he was so tired, he didn't awaken.

"Hey, Timmy, sweetie, let's go to my house. Your daddy isn't here yet, and I need to go home and cook dinner."

He opened his sleepy eyes and gave her a dazed look. "I'm hungry."

"If your daddy doesn't come soon, you can eat with me, okay?" She reached for his hand.

He nodded and let her help him to a standing position. Amanda had walked to work, so it took them awhile to get to her house, with Timmy shuffling his feet from exhaustion. Jerry and his dad had clearly worn him out.

Finally, an hour after Amanda and Timmy got home, Lacy and Brad showed up. "I am so sorry," Lacy said. "We went out in the boat, and I completely lost track of time. You should have been there, Amanda. It was beautiful!" She sniffed the air. "Did you cook spaghetti?"

"Yes, and I fed Timmy," Amanda replied. "I bet it won't be too hard to get him to go to sleep tonight. He's been a very busy little boy today."

"C'mon, sport," Brad said as he took his son's hand. "Let's go home and get you ready for bed."

Timmy obediently followed his dad out the door, pausing only to say good-bye to Amanda. As soon as they were gone, Lacy danced and twirled around the living room.

"I think I'm in love!"

Chapter Nine
....

"Um...Lacy, how long have you known Brad?" Amanda was pretty sure it hadn't been more than a couple of weeks.

Lacy frowned back at her. "It doesn't matter. I just know." She patted her chest over her heart. "I feel it."

Amanda sucked in some air and said a quick, silent prayer for help in getting through to her sister how important it was to go with more than the first two weeks' worth of feelings. Love took time. Love wasn't just a fluttering heart.

"We need to have a talk, Lacy."

"No, you just want to lecture me about something you don't understand. You hate when I'm happy." Lacy frowned and pouted.

Nothing could be further from the truth. "I want you to be happy, Lacy, but I also want you to understand what love really is."

"How can you tell me anything about love when you don't understand it yourself?" Lacy glared at her for a few seconds before continuing. "Even you said that when Eric left, it was for the best because you only *thought* you were in love."

"That's all the more reason you need to be careful about your feelings. When you first meet someone you're attracted to, it's easy to think that those fluttery feelings are love, when they're actually just a result of infatuation."

Lacy closed her eyes then opened them as she shook her head. "I know the difference between love and infatuation."

"I don't want you to make the same mistakes Mother made," Amanda said, her voice barely above a whisper. "She thought she was in love with our fathers."

Lacy shrugged. "Well, maybe she was."

"No, I don't think so. Love involves more than that little quiver in the stomach. You need to see all sides of a man before you can truly love him. How much do you really know about Brad?"

"I know plenty. He's good-looking, sweet, and fun. Timmy's mother was killed in a car crash a couple of years ago, so he's had to take care of the brat all by himself."

"That's another thing," Amanda said. "Timmy lost his mother at a very critical time of his life. He's not as much of a brat as you think."

"Maybe not, but he's always doing something bad."

Amanda reached out and touched her sister's hand. "Have you ever thought that all he needs is a little more attention?"

Lacy pushed Amanda's hand away. "How much attention does a kid need? Someone's always having to fuss at him."

"That's not the right kind of attention. Haven't you noticed that he's well-behaved around me?"

"You always did have it easy with kids," Lacy said with a shrug. "Maybe he's scared to misbehave with you."

Amanda laughed. "I don't think so. I just talk to him and let him know I care enough to listen to what he has to say. You should have seen him with Jerry's dad."

Lacy bobbed her head. "Jerry's dad isn't exactly Mr. Good-Behavior. In case you haven't noticed, that old man is grouchy!"

"He was actually pretty jovial with Timmy. They seem to do fine with each other," Amanda said as something dawned on her. "Maybe they both need attention, and they relate in a way no one else understands."

Now Lacy rolled her eyes. "Don't go getting all psychoanalytical on me."

Amanda chuckled. "That's the last thing I want to do."

"Let me enjoy my relationship with Brad, okay?" Lacy said as she averted her gaze. "Don't try to bring me down just because you can't find a man."

"Just do one thing for yourself, Lacy." Amanda paused until Lacy looked her in the eyes.

"What's that?"

"Talk to him about faith issues. I know you haven't gone to church in a while, but I believe…well, I want to believe your faith is still in there somewhere." Amanda patted her chest over her heart. "Discuss this with Brad. See how he feels. Do you even know if he's a Christian?"

"How should I know? That would be a rude question to ask," Lacy replied.

"Not if you're professing your love for each other." Amanda shook her head. "The most important thing in any relationship is a common faith. It'll hold you together when everything else fails—even when that flutter fades."

* * * * *

When Jerry and his dad got back to the condo, his mom had just gotten up from a nap. She smiled when his dad started whistling.

"I haven't heard him do that in a while," she said. "Timmy's really good for him."

"Yeah, I noticed," Jerry agreed. "I think they had a good time today. Maybe Dad just needs a guy to hang out with."

"Someone his age, maybe. I'm not so sure it's healthy for a man in his seventies to hang out with a little five-year-old boy."

Jerry thought about it for a minute and then turned to his mom. "If you think about it, though, Dad is at the age when he should be enjoying his grandchildren. Since Steven and Jennifer don't bring their families around much, he probably misses that."

His mom's chin quivered and she pursed her lips at the mention of her other two children who rarely made the effort to visit. She tried to force a smile, but she couldn't hold it.

Jerry reached out and pulled her to him. "I'm sorry, Mom. I know how difficult it's been for you and Dad."

She sniffed. "I don't understand it, Jerry. We tried to be good parents to all three of you. Where did we go wrong?"

Jerry held her at arm's length then touched her face and tilted her chin so he could look her in the eyes. He knew she didn't want him to see the tears, but he wanted her to know he meant every word he said.

"Listen to me." He waited for her to look him in the eyes before continuing. "You've been a fantastic mother, and Dad's always been there for us. Neither of you did anything wrong."

"I don't think they even bother going to church. We raised them to be Christians."

"Yes, I know, and I wish I could tell you what's going on with them." Jerry wanted to do something to fix things, but he was helpless. "All I know is that you and Dad did everything you could do. The rest is up to the Lord."

She sucked in a ragged breath then slowly let it out. Jerry watched his mother as her chest rose and fell. He made a mental note to contact both Jennifer and Steven when they got back home to tell them what was going on. They needed to know how their lack of attentiveness was affecting their mother. They also needed to understand that the parents who cared for them and loved them through everything—good and bad—were not in the best of health.

Suddenly his mom let out a little chuckle. "And now I wonder if we're doing right by you."

"What are you talking about?"

"I'm afraid we're keeping you from finding a nice girl and settling down."

"If I find a girl half as good as you, Mom, trust me, I won't let her get away."

"Amanda's an awfully sweet girl," she said. "You might want to give her a chance."

"We're on vacation, Mom." He hated having to repeat this over and over, but she needed to understand that he wasn't about to start a relationship he couldn't follow through with. "I don't want to get too involved with someone I'm not going to see again. That wouldn't be fair to her or to me."

Her chin stopped quivering, and she leveled him with a look he knew too well—a look that let him know she could see right through him.

"I'm afraid, son, that it's too late for that. You're already involved with Amanda. I've seen how the two of you look at each other."

Jerry took a step away from his mom and shoved his hands into his pockets. "We're friends, that's all. We both like the outdoors, and we enjoy each other's company."

"And you both love the Lord, and you have the same values," she added. "That's a very good start of a strong relationship."

His mother obviously didn't understand how he wasn't about to do what his sister and brother had done. His parents needed him more than ever right now, and he wasn't about to abandon them.

"You look peaked," she said as she lifted her hand and touched his cheek. "Are you feeling okay?"

"I'm fine. Just tired."

"Tell you what. After dinner, you can hang out here while your father and I go for a little ride on that bicycle you rented us. I'm thinking it might be good for us to get out of your hair for a while." She paused and smiled. "Give you some alone time."

He didn't argue with her. He wanted his parents to do things together as much as possible for as long as they could. And, being honest with himself, he really could use some time alone.

It was nice having two cheerful parents acting civil toward each other through the meal. Not only had his dad enjoyed the day, but his mother was rested from her nap.

"That Timmy kid is so cute," his dad said. "Rosemary, did I tell you what he said when I gave him the treasure chest?"

She nodded. "Yes. Several times."

"He wants to see me again soon. Maybe we can keep looking for treasure, or I can teach him how to build a really cool sand castle."

"Dad, I'm sure he knows how to build a sand castle."

"Nope. He told me his daddy was too busy to take him to the beach." He shook his head and put down his fork. "It's a crying shame for a little boy to live so close to the beach and not know how to build a sand castle."

Jerry hopped up from the table as soon as everyone finished eating. "I'll clear the table. Y'all go on and have some fun."

"C'mon, Harold," his mom said. "You heard him. Let's go have us some fun!"

His dad did a little dance shuffle with a step back then a double step forward, a silly little grin quirking the corners of his lips. When he lifted his eyebrows and lowered them quickly, Jerry laughed.

"Don't wait up for us," he said as he wiggled his eyebrows.

* * * * *

The next morning, Amanda cleared the way for one more clinic that would be the last of the season. These lessons had been the highlight of her summer season in past years, but this year, everything was different—very topsy-turvy. Even though Jerry had been a customer for a couple of years, she hadn't given him much thought after he left her shop in the past. Sure, she thought he was attractive, but she rarely saw him other than when he rented the tandem bicycle and then returned it before he left the island. This year, however, was a completely different story. All she could think about most of the time was Jerry.

She had all the chairs in place and the snacks on the table in the back when Matthew walked in, grinning. "If my clinic doesn't get their attention, the food will. You know the way to any boy's heart."

"I want to make sure they have all positive associations with my store," she replied. "Before the clinics, summer was sort of dead around here. But ever since we started these clinics, summer is my best season."

He shrugged as he lined up on the counter some of the equipment he would demonstrate. "That would probably happen anyway. Summer's when all the skateboarders are out in droves. They just didn't know you were here before."

"You've been a big—"

Something caught her eye, and she forgot what she was about to say. Straddling the bicycle-built-for-two were Jerry's parents, as they peered into her window. She knew the glare on the south side of the building prevented them from making out specific faces inside. All they'd be able to see were moving shadows.

"Isn't that your friend's parents?" Matthew asked.

"Yes." Amanda came around from behind the counter and headed for the door. "I wonder if everything's okay."

"While you're out there, tell the man to put his helmet on."

She smiled at Matthew. "Aye-aye, sir."

The second she opened the door, both Rosemary and Harold snapped their heads in the other direction, as if they didn't want her to know they were looking at her. She had to force herself not to laugh, they were so cute.

"Hey, Rosemary, Harold! Is there something I can do for you?"

Rosemary glanced over her shoulder with a half smile. "No, sweetheart. Harold and I were just taking a spin around town. It's such a beautiful day."

"It's a wonderful day." Amanda took a few steps closer and lifted the helmet off the back of the bicycle. "Harold, I'd really like for you to wear this. We've had some pretty bad spills on bicycles around here, and I'd hate for you to get hurt."

He made a noise, but he took the helmet from her and plopped it on his head. "Happy?" he asked.

"I will be as soon as we get the chin strap fastened."

Harold stood still but scrunched his face as Amanda snapped the chin strap in place. A couple of middle school boys walked by and lifted their hands in a shy wave. Amanda motioned for them to go on inside.

"There ya go," she said. "We're about to have our last safety clinic. It'll only be an hour. If you're still out and about, why don't you two stop by for some snacks? I always have way more than enough."

Rosemary shook her head, while Harold nodded. "Whatcha got?"

"Oh, Harold, you don't need Amanda's snacks. We have plenty of food at the condo."

He winked at Amanda. "Yeah, but I bet she has better stuff than we have."

Rosemary groaned. "Probably." She took a deep breath and slowly let it out as she looked back around at Amanda. "If we're still out, perhaps we'll swing by. I don't want to keep him out too long."

After they left and Amanda went back inside, she found herself actually hoping they'd come back. She liked Rosemary and Harold, even though they bickered constantly. She knew they loved each other and were just letting off steam.

Matthew was about to get started, but first he asked if everything was okay. "I'm glad he didn't put up too much of a fuss about the helmet," he added. "But I wouldn't be surprised if he took it off as soon as they left." He chuckled. "He didn't seem happy about it at all."

"Oh, I think he liked me fussing over him," Amanda said. "He just likes to growl. Makes him feel more manly, I think."

With a smile, Matthew turned and whispered, "Yeah, we guys do like to roar just to let our voices be heard every now and then." Then he turned to the waiting kids and introduced the clinic.

Amanda recognized about half the kids from the year before. Some of them had brought friends who were new to the area, and others had found out about the clinic through fliers she'd posted and left in other businesses.

As soon as the clinic was well underway, Amanda pulled out her order book and listed the items Matthew recommended. Then she switched over to her computer and clicked around to order as much as she could online. Her distributors were good about getting things to her quickly.

At the end of the class, she rang up a few sales and let everyone know when she'd have all of Matthew's recommended items in stock. He thanked her and ran to meet someone for private lessons. She was glad when she finally had the place to herself.

The day went by fairly fast and without anything major happening. Occasionally she walked over to the window and glanced up the street for a sign of Jerry or his parents. But she didn't see a thing besides the usual foot and car traffic. She sold two high-priced bicycles and several hundred dollars' worth of skateboard gear.

When she got home from work, Lacy was in the kitchen cooking on all four burners. That was odd. The only thing Amanda had ever seen her sister cook since the stew was something from a box—mostly frozen.

"So what's for supper?" Amanda asked.

Lacy frowned. "I was practicing cooking chicken and dumplings with all the sides, but I think I messed up."

"Why chicken and dumplings?" Amanda walked over to see for herself. "It doesn't look bad. What's the problem?"

"The chicken is still raw." She stuck the fork in and pulled out one of the pieces from the pot.

Amanda glanced at the knobs and chuckled. "Did you forget to turn on the burner?"

Lacy gave her a look of frustration. "See? I'm such a mess-up. I never do anything right."

"That's not true," Amanda said. "You know fashion and makeup better than anyone I know."

"Maybe so, but that won't accomplish anything when I promised Brad I'd come over and cook for him and Timmy on Saturday night."

Amanda walked over to the counter where Lacy had a couple of cookbooks open and a page she'd printed from the Internet. "Let me see if I can help you figure this out."

Lacy's face scrunched in concentration as Amanda gave instructions from the cookbook. "I don't know what I'd do if you weren't here."

"You'd eventually figure it out." Amanda pointed to the pot of green beans in the back. "Keep an eye on the water in that pot. After it comes to a boil, you'll want to turn down the heat." She glanced at the clock on the wall. "I need to go wash up, so why don't you just finish everything?"

"You're leaving?" Lacy looked frightened.

"No, I'll be in the house."

Amanda hadn't been away from the kitchen more than five minutes when she smelled something burning. She scurried back to the kitchen, where smoke billowed up from the pot of beans.

"What's going on here?"

Lacy looked at her with tear-glistened eyes, her chin quivering. "You said to turn down the heat, but I turned it up by accident."

Amanda grabbed the pot and removed it from the burner. When the smoke died down, she carefully lifted the lid. The beans were burned beyond saving. "We'll just have to steam a package of frozen mixed vegetables."

"I'm such a loser," Lacy whined.

"Stop it. This happens to everyone when they first learn how to cook. You're just learning a little later than most." The instant the words came out, Amanda realized how harsh she sounded, and she regretted it. "I didn't mean it that way."

Lacy shook her head. "No, you're right. I never really cared about cooking before, but now…" Her voice faded and she swallowed hard. "I really want to show Brad I can do this."

Amanda understood and nodded. "We'll work on it, but you won't be a great cook overnight. That comes with time."

For the first time that night, Lacy smiled. "I doubt I'll ever be a great cook. All I care about is getting a decent meal on the table."

The two of them finished cooking dinner, and even though it wasn't the best chicken and dumplings Amanda had ever had, it was okay. The vegetables were crisp, which was how Lacy said Brad liked them.

"At least he won't think I was lying," Lacy said as she scooped up some of the chicken and a dumpling and looked at it.

Amanda studied her sister for a moment. "Exactly what did you tell Brad?"

A grin flickered across Lacy's face before she glanced downward to aviod Amanda's glare. "I said I cooked all the time."

"Why would you say something like that? You never cook."

Lacy shrugged. "I want Brad to like me."

"He likes you whether you can cook or not. Did you enjoy doing all this?"

"Not really."

"Listen, sweetie." Amanda reached out and took Lacy's hand in hers. "Don't ever try to be anything other than who you are."

Lacy hopped up from the table, grabbed her plate, and carried it over to the counter. "I do need to learn how to cook at least a few things. You can't keep taking care of me for the rest of my life."

"True, but it's a slow process. You can't do it all at once. This was a tough meal to tackle, with all the different items. Maybe next time you can try something simple, like pasta and sauce, or meat, potatoes, and a salad."

"Well," Lacy began as she glanced around at the mess, "that would be three meals—this one and the two you said. If I can do a couple more things, then I'd have a week's worth of dinners. We can eat out on weekends."

"Sounds like you have something up your sleeve. What's going on?"

Lacy grinned and lifted her eyebrows. "I know for sure now that I'm totally in love with Brad, and if I'm reading him correctly, he's falling in love with me."

Amanda decided to skip the lecture. Besides, what could she add to what she'd already said?

"So you think you two might get married one of these days?"

"That's the plan," Lacy replied and turned toward the sink. "Wanna help me with this? I can't believe we made such a mess."

As much as Amanda wanted to tell Lacy to do it herself, she couldn't. So she took off her watch and started clearing the table. A half hour later, they finished wiping the cabinets, and everything was done.

"Now, that wasn't so bad, was it?" Lacy brushed her hands together.

* * * * *

The next morning, an hour after Amanda opened the store, Tiffany came strutting in. "You look mighty chipper today. What are you up to?"

"Your man said he wanted you to hang out with him and his parents today, so I figured I'd come in so you could have a little time with them."

Amanda tilted her head and squinted at the teenager. "Speak English, Tiffany. What are you talking about?"

Tiffany giggled. "You know. That guy you've been seeing. Jerry. The one who's vacationing with the old people."

"Okay, so what makes you think I need time with them?"

With a puzzled expression, Tiffany tilted her head. "He asked me if I was working today, and when I said I might, he said good, and I said why, and then he said—"

Amanda held up both hands to stop her. "Whoa, slow down. Where did you see Jerry?"

Tiffany glanced over her shoulder and pointed. "He was right around the corner getting his parents a treat. I'm sure he'll be here any minute."

"Okay, thanks for letting me know." She thought for a moment about what to do. There wasn't much going on today, and she did have Tiffany right here, willing and able to work. "How long can you stay?"

Tiffany shrugged. "As long as you need me. There's nothing else to do." She grunted. "Summer can be so boring."

The bell on the door jingled, and they both turned toward it. In walked Rosemary, looking like she had something up her sleeve.

"Hi, Rosemary. Where's the rest of your crew?" Amanda asked.

"Outside arguing. Jerry wants the four of us to do something fun, and Harold insists we should go looking for treasure. Honestly, I don't know what's gotten into my husband. He's always liked treasure hunting, but I used to be able to distract him. Not anymore. Nowadays that's all he ever wants to do. Can you believe he wants to get one of those metal detectors we see all over the place?"

"A lot of people use them," Amanda said in his defense. "I've heard they find some valuable stuff."

"I'm sure," Rosemary said with a frown. "But that just seems wrong. When people find valuable things, they should turn them in."

Amanda already knew that Rosemary had a strong sense of right and wrong, even if no one else understood it. "I don't mind hunting for treasure," Amanda said. "I'm up for a nice long walk anyway. It'll be good to go outside and get some fresh air."

"See, Rosemary?" They jumped at the sound of Harold's voice by the back door. He chuckled. "Did I scare ya? I saw the back door open, so I figured I'd slip in that way."

"I must have left it open when I took out the garbage." Amanda leaned forward and looked around.

"If you're looking for Jerry, he refused to follow me in the back door. He said he didn't think you'd like that."

Amanda was about to tell him it didn't matter when she heard the front door. The whole group of them turned around as Jerry walked in, a goofy look on his face.

"What?" he said.

"Took you long enough to get in here," Harold said.

Jerry rubbed the back of his neck and smiled at his dad. "I had to find a place to park your bicycle."

Rosemary stepped up. "I hope you found a safe place for it."

"We can see it from here." Jerry pointed outside. "So, Amanda, how's business?"

"Can you go out and play with us?" Harold asked.

Amanda laughed out loud. "I thought you'd never ask. But I have a question."

"Uh-oh." Harold took a step back. "Looks like one of us is in trouble now, and it's probably me." He made a grumpy face. "It's always me."

"No, you're not in trouble, but there are three of you and only two seats on the bicycle. How—"

"Jerry walked." Rosemary reached out and gave her son a pat on the back. "He only had to run a couple of times to keep up with us."

Amanda glanced around the store. "I have an idea."

"Everyone be quiet," Harold announced. "The lady has an idea, and we all need to listen."

Amanda was having more fun than she could ever remember—and it was just a bunch of people standing around acting lighthearted and goofy. She laughed.

"So, Amanda dear," Rosemary said. "What's your idea?"

"My other tandem bicycle came back from the repair shop yesterday, and it's not booked until sometime next week. If you don't mind…" She glanced at Jerry, who smiled. "Do you mind?"

"I'd be honored to ride with you on a bicycle built for two."

A lump formed in Amanda's chest. She hadn't ridden on a tandem bicycle since Eric—and she'd had to talk him into it because he didn't think it was a cool thing for a guy to do. Jerry obviously didn't mind in the least. There hadn't been a second of hesitation when she suggested it.

"Okay, Tiffany, you can hold down the fort while the rest of us go play. Anyone up for a treasure hunt? I think I know where we might find something cool."

"All righty, then, let's go!" Harold was out the door in two seconds flat. Rosemary joined him.

Jerry helped Amanda get the tandem bicycle from the back room. "I want to thank you for being such a good sport," he whispered. "I haven't seen my dad this happy in…I don't know…years?"

"He's on vacation. He's supposed to be happy."

Jerry muscled the back end of the bicycle around a rack and then rolled it toward the door. "Until he met Timmy, he'd been a grouch ever since we got here." He looked at Amanda. "You want front or back?"

"Since I know where we're going, I'll take the front first. Then we can switch on the way back."

"Good idea."

"Hey, listen!" Harold hollered. "Music!"

Amanda slowed down. "That's the clock tower."

"I like it," Harold said. "Especially the love song that's playing now."

Amanda wondered what Jerry was thinking. She couldn't see his face since he was directly behind her, but she could tell he'd slowed down his pedaling.

"Come on," she said as she pointed. "Let's go that way."

When they came to a stop at the next intersection, Amanda turned around and noticed that Harold wasn't wearing his helmet. She knew he hated it, but she'd also seen some bad accidents where helmets had saved lives.

"I think your dad forgot his helmet," Amanda said. "Did he leave it in the store?"

Jerry folded his arms, shook his head, and closed his eyes for a second. "Nope. He refuses to wear it. Says it's for kids."

"I have some extras in the store. Let's go back and get one."

He held up a finger then turned toward his parents. "Hey, Dad, will you wear a helmet?"

"I already told you, *no*!" Harold grabbed the handlebars on the back of the bicycle and motioned for Rosemary to start pedaling. "Let's go before they start treating us like kids."

"Harold, they're telling you this for your own good."

"I don't care." His tone sounded more juvenile than most teenagers. "If you want to wear a helmet, that's your business, but I've gone seventy-something years without one, and I do just fine."

Rosemary cast an apologetic glance at Amanda before pushing off and pedaling. "You two lead the way. We'll be right behind you."

"What do you think?" Amanda asked.

Jerry squared his shoulders. "I agree with you, but I don't want to make a scene. Dad's not gonna do anything he doesn't want to do."

"Okay, I guess since he's not going to change his mind, we might as well accept it." Amanda resisted the urge to call the whole rest of the bicycle ride off, but she didn't want to make everyone miserable. Besides, chances were, nothing would happen if they didn't go very far.

Jerry pedaled harder, while Amanda steered and did her share of pedaling. "The only time I've ever ridden one of these things is when I took Mom for a spin on the one we rented, and I was up front."

"Are you having trouble being behind me?" she called over her shoulder.

"Oh, yeah, I can handle being behind you any day."

Amanda resisted the urge to stop, turn around, and face him. His closeness reminded her of how easy it was to fall for a nice guy who said all the right things and was good-looking to boot.

Still facing straight ahead, she leaned back. "I thought we'd swing around by the bridge, come back to the clock tower and walk around, then maybe check out the beach."

"Sounds good. Let's go!"

"You two gonna sit there and talk all day, or are we going on a treasure hunt?"

"Have patience, Harold!"

Amanda and Jerry took off and maneuvered around Rosemary and Harold, who followed right behind. As they made their way down the street, people in cars slowed down and waved—something Amanda enjoyed about riding this bicycle built for two. When she was on a single, no one paid a bit of attention to her.

"This has always been such a friendly town!" Jerry shouted so she could hear above the traffic sounds.

Amanda laughed. "That's because we're on a tandem."

"Yeah, I figured as much."

As they approached the intersection, Amanda motioned to slow down. They were barely moving when a car from the adjacent street came barreling around the corner, turning right in front of them and not slowing down a bit. Her heart thudded at the close call. Suddenly she heard the screeching sound of brakes, and before she had a chance to turn around to see what was happening, the sound of Rosemary's scream pierced the air.

Chapter Ten

....

Jerry didn't waste a second in getting off the back of the bicycle. Amanda was right behind him.

"Dad?" Jerry leaned over his father, who'd fallen off the bicycle and obviously hit his head on the curb. "Can you hear me?"

A soft moan came from the elderly man, who was bleeding at the temple. He didn't appear to be injured anywhere else, but no one was sure, so they didn't try to move him. Amanda knelt down beside Jerry and Rosemary, whose panic-stricken face twisted her insides.

Jerry quickly pulled his cell phone out of his back pocket and requested emergency service. Amanda went through the motions of telling Jerry where they were so he could relay it to the operator, but she was numb with worry.

After Jerry flipped his phone shut, Amanda quickly assumed the role of comforter to Rosemary. She placed her arm around the elderly woman's trembling shoulders and whispered what she hoped were soothing words.

"I'm sure he'll be okay," Amanda said. "The paramedics will be here soon."

She nervously leaned over and glanced down the street, hoping to hear the wail of sirens. Jerry tried to assess the situation, but there was so much blood that, by now, it was hard to tell much. He cast a worried glance toward Amanda. She reached out and gently laid her hand on his shoulder.

Jerry closed his eyes. Amanda assumed he was praying, so she offered her own to the Lord. *Please protect this family, Lord.*

When the siren's shrill sound came blasting toward them, Amanda opened her eyes, as a sense of warmth washed over her. She gulped and took a step back so the paramedics could get to Harold, who'd opened his eyes.

"What's going on here?" Harold asked. He lifted his head, but the paramedic gently pulled it back down and held it.

"You had a nasty fall, Dad," Jerry said softly.

Harold tried to get up, and it took both paramedics to nudge him back down. "Let's get you to the hospital and make sure nothing's broken."

"I don't need to go to a hospital." Harold's voice came out in a rasp as he struggled to get up. But the paramedics were stronger, so he gave up. He glanced over at his son and smiled. "Glad you're here, Steven."

Amanda watched the color drain from Jerry's face at the mention of his brother's name. His very absent brother who rarely gave their parents the time of day. She considered trying to console Jerry, but she had no idea what to say.

It took several minutes for the paramedics to get Harold on a gurney and into the ambulance. One of them hung back and got pertinent information from Jerry. Rosemary asked to go with them. The paramedics exchanged a glance before looking at Jerry for assistance.

"Mom, I want you to go with us." Jerry's firm voice startled Amanda. She'd never heard him talk to either of his parents in such a stern tone, but she fully understood it.

"What if he needs me?" Her chin quivered, and she sniffed. "I should have been more careful."

Jerry gritted his teeth. "It's my fault. I should have insisted he wear his helmet."

Amanda felt her own share of guilt in the incident. If only she'd made him understand the necessity of the helmet, and if only she'd waited a couple of seconds longer to let them catch up. But too late for all that now.

"What hospital are you taking him to?" Amanda asked the paramedic.

"Palms of Pasadena."

She nodded. "I know where that is. We have to go back to get a car, but it won't take long."

Harold moaned. Rosemary's hand flew to her mouth. "M–my husband…"

"He's stabilized." The paramedic jotted something down then glanced up at them. "We have everything we need. You might want to give it about twenty minutes. It'll take that long to get him checked in."

Amanda took charge, now that Jerry agreed. "Let's get these bicycles back to the shop. We can go to my house and get my car; then I can drive to the hospital. I'm sure Tiffany won't mind sticking around for the rest of the day."

Jerry opened his mouth to speak, but Amanda gave him her no-nonsense stare that always worked with Lacy. She was relieved that he didn't argue.

Amanda used her cell phone to call Tiffany to explain what they needed to do. "We'll drop off the bicycles and leave right away. I hope you can stay until closing."

"No problem," Tiffany replied.

They were in and out of the shop in the time it took them to drop off the bicycles and for Amanda to grab her purse. "Let's go." She headed out the door, with Jerry and Rosemary right behind her.

Five minutes later they were in her car, on their way to the Palms of Pasadena Hospital. Once the hospital was in view, Amanda glanced over at Jerry to see how he was holding up. His jaw was set, and he stared straight ahead. He appeared to be in shock. Then she looked at Rosemary in the rearview mirror and saw that she wasn't any better than Jerry. Amanda knew that nothing she said would change anything, so she pulled up to the emergency entrance in silence. Once she stopped the car, she gestured toward the door. "You two go on in. I'll park the car and be there in a few minutes."

Jerry got out and held the back door for his mother. Then he leaned over and forced a half smile. "Thanks for doing this. If it weren't for you, well…"

If it weren't for her, Harold wouldn't have been on that bike, and he wouldn't have fallen. She gulped, nodded, and offered what she hoped was a comforting smile. "Go help your parents. I'll be there soon."

After she got the car parked and locked, she whipped out her cell phone to call Pastor Zach and request prayers for Jerry and his parents. He promised to not only pray for them but said he'd call the prayer group leaders and get the word out. Amanda knew it wouldn't stop there. The Treasure Island Community Church had the most generous members on the island and in St. Petersburg. She wasn't sure exactly what they'd do, but they'd come up with something, and it wouldn't take long. She'd been on the receiving end of it enough to know how loving they were.

* * * * *

Jerry had his arm around his mother and cradled her elbow to keep her from falling. Although currently shaky, she didn't normally have a serious balance issue—at least not yet—but her nerves were frazzled from the accident. Somehow she'd managed to stay upright when his dad had tumbled to the street. But immediately after she looked at his dad, her knees buckled and she had to be helped up.

As soon as they walked into the emergency entrance, they were greeted by someone in uniform, who asked if they needed assistance. Jerry gave their information, and then they were asked to wait. He guided his mother to the chairs and helped her into one of them. Nervous energy prevented him from sitting down beside her, so he was glad when Amanda walked through the automatic doors and joined them.

One of the things he appreciated about Amanda was her ability to quickly size up situations and immediately react in the most appropriate way. He suspected it had something to do with all the practice of looking after her sister.

"Any news?" she asked as she sat down next to his mother and took her hand. Jerry's heart warmed at how well his mother responded to Amanda's nurturing.

Jerry shook his head. "Not yet."

Amanda turned to his mother and squeezed her hand. "I called the pastor, and he's going to get the prayer chain going."

His mother managed a weak smile as tears glistened in her eyes. In spite of all the bickering, there was never any doubt that his parents deeply loved each other.

They waited another ten minutes before they were called to the desk. The nurse ushered them past the doors and into a room where his dad lay in bed, hooked up to monitors, with machines buzzing and beeping all around him. His eyes were closed, but the instant Amanda cleared her throat, he opened them.

Jerry leaned over the bed. "Dad?"

The elderly man blinked as though confused. "Steven?"

"No, Dad, I'm Jerry."

As his dad closed his eyes, a tear trickled down his cheek. The only signs of the accident were a bandage on his head where he had hit the curb and a large bruise on his forearm.

A lump formed in Jerry's throat as he tried to think of something to say. He was grateful when Amanda stepped up to his side and took over.

"You had a nasty spill, Harold."

His dad opened one eye and stared at Amanda for a moment. "Who are you?"

She sucked in a breath and carefully took his hand without disrupting any of the attached tubes. "I own the shop where your son Jerry rents the bicycle built for two that you and Rosemary like to ride."

He frowned then chuckled. "Oh yeah. I remember." His gaze moved from Jerry to Amanda; then he seemed to search for something or someone else. "Where's my wife?"

Amanda let go of his hand, took a step back, and gently guided Jerry's mother into his dad's line of vision. "Here she is."

Jerry put his arm around his mother and pulled her toward his dad. "Mom and I have been very worried about you." He didn't know what else to say. It was obvious that his dad still didn't recognize him, and he hated to admit, even to himself, that it broke his heart.

"Where does it hurt, Harold?" his mother asked.

His dad squirmed then grimaced in pain. A medical assistant rushed into the room to see what was going on.

"Stop fussing over me," his dad barked. "Just do what you gotta do so I can get outta here."

The young woman who looked barely old enough to be out of high school shook her head. "Sorry, Mr. Simpson, but we have to keep you overnight for observation."

"I'm not spending the night here."

"If you choose to check yourself out, we'll have to let the insurance company know, and they might not pay your bill."

Jerry whipped around to see his dad's reaction. He was surprised when all he got was a snort and a snide remark about how insurance companies ran people's lives.

After the woman left, Jerry glared down at his dad. "She can't help it."

"I know, but this is ridiculous. I fell down, and now they act like I might not live if I go home."

When the doctor arrived and asked to speak to Jerry and his mother, Amanda suddenly reappeared and took over with his dad. He was glad to have her there. She always knew what to do, what to say, and when to disappear.

The doctor led them to a small room nearby and offered them a seat. Jerry held his mother's hand, just in case the news was bad.

"How serious is it?" Jerry asked.

"We're not sure yet, but we think he suffered a concussion. I think he'll be fine in a day or two, but we need to keep him here to be sure." The doctor flipped the page on the chart in front of him. "He has a few bruises, but the brunt of the fall was mostly on his head." He glanced up and looked at Jerry's mother. "Can you give me a list of his prescriptions?"

She scrunched her forehead as she thought. "I can't remember the names of all of them."

"We have them at the condo we're renting," Jerry said. "Want us to go home and write down all the names of his medicine?"

The doctor nodded. "Better yet, if you can bring them in, we'll administer them while he's here." He looked up with a stern expression and added, "Perhaps we can make a few adjustments that might help."

Jerry nodded. "We can do that."

"Anything else I need to know about his health?" The doctor poised his pen above the chart and glanced up at his mother, who seemed too distraught to talk, so Jerry took over.

"He's been diagnosed with Alzheimer's."

"That explains a few things," the doctor said as he jotted a few things in the chart. "I wondered about that."

"Early stages. His memory is good at times, and others…" Jerry's voice trailed off.

The doctor chewed his bottom lip as he studied the chart then put it down. "This says they were riding a bicycle built for two."

Jerry nodded. "I always rent one so they can stay active."

"I understand that exercise is important for his health, but he needs to take all the safety precautions. Does he have access to a helmet?"

Jerry felt sick to his stomach. If he'd been stronger and made his dad wear the helmet, this wouldn't have been as serious. "He has one, but he hates wearing it."

The doctor smiled with a hint of sympathy. "My parents hate them, too, but I always insist." He stood up and gestured for them to go ahead of him. "If I had to wager a guess, I think he'll be well enough to go home on Saturday—unless something shows up in the x-ray."

"Just do whatever it takes to make him better," Jerry said. "I'll bring his prescriptions as soon as I can."

As they headed back to the small room, his mother babbled about how it wasn't Jerry's fault; it was hers. She was the one steering the bike.

His dad had a scowl on his face when they got to his room. "I wanna go home."

"Sorry, Dad, but you have to stay here for a couple of days."

"That's silly." He turned his head toward the window, away from Jerry and his mother.

"The next time you go out on the bicycle, you need to wear your helmet," Jerry said. "I shouldn't have let you go off without it."

His mother reached out and squeezed his arm. "It's not your fault, honey. I'm the one who wasn't careful enough."

Jerry argued for a moment and then figured there was no point. Everyone felt responsible, and nothing would change that. When his mom offered to stay in the hospital while he and Amanda went back for his dad's medicine, he nodded his agreement. At least if something happened to her there, someone would be able to help her.

Amanda didn't talk much on the way to the condo, and Jerry was glad. Not only was there not much to say, any conversation would seem trite and disrespectful under the circumstances.

* * * * *

She sensed that he needed his space, so Amanda remained quiet as she drove him to the condo. He said he'd go back to the hospital in his own car, so after dropping Jerry off, she headed straight home.

Her heart sank when she saw Brad's car parked at the curb. After all she'd been through, she didn't feel like socializing.

The instant she walked inside, Timmy accosted her. "Daddy said Gramps is in the hospital, and I wanna go see him."

Amanda glanced over at Lacy, who sat on the sofa beside Brad, both of them staring at her. "How did you know?"

Lacy stood up and walked toward her. "We went to see you at the shop, and Tiffany told us. Why didn't you call me?"

Amanda shut her eyes and said a short prayer for guidance and the ability to keep her temper in check. Then she took a deep breath and slowly let it out. "I haven't had a chance."

"Well, is he going to live?"

Lacy didn't have any tact, and she needed to be more careful around Timmy or she'd scare the poor child half to death. "I'm pretty sure it's not that serious."

"Tiffany said he hit his head and was gushing blood." Lacy scrunched her nose and shivered.

Brad stood up and took Lacy by the hand. "Sometimes it looks worse than it is." He glanced over at Amanda as if looking for affirmation.

"I'm pretty sure that's the case with Harold. He hit his head on the curb and suffered what the doctor thinks is a mild concussion. Hopefully, there won't be any long-term problems."

"Is Gramps gonna die?" Timmy's quivering voice let Amanda know they'd frightened him.

Amanda looked down at the little boy who stared up at her, wide-eyed and obviously worried sick about Gramps. She shook her head. "No, honey, he's not going to die—at least not anytime soon, from what we can tell. He fell and got a bad bump on his head."

"He's sick, Timmy," Brad added.

Timmy jumped up and down. "I don't want Gramps to be sick. Can I go see him?"

Amanda glanced over at Brad, who waited for her answer. "I can call Jerry and ask what he thinks."

Timmy grinned. "Gramps will wanna see me. He's my bestest friend in the whole wide world."

Brad looked helpless, so Amanda nodded. "I'm sure he'll want to see you, Timmy, but I'm not sure—"

"Hey, champ, why don't we head on home and let the ladies have a little time alone?" Brad reached for Timmy's hand.

Timmy's smile turned to a frown as he yanked away from his father. "No. I wanna go see Gramps."

Amanda didn't feel like dealing with this. "Let me try giving Jerry a call and see what he thinks."

Jerry answered his cell phone immediately. After Amanda explained that Timmy was adamant about wanting to see Gramps, he said he thought that might be an excellent idea. "I just hope Dad remembers Timmy."

"Maybe you can tell him Timmy is coming, and if he doesn't remember him, you can explain who he is."

"Good idea."

"This might be what both of them need," Amanda said.

"Why don't you give me about an hour with him before you bring Timmy?" Jerry asked.

Amanda hadn't planned to go back to the hospital, but she couldn't turn him down after all he'd been through. "Okay, but let me know if anything changes."

Timmy was ecstatic about visiting Gramps in the hospital. "Can we go to the store and get him something really cool?"

Brad cast another helpless glance in Amanda's direction. "What does he want?"

"I know what he likes," Timmy said. "Just take me to the store, and I'll show you."

Amanda nodded. "He's at Palms of Pasadena. Why don't we meet there in an hour?"

Timmy looked up at his dad, who nodded. "I'll take him to the store, and we'll meet both of you there."

Lacy narrowed her eyes, gave Amanda a cursory glance, crossed the room, grabbed her handbag, and headed for the door. "I'm going with you and Timmy. My sister obviously doesn't want me around."

Amanda's jaw went slack. How could her sister be so harsh when she was still in shock over what had happened to Harold? But she didn't have a chance to say a word before Brad, Timmy, and Lacy took off.

After they were gone, Amanda plopped down on the sofa and leaned her head back. This had been an unbelievable day. She'd felt pretty good that morning, but her pulse quickly shot up when Jerry arrived.

Every few minutes she looked at the clock, waiting for the time she needed to leave in order to meet Brad, Timmy, and Lacy at the hospital. After a half hour, she got up to splash a little water on her face to try to erase some of the visible tension. One look in the mirror let her know she needed more than a few drops of water.

She powdered her face then patted a little blush on her cheeks before applying a thin layer of lip gloss. It didn't do much, but she felt a little better for at least attempting to look human.

On the way, she spotted a guy on the street selling summer bouquets, so she stopped and purchased one for Harold. It wasn't much, but at least she wouldn't walk into the hospital empty-handed.

When she arrived at the emergency room reception desk, Amanda was directed to another wing. "They put him in a room," the receptionist explained. Then she gave detailed directions.

She pulled out her cell phone and called Lacy to let her know where to go. Once she got to Harold's wing, she waited by the nursing station for Lacy, Timmy, and Brad. They arrived about ten minutes later.

"I got Gramps his favorite thing," Timmy announced the instant he spotted her.

"What's that?" Amanda asked.

"It's a surprise." He beamed as he clenched the bag tightly in his fist.

The lady at the desk said Timmy couldn't go into the patient area. He scrunched his face and started wailing.

Amanda gestured for the nurse to step away. "Gramps really loves little Timmy. Can't you make at least one exception? I think it'll make him feel so much better…." Amanda paused for a couple of seconds before adding, "It'll give Gramps something to look forward to, and he'll be much happier."

The nurse pondered for a moment and finally nodded. After the nurse directed them to Harold's room, the four of them headed down the hall. Amanda could only imagine what the medical staff thought.

When they were halfway there, Amanda heard Harold bellowing about wanting to go home and then Rosemary telling him to be quiet. Well, at least things were back to normal.

Timmy yanked free from his dad's hand and bolted toward Harold's room before anyone could stop him. "Timmy, come back here!" his dad yelled. "You can't run in a hospital!"

The little boy ignored his dad as he darted into the room. "Gramps! I brought you something to make you feel all better!"

By the time Amanda, Brad, and Lacy got to Harold's room, Timmy was already up in the bed beside him. To Amanda's surprise, Harold's face was the picture of pure joy.

"What took you so long to get here?" Harold asked. "I figured you'd come right away and spring me from this awful place."

Timmy beamed right back at him. "Here, Gramps." He shoved the bag toward Harold. "Daddy took me to the store, and I picked these out just for you."

Harold grinned as he looked around the room at everyone. Then he settled his gaze on Timmy. "You did this for me?"

Timmy nodded. "It's all yours. Open it."

As Harold slowly opened the bag, Timmy bounced beside him on the bed. Brad reached out to still him, but Jerry shook his head and gestured to let him be.

"Oh, wow!" Harold pulled out a stack of baseball cards. "This is perfect!" He chuckled. "Who all is in here?"

Timmy helped him open the packs of cards, and they made all kinds of joyful sounds as they flipped through the stack. Amanda watched in awe as she realized that until Timmy had arrived, Harold was grumpy and completely out of sorts. Now that the little boy was beside him, the whole room seemed charged with positive energy.

"Here, let me take that." Jerry reached for the flowers in Amanda's hand. She'd forgotten she had them. "Dad, Amanda brought you some flowers."

Harold barely glanced up. "That's nice." Then he turned all his attention back to Timmy.

Amanda looked around for her sister. Lacy hung back by the door looking bored, while Brad looked awkward and bewildered by everything around him. He stepped back and took Lacy's hand.

"When I get outta this place, we're gonna go on a great big treasure hunt," Harold whispered loud enough for everyone in the room to hear. "One of the nurses said she knew where we might find some secret stuff."

Timmy turned and looked at his dad, who nodded. Then he turned back to Harold. "The man at the store told me about a really cool place I want to take you."

"Where's that?"

"Babe Ruth's house!"

Chapter Eleven
....

"Babe Ruth's house?" Harold whistled. "Don't tell me he lived on Treasure Island."

Brad pulled away from Lacy. "Apparently he had a bungalow in a neighborhood not too far from Amanda's shop. The house has been renovated like most of them in the area."

"That, I gotta see." Harold extended his hand that wasn't hooked up to monitors and tousled Timmy's hair. "Thanks, little buddy. I can't wait to see Babe Ruth's place."

Amanda could tell that her presence didn't mean much, so she walked up to Harold and patted his arm. "Take care, Harold. I'll see you later."

He waved but never took his eyes off Timmy. She was amazed at how strong the connection was between them.

Jerry joined her as she left the room. "I'll walk you to your car."

This had been an emotionally charged day, and Amanda felt the effects with a stiff neck and numbing thoughts. Jerry seemed to sense that she wasn't in the mood for conversation. They rode down in the elevator in silence.

When they got to her car, he took her key, unlocked the door, and opened it for her. "I appreciate all you've done for my family, Amanda. It means the world to me."

She looked up at him and instantly felt a thudding sensation in her chest. She had to quickly glance away.

"Amanda?"

She looked back at him and away again, doing everything in her power to guard her heart. "Yes?"

Without any warning, he cupped her chin in his hand and tilted it enough to force eye contact. As he lowered his face to hers, she was certain he could hear her heart pounding out of control.

The kiss was light and brief, but she felt as though she'd been struck by something she couldn't describe. When she looked into Jerry's eyes, she knew he felt it, too.

"I'll call you," he whispered before letting go.

She watched him walk back toward the entrance to the hospital, and she felt as though he took a part of her with him. Once he disappeared through the electric doors, she leaned her head against the car window and pressed her hand onto the warm steering wheel. All sorts of crazy thoughts flitted through her mind. *This can't be happening*, she thought.

After Eric, Amanda had walked around in a numbing stupor, barely going through the motions of day-to-day life. Without her faith, she wasn't sure what she would have done. Fortunately, after months of prayer and listening to the Word, she had managed to overcome the deepest grief she could ever imagine experiencing.

She'd stopped thinking about Eric after time passed. The bicycle shop took up most of her time, and she threw herself into church-related activities. Pastor Zach knew he could count on her to do things no one else had time to do, and she liked it that way. Not having time for another romantic relationship kept her from being too involved in anything that could hurt her personally.

And now she'd gone and fallen in love again.

As she crossed the causeway that led from St. Petersburg to Treasure Island, she looked out over the water. A motorboat sped past a tiny sailboat, reminding her that everything had its own course and timing. She was like the sailboat, leaning and following the wind. If she continued to allow herself to drift in directions determined by other people, she might never experience all that love had to offer. However, if she became more like the motorboat, she might find herself going too fast and hitting a wall.

Now that she was older, more experienced, and hopefully wiser, she should be able to prevent something like that from happening again. But could she? Would Jerry be the force that shifted the world beneath her again?

Focusing on the road in front of her, she appealed to God and asked for help. *I'm not trying to tell you how to do Your job, Lord, but please keep me from getting hurt again.* She continued praying for help in avoiding a relationship with Jerry because she didn't think she could handle it after what had happened in the past.

As soon as she finished praying, she swallowed hard. The very fact that she'd prayed so specifically about protecting her heart reminded her that it was in jeopardy of being lost to Jerry. He was everything she could possibly want in a man. He was intelligent, kind, fun, and family-oriented. And most of all, he was a Christian. If she could have built the ideal man for herself, he would have been it. But she didn't want that in her life. She had everything just like she wanted it. Didn't she?

Well, there was one exception, the issue of him being here on vacation. As she pulled up in front of her house, she thought about how insane she was to let herself fall for a tourist. That was exactly what her mother had done—twice that Amanda knew about—and now she was the loneliest woman Amanda had ever known. Granted, her mother had given herself completely to the men she'd fallen in love with, and Amanda wasn't about to do that. However, the simple fact that she cared so much for Jerry was more than she could handle at the moment.

She got out of her car and walked up to the front door, thinking about how she'd gotten herself into this mess. Once inside, she dropped her handbag on the table by the door and walked through the house flipping on lights and talking to herself.

The clock in the hallway chimed the hour, which reminded her that she'd left Tiffany in charge of the store. She went to the kitchen and called the shop from the house phone.

"Hey, Tiffany, everything okay?"

"Yes, we only had a couple of customers all afternoon. I sold that bicycle you had on sale, and the rest was about skating stuff."

"I just wanted to make sure you were okay. Want me to come lock up?"

"No, that's okay. I'll do it. How's Mr. Simpson?"

"Looks like he'll be fine. Just a mild concussion."

"That's good. Let me know if you need me again. I'm trying to save some money for college. Mom said she'll help me out, but she can't pay for everything."

Fortunately the shop did well, regardless of the economy, so Amanda was able to hire some extra help. "I'll probably need you a few more hours this week. Thanks, Tiffany. I don't know what I'd do without you."

Tiffany giggled. "Maybe you can write me a reference…you know, for the future."

"I'll be glad to," Amanda said. She heard the sound of car doors slamming, so she walked over to the window and separated a slat of the vertical blinds. Lacy was home. "Just let me know when."

She headed to the kitchen to return the phone to the docking station. When she came back, Lacy stood at the door, chin jutted, eyes narrowed, and looking ready to hurt someone.

"What happened to you?"

Lacy growled and shook her head. "I can't believe what Brad just told me."

"Obviously something you didn't appreciate."

"He said I was a spoiled brat." She tossed her purse onto the sofa and stomped into the kitchen. "What's for supper?"

"I don't know, Lacy; I just got home."

Lacy's eyebrows came together as she pouted. "I'm starving. Maybe you can go out and get us something."

Brad might have a point. Amanda nodded. "I'll fix dinner. Come on into the kitchen and tell me all about it."

Lacy sat at the kitchen table while Amanda perused the refrigerator and cupboards for something quick and easy. She settled on grilled cheese sandwiches and canned soup while Lacy told her how she'd wanted to leave the hospital but Brad said he wanted to give Timmy a little time with Gramps.

"That sounds reasonable to me," Amanda said.

"Reasonable?" The shrillness in Lacy's voice sent a stabbing pain through Amanda's head. "He's supposed to care about how I feel. I was bored stiff just standing there while an old man got all excited over some stupid baseball cards."

Amanda slammed the pot down on the counter and turned to face her sister. She'd put up with enough, and it was about time to let her know how selfish she sounded.

Lacy's eyes widened. "What was that all about?"

"You really don't know, do you?" Amanda leaned against the cupboard and stared at her sister.

"Don't stop cooking," Lacy said. "I'm hungry."

"So am I, but you need to listen to me, Lacy. I've been taking care of you almost all our lives, and it looks like I haven't done such a good job."

"What are you talking about?"

"When we were kids…" Amanda had to pause to settle her shaky voice. "When we were kids, I knew Mom couldn't deal with two daughters, so I pretty much took over. I had no idea what I was doing. All I knew was that I was responsible for you and everything that happened to you. I did the best I could, considering the fact that I started trying to be your mother when I was barely a teenager."

Lacy squeezed her eyes shut. "Stop it, Amanda. I don't want to hear this."

"Too bad, because you're going to listen to me."

Lacy stood up, but when Amanda took a step toward her and pointed to the chair, she sat back down. "Okay, okay, just get it over with and cook us some dinner."

Amanda's jaw tightened, but she knew she had to continue or Lacy would never get what she needed. "You were like a live doll to me. I made sure you had clothes to wear and food to eat and that your teeth were brushed. Then when you graduated from high school, it was obvious that you weren't ready for the real world, so I paid your tuition to college—and it wasn't easy because I was barely making ends meet when you started. It's time you begin acting like a mature adult."

Lacy rolled her eyes. "This is so lame, Amanda. What's your point?"

"My point is…you need to realize that you're not the only person with needs. Brad clearly cares about you, but his first priority has to be his little boy."

"Timmy is such a brat." Lacy scowled.

"C'mon, Lacy, even you have to understand what's going on with him. He lost his mother, and his dad barely has time to take care of his basic needs."

"He's not the only kid who only has one parent. You and I—"

"You and I had each other." Amanda leveled her sister with a look that she knew would get her attention. "Timmy has no one but his dad."

Lacy lifted one shoulder and let it drop as she looked around the room to avoid Amanda's glare. Finally, she clicked her tongue. "Okay,

okay, I get it. Timmy has issues. So finish cooking so we can eat. I'm so over this."

"No, you're not. If you don't accept the fact that Timmy is a little boy and needs every ounce of energy and attention his father can give him, you need to stop seeing Brad."

Lacy stood up. "I don't need this right now. You sound just like Brad. Call me when supper's ready." She stormed out of the room, leaving Amanda standing there with her mouth hanging open.

Amanda managed to pull herself together long enough to cook dinner and put it on the table. She called for Lacy, who came without having to be told a second time. They ate in near silence, with only a few insignificant words exchanged through the entire meal. When Lacy was finished, she carried her plate and bowl to the sink and left the kitchen.

For once, Amanda didn't mind that Lacy didn't offer to help clean up. She needed to be alone, and she was grateful for the silence. Her mind raced through the events of the day until she finally had the last plate in the dishwasher and the rag draped over the faucet. She went to her room and got ready for bed.

When she arrived at the shop the next morning, a young woman wearing spandex stood at the door. Amanda was more than happy to start out the day busy and maintain a steady pace until closing. When she got home, she found that Lacy had already ordered pizza and left the half-empty box for her on the kitchen counter.

* * * * *

Jerry was happy to have his dad home, but he wasn't nearly as happy as his dad was to be home. They didn't even have his bags unpacked when his father started pacing.

"What's wrong, Dad?"

"I'm bored."

"You haven't been home more than ten minutes. How can you be bored?"

"Don't know. I just am."

"Why don't you rest for a little while and then we'll think of something to do."

His dad turned to him and lifted his hands. "I don't wanna rest. That's all I've been doing for the past couple of days."

"You're not supposed to exert yourself!" his mother hollered from the kitchen. "Doctor's orders."

"That doctor's just a kid. What does he know?"

Jerry couldn't help but laugh. "Okay, so what do you want to do?"

"Call Timmy's father and see if he can come over."

"I can't do that, Dad. It doesn't seem appropriate."

"That's ridiculous. What's not appropriate about an old man enjoying the company of a boy?"

Jerry couldn't think of anything wrong with his dad talking to Timmy because he knew where his heart was. "Tell you what I'll do. Later on, I'll call Amanda and see if she can get her sister to arrange for us to meet at her store sometime next week."

His dad narrowed his eyes and turned back to look out the window at the Gulf of Mexico. The sun still hung above the water, but it wouldn't be long before it set. As he turned back to face Jerry, his expression changed to a look of resignation.

"Okay." He paused for a moment. "Do you think Timmy might be in church tomorrow?"

Jerry wasn't sure, but he didn't remember seeing either Timmy or Brad in church. "I really don't know, but I doubt it."

"That's sad. Timmy needs a good Christian upbringing—like you had."

"Yes, I agree."

"Harold, I hope you don't get between Timmy and his father about church." Jerry's mother stood in the opening between the kitchen and the living room, wiping her hands on a towel. "You know it's none of our business what they choose to do."

"I disagree, Rosemary. If he's not getting any Bible teaching at home, someone needs to talk to him about the Lord."

She headed back into the kitchen, mumbling under her breath. Jerry saw both sides, but he kept his mouth shut. Deep down he agreed with his dad, but he was sure his dad was spoiling for an argument, and he wasn't about to add the fuel.

"Let's go out onto the balcony and get a little fresh air, Dad. You've been cooped up inside way too long."

* * * * *

Sunday morning, as Amanda got ready for church, she wondered if she'd see Jerry and his folks. She was torn between wanting them there and wishing she'd never told them where she worshipped. Then she had a flash of guilty conscience.

Once she was dressed and ready, she rapped lightly on Lacy's bedroom door. "Lacy, are you awake?"

"What do you want?"

"Are you okay?"

"No. Leave me alone."

Amanda hadn't seen her sister in a couple of days—not since Brad had called her a spoiled brat and the two of them had talked about it. Amanda wondered if she'd gotten through to Lacy. Until now, she'd avoided confronting Lacy with her feelings, but it was time to face reality. Lacy needed to grow up and accept that the world didn't revolve around her.

"I'd like for you to go to church with me, Lacy."

"It's not doing you any good."

Amanda shook her head. "That's not why I go to church, and you know it."

"Just go and leave me alone."

With a heavy heart, Amanda left her sister alone in the house. Lacy was hurting, and Amanda had no idea what to do to help her.

All the way to church, she thought about how she could have handled the situation differently, and she couldn't think of a single way that wouldn't bring them right back to where they started. If she continued to coddle Lacy, nothing would change. It was time to make some major changes. Lacy had a college degree and a job, but she didn't have any major responsibilities. Amanda paid her mortgage and all the utilities. Occasionally Lacy helped out with food, but most of the time her entire paycheck went to designer clothes, handbags, shoes, and whatever else her heart desired—and that never involved anything outside herself.

Amanda decided right then that it was time to start charging her sister rent. Even though she didn't need the money now, Lacy needed to assume some of the responsibility of being a full-fledged adult. Until that happened, she'd remain in a fairy-tale world.

She managed to put Jerry out of her mind until she spotted him walking into the church with his parents. Her heart pounded hard against her chest, and she found herself short of breath.

Why had she let this happen? Before getting out of her car, she closed her eyes and asked the Lord for the strength to face Jerry without going to pieces and losing her heart to another man. Once she managed to calm herself down, she got out, turned toward the church, and put on her game face.

"Hey, Amanda!"

Matthew's voice was a welcome sound. She turned and smiled.

"Hey, Matthew. Have you seen Suzanne?"

"I think she went on vacation. Wanna sit with me?"

"Sure." She was thankful not to have to sit alone with Jerry in the sanctuary.

Unfortunately, knowing that Jerry and his parents were in the church prevented her from totally focusing on the sermon. Every now and then, Matthew glanced over at her and offered an understanding smile.

Once church was over, he chuckled. "Looks like you've got it bad, Amanda."

She bobbed her head but couldn't directly face him. "What are you talking about?"

"Oh, I think you know exactly what I'm saying. You have a thing for Jerry. Take my advice, and don't deny it."

Amanda felt her shoulders sag. Matthew could see right through her, so there was no point in continuing to pretend. "What am I supposed to do after he leaves?"

Matthew took her hand. "Don't look for problems before they happen. Pray about the relationship, and if it's something the Lord wants for you, He'll show you how to get it."

That sounded good, and if she'd been in his position talking to a friend, she might have said the same thing. But Matthew didn't grow up without a father, and he wasn't left at the altar. He had no idea what it was like to be abandoned.

"I don't know." She glanced over her shoulder and spotted Jerry talking to the pastor, who'd made his way to the back of the church. "It's just difficult knowing he's here on vacation and he hasn't given any indication that anything will change."

"Maybe you're not looking at the same thing I am." Matthew glanced back at Jerry then turned to face her again. "From my perspective, it looks like he's open to a relationship. I think he might just be waiting for a sign from you."

"A sign?"

Matthew nodded. "Yeah. Guys don't like rejection. We look for some kind of sign that the lady is as interested in us as we are in them before we make our move."

Amanda couldn't hold back her laughter. "You're kidding, right?"

"No." Matthew twisted his mouth and shook his head, making her laugh even harder. "Before a guy says 'I love you,' he wants to be pretty sure he'll hear it back. In fact, coming from a guy, it's more of a question than a statement."

"I never realized that."

"It's true." Matthew looked back at Jerry again. "I also know that he doesn't like you sitting next to me because he thinks you and I are…" He let out a nervous chuckle. "Well, you know."

She gave him a gentle shove. "He doesn't think that."

"Based on the way he keeps looking at us, he's not happy at all."

She quickly changed the subject. "Are you going to the Bible study today?"

"Yep. In fact, I'm leading it. The pastor has a family commitment, and he asked if I'd take over."

"Cool," she said out of the corner of her mouth. "This should be interesting. Will it involve skateboards?"

"Hey, give me some credit. I've been working hard on this lesson all week."

"Sorry." She knew that in spite of all his quirkiness and kidding around, Matthew took his walk with the Lord very seriously. "I'm sure it'll be wonderful, and I can't wait to get there."

"Okay, don't overdo it on the praise, either. I don't need that kind of pressure."

"I'll see you there in a few minutes, okay? I need to talk to Jerry's mother and see how things are going now that Harold's home from the hospital."

Matthew smiled and winked as he edged toward the aisle. "Great idea! Don't be late to class."

Some of Amanda's enthusiasm waned and turned to apprehension as she approached Rosemary. Rather than the cheerful greeting she normally received, all three of the Simpsons acted cool toward her. She regretted making such a big point of going all the way over to talk to them, but she couldn't turn around at this point.

"So how are you feeling, Harold?" The formal tone of her own voice startled her.

A frown wrinkled his forehead. "Like I fell on my head."

A nervous giggle escaped, so she forced a cough to recover. "I can imagine. I'm just glad it wasn't more serious."

She caught Rosemary casting a glance over toward Jerry, who took a small step back—almost as though he wanted to get away from her. This bothered her more than she ever imagined it would.

"Are you up for the Bible study?" She looked directly at Jerry, hoping he'd make more of an effort to talk to her. As it was, she wanted to run to the nearest dark corner and hide. Then Matthew's comments played through her mind, and that gave her strength.

Jerry opened his mouth, but Rosemary took charge of the situation. "I'm sorry, Amanda, but he needs to take us back to the condo. Why don't you come over this afternoon, and we can visit then?"

"Um...I don't know," Amanda began as she looked to Jerry for confirmation that it was okay. When he nodded, she felt an overwhelming relief. "Okay, I can stop by for a little while."

"Let's plan on having dinner together, okay?" At least Rosemary was trying.

"That sounds great."

"I'll have some hors d'oeuvres ready around four." Rosemary turned to Jerry and smiled in such a way that Amanda knew there was some unspoken communication going on between them. "Why don't we go to Captain Kosmakos for dinner?"

Amanda nodded. "Perfect! I love seafood."

Jerry offered a good-bye grin, while his mother gave her a hug then quickly took him and his dad by the hand to lead them away. Amanda felt as though something had happened between them, and it didn't seem good. At least she'd see them later, and hopefully whatever was going on would come to light. Was it possible that Matthew was right? Could Jerry be jealous? She didn't think so, but maybe....

* * * * *

"Don't assume anything, son," Harold said. "Just because she sat next to that boy doesn't mean there's something going on between them."

"It really doesn't matter if there is." Jerry stared straight ahead at the road. "What they do is their business."

"You expect me to believe you mean that?" Harold belted out a loud snort. "You're so in love with that girl, you're impossible to be around."

"Harold, stop it. Don't embarrass him."

"I'm not going to stop, Rosemary. I don't know what's going on with our youngest boy, but it's time he stopped trying to run our lives when he still has his own to deal with."

Jerry glanced in the rearview mirror and caught his dad staring directly at him. "Dad, I admit I do like Amanda. Very much. But we're leaving, and I probably won't see her again until next year."

"If there is a next year," his dad retorted. "We don't know what will happen the next day, let alone next year. You'd better seize the opportunity while you have it, or it might be gone. Even if she is involved with that boy, I think she's sweet on you."

Jerry grinned in spite of the jealous gnawing at his gut. "Thanks for the advice, Dad." He had no intention of taking it, but he wanted to end the argument.

"You're welcome."

His mother remained silent, so he turned to her. "Captain Kosmakos, huh?"

"I'm craving seafood." Her answer was so abrupt, he almost laughed.

"Not to mention the fact that it's always been my choice for comfort food."

She slowly nodded. "Yes, well, there is that. I figured you might be able to use a little comfort food."

"Thanks, Mom." He inhaled deeply and slowly blew it out. One thing Jerry always knew was that his parents were on his side—no matter what. Even when they thought he was blowing a major opportunity for love.

After they got his dad settled back at the condo, his mother handed him a shopping list. "Make sure you get everything I wrote down."

"I thought we were going out for dinner." He glanced at the list and looked back up at her. "You have something on here from almost every department in the grocery store."

"I promised her hors d'oeuvres, and I don't know what she likes."

Jerry knew better than to argue. His mother had always been a people-pleaser, from as far back as he could remember. When he had played high school football, she was the mom who brought snacks onto the field after the games. The guys had dubbed her "Team Mom," and she'd loved it.

"Okay, I'll get everything on the list." He made sure his dad was situated in the recliner before he left. Then he instructed his mother to call him if she needed anything else. Once he was alone, he had time to reflect.

His parents had nearly convinced him that he and Amanda were meant to be together. But seeing her sitting next to Matthew reminded him that there were quite a few things about her he didn't know.

She'd told him she and Matthew were just friends, but they seemed awfully cozy. They had an unspoken language between them that husbands and wives often had after years of marriage. He certainly couldn't compete with that. Besides, why should he? She lived here. He and his parents were on vacation, and they'd be going back to Atlanta soon.

He parked in the Publix parking lot, ran in, and picked up everything on the list. After he paid, he headed straight to the condo. When he arrived, his mother was grinning from ear to ear.

"What's up with you, Mom?" he asked.

"Oh, nothing." She headed for the door. "I think I'll go for a walk on the beach and get some fresh air. See you in a little while."

"Don't be gone long. Amanda will be here soon."

Chapter Twelve

. . . .

Amanda got to the Simpsons' condo a half hour early, so she decided to walk on the beach until she was supposed to arrive. She'd no sooner gotten to the edge of the water when Rosemary joined her.

"Hey, Amanda. Why don't you come on up?"

"I don't want to intrude. I'm way too early."

Rosemary waved her hand. "Don't worry about that. Jerry just got back from the grocery store, and he's putting things away. Harold fell asleep in his chair, so you and I can have a nice chat."

Amanda wasn't sure if that was a good thing, but how could she argue with the woman now? "If you don't mind…"

"Of course I don't mind. Come on. I'll fix you something to drink. Do you like sweet tea or lemonade?"

"Tea is fine." Amanda walked beside Rosemary until they got to the condo elevator. She was glad Jerry's mom had gotten over whatever had upset her earlier. Rosemary's cold shoulder at church had been disconcerting.

"Have you ever lived anywhere besides Treasure Island?" Rosemary asked.

"Only when I went to college, but that was just for a semester, I'm afraid."

"That doesn't count." Rosemary paused, turned back toward the water, then spun around to face her. "Just remember that sometimes moving to a new place is good for a person. It enables them to start over."

Amanda was speechless. She wasn't sure where Rosemary was going with that comment, and she didn't think she wanted to pursue the angle.

As soon as they stepped into the elevator, Rosemary turned to her and smiled. "So how long have you been going to Treasure Island Community Church?"

"About twenty years." Amanda braced herself for more interrogation.

"Is that where you met that young man you were sitting with this morning?"

Rosemary hadn't wasted a single second. "No, I've known Matthew since high school. We've been good friends for a long time."

"How good of friends are you?" She stopped, angled her head, and waited, giving Amanda a look that made her feel like if she didn't answer correctly, there might be repercussions.

"He tells me about his girlfriends and asks for advice. When my former fiancé left me at the altar several years ago, Matthew was there to console me."

Rosemary nodded her understanding. "I see. So how did he console you?"

"He was there when I needed to talk." Amanda felt very uncomfortable, but she didn't want to be rude, so she tried to give brief answers and hoped that Rosemary would change the subject.

But she didn't. The woman was like a shark.

"I'm sure he wanted to date you." Rosemary forced a smile. "You're such a sweet, pretty girl, I have no doubt he wanted more than friendship."

"Actually, that's not the case. Matthew likes a different type of girl—more the surfer type—and he's not ready to settle down. He's a professional skateboarder, and he plans to stay with that until he's too old to do it. That kind of lifestyle is very difficult on a relationship."

"So you've thought about it." Rosemary changed her position and looked at her from beneath hooded eyebrows.

"Not really." Amanda needed to end this conversation, since Rosemary obviously wasn't going to. "I'm just not attracted to him in that way. Matthew is only a friend, and that's how it's going to stay." She paused and gave Rosemary a firm stare, letting her know she was serious. Then she smiled. "I haven't been to Captain Kosmakos in a long time, and I'm really looking forward to it."

Suddenly Rosemary stopped, so Amanda followed suit and turned to the older woman, whose expression had turned to one that was disquieting. Amanda had a strange feeling in her gut.

"Tell me something, Amanda," Rosemary said softly but with resolve. "Do you always change the subject when you don't like what's being discussed?"

Amanda let her head fall forward as she expelled a burst of air. Leave it to Rosemary to cut to the chase. "I don't know...."

"I don't mean to upset you, dear, but my son is emotionally involved, and I don't want him getting hurt."

When Amanda looked back up at Rosemary, she simply shook her head. "I don't want anyone to get hurt—Jerry or me."

"I understand that." Rosemary reached for Amanda's hand and grasped it firmly between both of hers. "Harold and I were kind of hoping...well, we were thinking that something might develop between the two of you."

Amanda didn't say a word. What could she say? Even though she suspected as much, she was flummoxed by Rosemary's ready admission.

"Okay, I think it's time to lighten up," Rosemary finally said after a couple of minutes of silence between them. "Jerry should be done with the groceries by now, and hopefully he woke his father. Perhaps you can help me get the appetizers ready."

"You didn't have to go to all that trouble for me," Amanda said. "But I'll be glad to help you with anything you need."

"I want to say one more thing, and then I'll quit being so annoying."

Amanda waited for a few seconds, and when Rosemary didn't continue, she turned toward her. "What do you want to say?"

"You remind me of myself when I was younger. I did everything for everyone, and I rarely looked after myself. When our first two children were born, I wore myself out. Steven came first, and then three years later, we had Jennifer. As soon as she started kindergarten, I went back to work part-time, and that was the first time in my adult life I had my own life."

"When did Jerry enter the picture?" Amanda asked.

Rosemary smiled and shook her head. "About two years after we'd decided it was too late to have more children."

"I bet you're happy he came along."

"Oh, absolutely." Rosemary guided her toward the high-rise condo then took the lead to the elevator. "Jerry was the light in our lives during his entire childhood. After the other two were grown and gone, Jerry stuck around and made sure we weren't lonely."

Amanda detected a note of consternation in Rosemary's voice. "Where are Steven and Jennifer now?"

Rosemary punched the elevator button then turned to face Amanda while they waited. "Steven's company transfers him every couple of years. He's in Alabama now. Jennifer and her husband moved to North Carolina shortly after their daughter, Isabelle, was born."

"I bet you miss them."

"You bet right." The elevator door opened, and Rosemary got on and moved over for Amanda. "Jerry makes sure they call us every week, but he thinks we don't know he's behind the calls."

It sounded as though Jerry was quite a bit like Rosemary and Amanda—only in a much more masculine way. He didn't mind being a protector while at the same time taking care of everyone's feelings.

Unfortunately, that elevated him to a new level in Amanda's mind and made her care about him that much more.

The elevator came to a stop and dinged, and the door opened. Rosemary stepped out and headed toward the condo. "We don't need to tell anyone about our little discussion, okay?"

"Sure," Amanda agreed. "It's just between you and me."

"I knew you'd understand." When they got to the door, Rosemary reached for the knob and opened it. "I hope you're hungry."

Jerry greeted them as soon as they walked inside. "I already put a few things out on the dining room table, but I wasn't sure what you wanted with some of it."

Rosemary shooed them out of the kitchen. "I'll finish with the hors d'oeuvres. Why don't y'all go out on the balcony and chat? It's such a nice evening."

Amanda looked at Jerry, who appeared to be uncomfortable. "We don't—" she began before Jerry interrupted.

"Come on, Amanda." He gestured toward the sliding glass doors that led to the balcony. "We need to talk."

As soon as they stepped onto the balcony, Jerry slid the door closed behind them. She walked over to the railing and inhaled deeply.

"So what did you and Mom talk about?"

Amanda glanced over his shoulder and tried to act nonchalant. "Just regular stuff."

He chuckled. "I know my mom. She has an agenda, but I also know she probably swore you to secrecy. Please forgive her for being so aggressive."

There was no point in acting coy, with Jerry being so intuitive and direct. "Your mother means well, I'm sure."

"Yes, she does. But that's still not a good reason for putting you on the spot." She turned around and saw that he'd folded his arms, physically closing her off. His coolness was disarming.

"She asked me about Matthew."

Jerry looked like someone had punched him in the face. His jaw dropped, but he quickly recovered.

"Matthew and I have been very good friends for years. That's all. We've been there for each other when things have gotten rough."

"Isn't that the foundation of a strong relationship?"

She nodded. "Of course, but neither of us wants more than friendship with each other. I really don't like when people assume more than that."

Jerry frowned as he joined her at the railing and looked out over the Gulf. When he finally turned toward her, he offered a slight smile. "Trust me, I understand."

"My mother hasn't been the model parent...." Amanda paused and turned to see Jerry's reaction. He looked at her, waiting. "Not like your parents, anyway. She relied on me to help with Lacy. It wasn't easy—especially when I was in my last couple of years of high school and later, when Lacy started acting out in middle school. Matthew was a skateboarder and surfer, and I was more into school sports, like track and volleyball. We started out talking about sports, and then the conversations turned to more personal things. He had problems at home, so he started hanging out at my house to get away. Even back then people assumed he and I were an item, but the chemistry wasn't there."

"Did you even try?"

She shook her head and smiled. "Not really. Neither of us wanted to ruin a good thing. I think he might have had a crush on Lacy a few years ago, after she graduated from college, but her whining eventually got on his nerves. He's the one who helped me with her and my mother."

Jerry had one fist planted on a hip and the other hand on the rail. He turned to her and smiled—this time with warmth. "I'm glad you had someone to help you."

"You're fortunate to have such great parents," she added.

"Yes, I know. That's why I never want to let them down. Since we seem to be in the confession mode, I might as well let you know that I've been disappointed in my sister and brother. They don't come around as much as they should."

Movement inside the condo caught her eye. They both turned in time to see Rosemary gesturing for them to join her and Harold.

By the time they left the condo for the restaurant, Amanda was no longer hungry. Rosemary had added spicy meatballs and stuffed celery to the platters of vegetables, chips, and nuts Jerry had already put out. All she ordered at Captain Kosmakos was a Greek salad. She wasn't even able to finish that, so she asked for a to-go box to take the rest home.

When they got to the condo parking lot, Amanda said good night and went to her car. The evening had been nice but packed with emotion, and she needed to be alone.

The next morning, she'd barely opened the store when Tiffany arrived. "Need me today?"

"Why? Do you still need the hours? Don't you want to take a little break and hang out with friends?"

Tiffany looked embarrassed as she shrugged. "Yeah, well…"

"You know I can always use a couple of extra hands—especially on Mondays."

"Good!" Tiffany walked to the back room to put her purse down then came back out front. "What would you like me to do first?"

They reorganized the shop, stopping only when customers came in. By noon, everything looked good. "I appreciate your coming in, but I don't want to keep you cooped up too long on such a pretty day."

"It's hot out there," Tiffany said. "I'm glad to be in the air conditioning."

Amanda had met Tiffany's family in church a few years ago. After the service, Pastor Zach had pulled her aside and let her know how the family struggled and how he wanted people to remember them in their prayers. A group of men had gone over to repair the roof of their small bungalow, and Amanda had hired Tiffany part-time as soon as the girl turned sixteen. At the time, Amanda only did it to help Tiffany, but she turned out to be a quick study who didn't mind doing whatever needed to be done—from renting out equipment to showing customers how to use it. Fortunately business was good, and Amanda loved having Tiffany there for backup.

"Hey, look who's coming!" Tiffany pointed at the window.

Amanda spun around in time to see Jerry's mom and dad round the corner and open the door. She looked back at Tiffany, who smiled and quickly glanced down at the counter.

Harold led the way and stopped a couple of feet from Amanda. "Wanna go for a walk?"

"I told him you had to work, but he wouldn't listen." Rosemary looked contrite as she stood with her hands clasped in front of her.

Tiffany cleared her throat. "If you wanna go, I'm cool with that."

Amanda thought for a couple of seconds then nodded. "Sure, but I don't want to be gone long."

"He's still on that treasure-hunt kick." Rosemary rolled her eyes.

"One of these days you'll be glad." Harold puffed out his chest. "I'll find the treasure, and everyone will be happy."

"I'm sure." Rosemary shook her head.

"Where do you want to go today?" Amanda asked.

Harold rubbed his chin in thought then beamed. "How about we head toward John's Pass?"

"Sounds good. Let me get out of these sandals and put on some walking shoes. Be right back." She took off for the back room then came out a couple minutes later in time to see Harold looking at the helmet display.

"We just picked up a new line. See any you like?"

"Harold doesn't need a new helmet. He already has one that's practically new."

"It's boring," he said, as he lifted one of the new ones with red-and-orange flames off the shelf. "I like this one."

"Why don't you take it and have Jerry bring back the last helmet he bought? I saw it still in the box on the table by your front door last night."

Harold's eyes lit up. "If I could have this helmet, I'd wear it all the time." He gave his wife a puppy-dog look. "I promise."

Amanda looked at Rosemary, hoping the woman wouldn't be so practical. She was relieved when Rosemary nodded.

"Okay, but I expect you to wear it."

"I promised, didn't I?"

Amanda got one of the boxes below the display and carried it over to the counter. "Put this aside for Mr. Simpson. He can pick it up when we come back."

Tiffany grinned and did as she was told. Then she turned to Rosemary. "Where's Jerry?"

"He's working on his computer today." Rosemary cast a glance in Amanda's direction as if to make sure she was listening. "He can work anywhere as long as he has his laptop with him."

Amanda took a couple of strides to the door then stopped and held it open for Rosemary and Harold. "I'll be back in about an hour, unless you need me beforehand. I'm taking my cell phone."

"Take your time," Tiffany said. "Don't worry about a thing."

"You've got a good thing going here," Harold told her as they left the building. "Business seems good, and you have that young lady who seems awfully good at what she does."

"Yes, I'm blessed." She sensed that something else was behind Harold's words.

"I think you could probably have a successful business no matter where you were," Rosemary interjected.

Time to change the subject. "So we're supposed to be looking for treasure, right?" She focused on Harold, who didn't look her in the eyes.

Rosemary grunted. "She's talking to you, Harold."

"I know she is. I'm just thinking."

"What's there to think about?" Rosemary sniped. "Either you're looking for treasure or you're not."

Amanda was about to say something when Harold spoke out. "Sometimes treasure is in the most unexpected places. And it doesn't always look like what you would think."

"What are you talking about?" Impatience was evident in Rosemary's voice.

"What I'm saying is…" He stopped and planted a fist onto his hip as he turned to Amanda. "It's not always about things."

"Oh, brother." Rosemary offered a sympathetic smile to Amanda. "Please excuse my husband." She twirled her finger around her ear. "Sometimes he's not altogether there. It's the Alzheimer's."

Her voice had dropped to a low whisper, but Amanda suspected Harold knew exactly what she'd said. He clamped his mouth shut, jutted his jaw, and took off walking ten paces ahead of them.

They were about a quarter of a mile from the shop when Amanda couldn't take the suspense any longer. Harold had dropped back and was only a couple of steps ahead. Finally, she simply had to ask.

"Did you and Harold need to discuss something with me?"

Rosemary tilted her head and forced a look of innocence. "Whatever do you mean?"

"I figured the two of you came without Jerry because you wanted to talk about something."

"Well…" She glanced ahead at her husband, who'd stopped and turned to face them.

"C'mon, Rosemary, she's on to us. Don't lie to the girl."

Rosemary gasped. "Why, I'd never lie."

Harold chuckled and shook his head. "We're heading back to Atlanta in a few days, and we wanted to see what you thought about our son. You have my wife convinced that you and that skateboard fella aren't romantically involved."

"That's true," Amanda said slowly. She wasn't sure how much to tell them about her feelings toward Jerry. If she said she wasn't interested, she'd be lying. However, if she told them that the chemistry between them crackled every time they were together, she'd be telling them too much.

"So out with it." Harold folded his arms and waited.

"I…uh…" She gulped as her face heated with a blush. "Jerry is one of the nicest guys I know."

"That's not what we're asking." Harold progressed to foot tapping.

Finally Amanda decided to tell them exactly what was on her mind, even if it wasn't what they wanted to hear. "I've lived in Treasure Island almost all my life, and this is where I want to stay. I have my shop, a house I like, and my church."

"But are you happy?" Harold was relentless.

Rosemary closed the gap between herself and her husband and gently put her arm around his waist. "That might be too personal, Harold. Let's not make her uncomfortable."

"That's ridiculous." He squinted at Amanda. "Are you gonna tell us if you think you could fall in love with our son?"

A nervous giggle escaped Amanda's throat. "I think that's a moot issue, since the three of you are leaving soon."

"Okay, that's enough," Rosemary said in her typical take-charge manner. "We're supposed to be on a treasure hunt, and that's what I aim to do."

He made a face and shook his head. "I'm suddenly not in the mood to hunt for treasure anymore. Let's go home."

They walked Amanda back to the shop, where she got the new helmet with red and orange flames. Rosemary promised she'd have Jerry drop off the unopened one and pay her the difference, even though Amanda said it would be an even swap.

After they left, Amanda felt as if someone had knocked all the air out of her lungs. She leaned against the wall in the back room and closed her eyes.

"That bad, huh?"

Amanda opened her eyes and saw Tiffany standing a few feet away. She nodded. "Yeah. They wanted to know my intentions with Jerry."

Tiffany grinned. "Isn't that the job of the girl's family to ask the guy?"

Amanda lifted a brow and snickered. "Can you imagine my mother doing that?"

"No way. So what did you say?"

As tired as she was about discussing this, she didn't want to hurt Tiffany's feelings. "I told them that a long-distance relationship would be difficult." The sound of the bell on the door caught their attention.

Tiffany bobbed her head as she glanced over her shoulder toward the showroom. "I'll be right there." Then she turned back to Amanda. "I'll take care of the customer while you pull yourself together."

Amanda started to argue with her, but Tiffany's no-nonsense expression let her know not to argue. After her young employee left her alone, she chuckled to herself about how a teenager was more astute than her own mother.

Once the customer was gone, Tiffany returned. "So did they argue with you?"

"No, not at all."

"I hope you don't move to wherever they're from." She made an exaggerated pout. "I'd really miss you."

Amanda smiled. "Trust me, I like it here and I don't plan to move."

The rest of the day was business as usual at the shop. Tiffany left about an hour before closing. By the time Amanda locked the door to head home, she was emotionally exhausted. Fortunately, Lacy had said she'd be out with friends, so Amanda wouldn't have to deal with more turmoil later.

However, when she opened the door to her house, the first thing she saw was Lacy sitting there staring at the wall, tears streaming down her cheeks.

Chapter Thirteen

....

Amanda dropped her things by the door, rushed over to the sofa, and sat next to her sister. "What happened? I thought you were hanging out with friends."

"My friends canceled on me, so I called Brad." Lacy sniffed and gulped. When she looked Amanda in the eyes, she started sobbing. "It's over."

"You and Brad?"

Lacy nodded. "He told me he had plans."

"That doesn't mean anything."

"If he really loved me, wouldn't he want to be with me all the time?" Lacy asked.

"Not necessarily. Did he tell you what his plans were?"

Lacy shrugged. "Just something stupid with Timmy."

"At least he's spending time with his son. That's a good thing."

"I told him what you said, and that's when he got mad."

Amanda thought back and tried to remember what she'd said, but she couldn't remember anything that would upset Brad. "How did anything I say come between you and Brad?"

"You said he didn't have enough time for Timmy." Her chin quivered, and she covered her face with her hands. "That's when he told me he's doing the best he can and I expect too much from him."

Amanda gasped. "You took what I said completely out of context, Lacy. You know that's not what I meant."

Lacy lowered her hands. "You did say that. I remember."

"What I meant was…" What was the point? Lacy would take anything and twist it to her advantage, only this time it wouldn't work.

"Why don't you call Brad and ask him to come over here? I'd like to talk to him."

"I don't think he wants to talk to you right now."

"This is a huge mess, Lacy. If you ever want a chance at a relationship, you need to learn to talk through things."

"That's what I thought we were doing."

Amanda stood up, picked up her things by the door, and started for her room. "I'm too tired to deal with it now. Let's talk about it tomorrow."

"You talk about Brad not having enough time for Timmy. Well, I think you're guilty of that yourself."

Amanda stopped in her tracks. "What?"

"You don't give me enough of your time. All you do is lecture me and boss me around."

"Give me a break, Lacy. You're a grown woman. Now act like it."

As soon as she closed her bedroom door behind her, Amanda felt sorry for the outburst. But she'd let all those feelings build up inside her for so long, they'd come out in an explosion. She rubbed her forehead and closed her eyes. *Lord, why do I keep messing everything up?*

Amanda rubbed her temples and prayed for enough energy to get through to her sister. She waited a few minutes before leaving her room. Lacy had gone into the kitchen and was banging around some pots and pans in the cupboard. "Where's the pasta pot?"

"Behind the skillets. Are you cooking dinner?"

Lacy stood up and gave her a look that answered her question. "You know I can't cook."

"But you can boil pasta and heat up some sauce."

"Yeah, I can do that." Lacy bent over, reached behind the skillets, and pulled out the large pot. "Is that what you want me to do?"

"That would be nice. Maybe after we eat we can talk about a few other things you need to start doing."

"No lectures."

Amanda shook her head. "I'm too tired to lecture. All I want to do is discuss a few things. Maybe I can help you with Brad."

Lacy's lips quivered into a smile. "You'll do that for me?"

"Yes, of course I will." She grabbed a bag of bread from the counter. "Want me to make garlic toast?"

The evening was much more relaxing than Amanda could have expected. The simple mention of helping Lacy work through her issues with Brad had brought a smile to her sister's face. Unfortunately, Amanda worried that Lacy assumed she'd be able to fix everything, as she'd somehow managed to do in the past. But this was out of Amanda's control. Relationships couldn't be fixed that easily. Lacy would have to put forth much more energy than she might be willing to do, once she realized how painful it could be.

After dinner, Lacy started to sit, but Amanda gave her *the look*, something she'd mastered years earlier. Lacy joined her at the sink, and together they cleaned up their mess.

"So what can I do to make Brad love me again?" Lacy asked as she wiped her hands on the kitchen towel.

"I don't think you can do anything to make another person love you. If he loved you before, I'm sure he still does."

"If he loved me, he wouldn't have hurt my feelings," Lacy whined.

"I hurt your feelings all the time, and you know I've always loved you." Amanda leveled her sister with a stare. "Sometimes it's the people you love who hurt you the most."

Lacy scrunched her face and stared up at the ceiling for a couple of seconds before nodding. "True. I never really thought about it that way."

Amanda finished her work and led the way to the living room, where they sat down—Amanda on the chair and Lacy on the sofa. Lacy reached for the remote, but Amanda shook her head and pointed to the gray box in Lacy's hand.

"I refuse to have this conversation between commercials."

"But there's a show on the Fashion Channel—" Lacy stopped abruptly when Amanda stabbed her finger at the table, indicating that was where she wanted the remote. She made a face then leaned over and put it down. "Okay, so talk."

Amanda bent forward and looked her sister in the eyes. "If you want to be loved, you have to love."

Lacy frowned. "I love him; you know that."

"Have you ever considered what all is involved in a loving, romantic relationship?"

"What are you getting at, Amanda? Are you saying I don't do enough?"

"It's not that you're not doing enough. I'm talking about your attitude toward the other person." She paused for the right words before continuing. "How do you see your relationship with Brad?"

"Well…" Lacy chewed on the lower edge of her bottom lip before smiling. "Brad and I have fun together, and he's a really good kisser."

"That's great, and it's a start, but that doesn't show love."

Lacy's smile quickly turned to a frown. "I don't get it."

Rather than risk preaching at her sister, Amanda stood up and crossed the room to the bookshelf, where she found one of her Bibles. She knew Lacy had always avoided learning scripture verses, so she figured the best place to start was with John 3:16. At least Lacy was somewhat familiar with it.

Her attention span was a little longer than usual. She nodded her understanding as Amanda expounded on the magnitude of what God did by giving His only Son. Eventually, though, she held up her hands and shook her head. "Enough."

Amanda reached out and took one of those hands in hers. "Let me finish up with a prayer, okay?"

Lacy slowly nodded then closed her eyes. Amanda kept her prayer brief, but she made sure she hit all the points of concern—mainly to do the Lord's will. When she opened her eyes, Amanda saw that Lacy had a tear trickling down her cheek. At least she felt something.

The next day was a typical day at the shop. She was busy as usual but not to the point of feeling pulled in too many directions, for a change. Each time the bell on the door jingled, she looked up but felt disappointment each time she realized it wasn't Jerry. She needed to get him out of her mind.

On Tuesday she arrived at the shop with the resolve to put Jerry completely out of her mind. However, he walked in shortly after she flipped the OPEN sign on the door. So much for good intentions.

Her first reaction was instant anxiety. Her stomach roiled, and her heart beat double-time. Then annoyance kicked in. The bicycle had been back in the store since the accident, so he didn't have any real reason to be there.

"How's everything going?" he asked as he walked around with his hands in his pockets, looking at one of the wall displays.

Since he was a paying customer, she had to hide the fact that his very presence bugged her simply because he'd made her fall for him and his family, in spite of the fact that it was always his plan to take off. She squared her shoulders and came around from behind the counter.

"Did you see your dad's new helmet?"

Jerry snapped his fingers and backed toward the door. "I knew I forgot something. Mom put the other one I bought in the car and said to bring it back. I appreciate how you've been with them." By now he had his hand on the door. "I'll go get it now."

Amanda stared after him, as he didn't waste time leaving. At least she had a moment to regroup before he walked back in.

By the time he came into the store with the helmet, she'd found something to put between them. He smiled at her then glanced down at the bike ramp and pointed.

"What's that for?"

"Boys who think they're Evel Knievel in the skateboard world. It's a ramp for stunts."

Jerry walked all the way around it, staring at it as though he might consider using it himself. When he looked back at her, there was something else in his eyes—sort of a pensive look. "Is this something Matthew would use?"

Amanda felt a flicker of confusion at his response. She nodded. "Yes, this is one of the many ways he makes a living playing with his favorite toy."

"Do you like the dangerous, adventuresome type?"

It suddenly felt as if the air had been sucked out of the room. Amanda reached out and steadied herself by gripping the rack behind her.

"I like Matthew. Why?"

He pursed his lips then forced a smile. "I'm not one to take life-threatening chances. I like to know where I'm going, and I don't want to test gravity."

"Yeah, me, too," Amanda agreed as she forced herself to look away. "Riding a bicycle is as dangerous as I want to get."

"And after what happened to my dad, we both know how dangerous that can be." He held his gaze steady on her.

Amanda understood, and she had the feeling that their conversation was irrelevant. Jerry was in her shop for a different reason she'd probably never know.

Finally he closed the distance between them. "We're leaving in the morning around sunrise. I just wanted to stop by and let you know how much I enjoyed...well, I enjoyed everything."

"I did, too. I wish you and your parents the best." She tried to keep her voice from cracking, but she slipped and had to recover with a cough.

"They really like you, Amanda."

"I like them, too."

"And I like you. A lot."

Why was he doing this? Why didn't he just leave after the comment about enjoying everything?

Jerry licked his lips then swallowed. Amanda had a strong urge to kiss him. In fact, if he'd taken her into his arms, there would have been no stopping her—but that wouldn't be good, so she took a step back.

He blinked and smiled again. "I guess I'd better head on back to the condo and help them pack. See ya."

"Yeah, see you." After he left the store, she whispered, "Next year."

Amanda's mood was sour the rest of the day. She forced herself to greet customers with a smile, but she was glad when people made their purchases and left. By the end of the workday, she was exhausted from trying so hard to be pleasant when she felt so awful. Pent-up emotional energy had her pacing, until she realized what she was doing. Then she forced herself to stand behind the counter. More than once she caught herself gnawing on a pencil.

How could she have let another man get to her like that? She should have learned her lesson from Eric.

The weather had been nice that morning and there was no rain in the forecast, so she'd walked to the store. Now she was glad she had because she needed to work off some of her energy. By the time she got home, she wasn't nearly as jittery as when she'd left the shop, but she was still on edge.

Lacy wasn't home when she walked into the house. At least Amanda wouldn't have to talk to anyone right away.

Since Lacy obviously wasn't coming home for dinner, she popped a frozen dinner into the microwave, ate it, and went to bed with one of her bicycle magazines. When she felt like she might be able to sleep, she closed the magazine, reached for her Bible, and opened it to the first page of the New Testament. She'd been meaning to reread the New Testament from the beginning to the end, and now was a good time to start. It was always good to close one chapter of her life by beginning something new.

The next day, Amanda felt a little better—as long as she was too busy to think about Jerry. She'd awakened a couple of times the night before, but she'd managed to go back to sleep fairly quickly. The store had a steady stream of customers, and the man who repaired her equipment stopped by and took the wrecked tandem bicycle to check it over.

Thursday was a little more difficult. The fact that Jerry wasn't on the island anymore had sunk in, and Amanda wasn't getting much sleep. A couple of nights being awakened by thoughts of Jerry had taken its toll on her. Her eyes burned, and she couldn't get past the way she felt every time either Jerry or his parents popped in and surprised her. Now that they were gone, that wouldn't happen. By noon, she knew that she couldn't last a whole day without shedding a tear or two.

She called Tiffany and asked if she could work for a few hours while she tended to some pressing needs. Although Tiffany jumped at the chance for more hours, her sleepy voice alerted Amanda that she'd awakened the girl.

By Saturday, Amanda felt a little better knowing that she only had to work until closing and then she'd have a whole day off to recover. Business was brisk, with a combination of locals, tourists, and some of her loyal customers from St. Petersburg.

Lacy stopped by and asked if she wanted to do something after work. Amanda was fully aware that she was Lacy's last choice, but that didn't matter. She was used to it.

"Sure, what do you have in mind?"

Lacy shrugged. "I dunno. I was thinking maybe we could go bowling."

Amanda lifted an eyebrow and studied her sister. "Since when do you like bowling?"

Lacy turned toward a rack of goggles and flipped through them, avoiding eye contact. "I need to try new things."

"Last time you and I went bowling, you said you never wanted to set foot in another bowling alley as long as you lived."

"That was a long time ago," Lacy reminded her. "Things are different now."

Amanda would have been willing to bet the bicycle shop that this had something to do with Brad. In fact, she remembered Timmy mentioning that he and his dad liked to go bowling on Saturday nights.

Finally, Lacy turned and looked at her. "Well? Do you want to or not?"

"I'd love to. It's been a long time since I've been bowling, and I could use a distraction."

Lacy stared at Amanda and studied her for several seconds. "You miss Jerry already, don't you?"

There wasn't any point in denying her feelings, so Amanda nodded. "I know it's silly, but I do."

"You can't help how you feel."

"I knew from the start that he was on vacation and he'd be leaving. You'd think I'd know better."

Lacy gave her a dreamy look. "Love does that. You can't put your feelings on vacation. Plus, it's the whole package with Jerry. You not only like him, you feel connected to his parents. That makes it even more difficult."

In her own way, she made sense. And she sounded like a woman speaking from experience. "Is that how you feel about Timmy now?"

Slowly Lacy nodded. Her normally pouty, fully glossed lips looked dry and thinner than usual. "Strange, isn't it? That little boy gave me more grief the second half of the school year than the rest of my class combined. But after I got to know him better, I understood him. In fact, I think he and I might have more in common than I realized."

"How so?" Amanda couldn't imagine what Lacy and Timmy had in common.

"I've always wondered about my father—what he looks like and what he likes to do. I think Timmy has a few vague recollections of his mother, but he's forgotten quite a bit. I'm sure he must think about her an awful lot."

That was very mature of Lacy to even consider. Amanda smiled and reached for her sister's hand. "I think everyone has issues of some sort. I wonder about my father, too."

Lacy leaned over the counter. "Do you think Mother has lied about some of our past?"

"Who knows? Mother lives in a make-believe world. She's always been gullible, and she's never really been happy."

"I'm afraid I might have some of those traits," Lacy admitted. "I don't like it, but I'm not sure how to change it."

Amanda held her breath for a few seconds before she decided the timing was perfect to share what was on her mind. "I'd really like for you to go to church with me tomorrow, Lacy. The pastor is really interesting, and the people who go there are very welcoming. I think you'd find some comfort among Christians, and the message might help you sort out a few things."

She'd half expected Lacy to turn her down again, point-blank. But she didn't. Instead, she had a pensive look on her face as she stared at something behind Amanda before looking her in the eyes.

"I think that would be fair. After all, you are going bowling with me. The least I can do is go to church with you."

"How about the adult Bible study afterward?"

Lacy crinkled her nose. "Is that like Sunday school?"

"Yes, only for adults."

"I don't know about that. I never really liked the way those women used to talk to us."

Amanda knew exactly what Lacy was referring to, and she agreed. The women who taught Lacy's elementary Sunday school class had annoying voices and didn't relate to kids very well. "This is different."

"Well, I'll think about it. We can take two cars, and if I decide not to go, I'll just come on home."

"Okay," Amanda agreed. She was happy she'd gotten Lacy to agree to church. She didn't want to press her too hard.

They went bowling and had a wonderful time. Amanda started out making gutter balls, but by the end of the second game, she'd made a strike and a bunch of spares. Even Lacy's game improved. Each time she knocked more than half the pins down, she jumped up and down, squealing.

"It doesn't take much to make you happy, does it?" Amanda asked.

"Not anymore." Lacy twisted her hair and clamped it on the top of her head with a barrette.

Amanda took a long look at her sister and realized she was finally growing up. Her maturity level had escalated, dipped, then spiked over the past couple of months—something Amanda hadn't realized until this moment.

They took a break and had hamburgers in the bowling alley snack bar. Amanda was ready to bowl another game, but Lacy shook her head. "I'm getting tired. I need to go home and get some sleep if I'm going to get up on time for church in the morning."

They turned in their rented shoes and headed home. Amanda went to bed with her Bible, feeling a little better in knowing that her relationship with her sister seemed to be improving.

To Amanda's surprise, Lacy was up and ready to go a half hour before it was time to leave. She was in the kitchen sipping coffee when

Amanda joined her. "I'm glad I don't have to wear those silly dresses you used to put on me."

Amanda tilted her head back and laughed. "The ones with the round collars and buttons you complained about all the time?"

"Yeah." Lacy wrapped her fingers around her own neck and made a face like she was being strangled. "I couldn't breathe. I never understood why I had to be miserable just to go to church, but you made me do it."

"I know," Amanda admitted, "and I don't understand why either." She poured a half cup of coffee, dumped in a couple of spoonfuls of sugar, and stirred it before taking a sip. "I guess it just seemed like the thing to do at the time. I was a kid myself. What did I know?"

Lacy smiled. "You knew more than anyone else your age. I always forgot how young you were because you were more like a parent to me than our own mother was."

That was a sad fact Amanda would have liked to forget, but she knew Lacy meant it as a compliment. "I wanted what was best for you. Still do."

"Yes, I know." Lacy glanced at the clock before moving toward the door. "Let me see if I can find my Bible."

"If you can't, I'll share mine."

As they walked outside, Amanda fully expected Lacy to get into her own car, but she didn't. Instead, she went to the passenger door of Amanda's car.

"I thought you were driving."

Lacy slowly shook her head. "No, I'm cool with going to Bible study. I thought it over last night and came to the conclusion that if they made it miserable, no one would show up—because they don't have someone forcing them to attend."

Amanda couldn't help but giggle. "True."

* * * * *

The next week was slightly better for Amanda. She still missed Jerry, but Lacy had gone to church, and at the Bible study, she'd asked questions. Pastor Zach seemed delighted to answer all of them, and she felt Lacy's resistance wane.

All the way home, Lacy talked about the Bible study and how much she'd never thought about things the way they were discussed. Amanda smiled and made an occasional comment to acknowledge her sister, but for the most part, she just listened. It was nice having Lacy so enthusiastic about something close to Amanda's heart.

When they pulled up to the curb, Amanda spotted a car behind them coming to a stop. "Don't look now, but I think Brad's coming for a visit."

In spite of Amanda's advice, Lacy spun around. "What's he doing here?"

"Aren't you happy to see him?"

Lacy frowned. "I would be if he hadn't made me feel so bad."

"Maybe he wants to talk things over. Why don't you at least listen to what he has to say before you assume anything?"

Lacy bobbed her head, blinked, and smiled. "Okay, you're right as usual."

Before Amanda had a chance to say another word, Lacy got out of the car and ran back to greet Brad. She didn't act the least bit put off in front of Brad.

Just when Amanda thought all might be good in her sister's world, Lacy suddenly took a step back from Brad, stared at him for a couple of seconds, then turned and ran inside the house. Brad stood there watching her, his jaw set and his body rigid.

Amanda tried to force herself to stay out of it. She'd already interfered enough. Lacy was a grown woman, and she could handle her own life.

But the look on Brad's face was one of pain, bordering on torture. She couldn't just stand back and let it go—not if there was something she could do about it.

Amanda shut the car door, paused, and walked slowly toward Brad. He didn't look at her right away; he was too busy looking at the house. Finally he turned to face her.

"What happened, Brad?"

He shook his head and rubbed his eyes. "I'm not sure. I just stopped by to pick up Timmy's ball cap, and she went ballistic."

"Did you say anything to upset her?"

"Not that I know of. We had a little disagreement the other day, and I told her we needed to have a little space between us while I sort things out."

Amanda understood both sides, but she had an allegiance to her sister. "You obviously don't understand women. Wait here. I'll go get Timmy's cap. Do you know where he might have left it?"

"I think it's by your bicycle display."

"Okay, I'll be right back."

Amanda wasn't sure what she'd face when she went inside, but she didn't have to worry. Lacy was nowhere in sight and her bedroom door was closed, which probably meant she was in there crying.

The ball cap was right where Brad said. Amanda grabbed it and headed outside. "I have some advice, Brad—if you're interested."

He snickered. "I guess I probably need all the advice I can get."

"Unless you're ready to talk things out with Lacy, try not to pay her any more surprise visits. If you think of something else either you or Timmy might have left here, call me at the shop, and I can have it waiting there for you the next day."

Brad offered a quick nod. "That sounds like a good idea. I didn't mean to upset her like that." He lifted his free hand in a wave. "Thanks, Amanda." Then he got into his car and drove away.

Amanda went back inside and knocked on Lacy's door. "He's gone. I'm going to fix some lunch, so come on into the kitchen in a few minutes, okay?"

"I'm not hungry." She sniffed and blew her nose. "I just want to be alone."

Come to think of it, Amanda wasn't hungry, either. She decided it wouldn't hurt to miss a meal—or at least have it later when her stomach wasn't in such a knot. This was the perfect time to go for a walk.

She went to her room to put on some workout clothes. On her way out, she heard the phone. She considered letting her voice mail pick up, but then thought it might be an emergency.

"Hello, Amanda dear."

Chapter Fourteen

....

Amanda's heart raced at the sound of Rosemary's voice. "Is everything okay?"

The older woman chuckled. "Yes, of course. Everything's fine, except that we miss you." She paused then added, "Especially Jerry."

Amanda suspected there was something else going on, but rather than ask, she decided to wait until Rosemary was ready to tell her. "So how is Atlanta?"

"Big and noisy, and the traffic is awful. I miss Florida."

A couple seconds of silence fell over the phone line. "You'll be back next year, right?" Amanda couldn't think of anything else to say.

"Next year is an awful long way away. I'm working on a plan."

Uh-oh, here it comes. More matchmaking. "So what is your plan?"

"I'm not sure yet. Like I said, I'm working on it. I just thought I'd give you a call to see how you're doing. Did you have the bicycle we crashed looked at?"

"Yes, and it's fine," Amanda replied.

"That's good. If you let me know how much it cost to have it looked at, I'll send you a check."

"No, that's okay, Rosemary. It's just routine maintenance—part of doing business."

"I guess you must be busy today, since it's your only day off. I'll let you go now." Amanda heard a voice in the background. "Oh, and Harold said to tell Timmy to keep hunting for treasure."

Amanda laughed. "I'll do that."

After they hung up, Amanda had no doubt there was quite a bit more to Rosemary's call than what she let on.

* * * * *

Rosemary lowered the receiver as Harold came up behind her. "Does she miss him yet?"

"I couldn't tell." Rosemary turned around and faced her husband. "I've been trying to figure out a way to talk to Jerry about our plans."

Harold laughed out loud. "I bet we worry more about how to break news to him than he ever does with us."

"I know." Rosemary walked over to the stack of brochures on the foyer table. "I've even thought about showing him these."

Harold shook his head. "He'll just argue."

"Or we could *accidentally* leave them out and let him figure it out for himself."

"That's too easy," Harold said. "And you've never done things the easy way."

"Easy isn't always the best way." She chewed on her lip as she thought about what she wanted to do. "I think we just need to sit him down and tell him what we want."

"If you want me to, I can have a father-son talk while you wait in the car."

"No," she replied, "I can't do that to either of you. It's best if we're both there."

"When do you think we should do this?"

She slowly moved her head from side to side. "I'm not sure. Maybe in a week or two?"

* * * * *

Jerry found it hard to keep his attention on work. Thoughts of Amanda continued to flow through his mind, even daring to pop up in front of the spreadsheet of vendors. He snorted. *Bet she wouldn't appreciate having her face smack-dab in the middle of a bunch of vendors whose names I can't pronounce.*

After a few hours of forcing himself to focus on work, Jerry finally got up and put on some clothes to go to the gym. He needed a good hard workout to redirect his brain.

Two miles on the treadmill, a half hour on the elliptical, and a couple dozen sets of weight lifts later, Jerry finally settled into the stretching segment of his routine. And Amanda was still front and center in his mind. There was simply nothing he could do to get rid of her image.

Maybe he should talk to someone—but who? Most of his friends were married, and they would love nothing better than for him to find a nice Christian girl and settle down—even if it meant picking up and moving. He knew exactly where his parents stood on the subject. They loved Amanda, and they wanted him to be happy. But how could he, considering their age and medical conditions? They were okay without him most of the time right now, but their doctor had said that over the next couple of years, both of them were likely to experience some deterioration.

They needed him. There was no way he'd ever abandon the people who'd always been there for him—no matter what, even if it meant sacrificing time and the prospect of a future with Amanda.

He picked up his laptop and tried to focus on his latest round of orders from Korea, but he couldn't concentrate. So he finally gave in, picked up the phone, and punched in Amanda's number at the shop. She didn't answer, so he tried her house phone. Lacy picked up.

"Hey, Jerry," she said in her squeaky little-girl voice. "How's Atlanta? Crazy, I bet."

"To be honest, I don't get out much, since I do most of my work on the computer in my den. But you're right—Atlanta generally is a little crazy with the traffic and all." He paused for a moment. "May I speak to Amanda?"

"Amanda isn't here right now. She and Matthew ran down to a warehouse in Pinellas Park to look at some new bicycles."

Jerry felt as if he'd been kicked in the chest. Amanda almost had him convinced that she and Matthew were just good friends, but it still bugged him that they spent so much time together.

"Want me to have her call you when she gets in?"

"Sure, that's fine." He gave her his home number then hung up feeling much worse than before he'd called.

By ten o'clock that night he figured it was too late for Amanda to return his call, so he finally crawled into bed and clicked off the light. His mind still raced, and he had a hard time going to sleep. When he awoke at the crack of dawn, he remembered looking at his clock shortly after midnight. When he wasn't even sleepy.

All he could think about was Amanda not calling. He downed a couple of cups of coffee and tried to get some work done, but his mind kept buzzing with all the possibilities of what could have happened to Amanda.

Finally, when the hall clock struck ten, he picked up the phone and called her store number. She was breathless as she answered right away.

"Hey, Jerry! What's up?"

"I waited for your call last night." The instant he said those words, he knew he probably sounded like a jealous boyfriend, so he tried to laugh it off. "Let me rephrase that. I called to see how you were doing, and Lacy said she'd have you call me back when you got in."

* * * * *

Annoyance flooded Amanda. Even though Lacy had been improving and maturing lately, she still didn't relay messages.

"I'm sorry, but I didn't know you called. Is everything okay?"

"Yes." She heard him sigh. "Everything's fine. I just wanted to see how everything's going. How's business?"

"Steady." She sensed some unspoken thoughts, but she didn't want to push.

"I understand you were looking at new bikes. See any good ones?"

"I'll probably pick up a new line soon. So how are your parents?" She wondered if he was aware that his mom had called her.

"Now that you mention it, they're up to something." He paused before adding, "Something seems strange."

No doubt. "Why do you say that? What are they doing?"

"I've been to their place a few times since we got back, and when I mention anything about Florida, they give each other a look and then giggle."

"Sounds like a typical married couple thing to do."

"Not my folks."

"Maybe you should come right out and ask if they're up to something."

"I tried that," Jerry admitted. "Dad told me that if I needed to know something, he'd be the first to tell me."

"Then I guess there's nothing else you can do but wait until they decide to let you in on their little secret."

"Yeah, I guess you're right." He cleared his throat. "Oh, there's one more thing. On the way home from Florida, we talked about coming down more often."

Her pulse quickened, but she squelched the urge to let him know how happy that made her. "Just let me know when so I can have the bicycle ready."

"Yeah, I'll do that."

After they said their good-byes and got off the phone, Amanda felt like there was something else he wasn't telling her. He was as bad as his parents.

* * * * *

Later that week, Jerry's mom called and said she was coming over with some food. "I'm worried about you."

"You don't have to worry about me," he said. "I can cook my own food."

"Are you saying you don't want me to come over?"

"No," he replied quickly, "I'd never say that. Come on over, but don't think you have to bring anything."

"I'll be there in a half hour."

The second he got off the phone, he grabbed a laundry basket and ran through his apartment, decluttering. Normally he was neat, but lately he hadn't been motivated to keep everything in order.

His mother arrived ten minutes early. He let her in and she made her way straight to the refrigerator, where she put bags of homemade food. After she had everything put away, he got them both glasses of tea and sat down in the living room across from her.

"Jerry, you can't just sit around all day." His mom crossed her arms and scowled. "You need to get out and get some fresh air."

"Is that what you came over to tell me?"

"No, but now that I'm here, I can't let you continue to mope around."

"I work out at the gym three times a week."

She rolled her eyes. "You know that's not the same as getting fresh air and being around people."

He grinned at her. "I have you and Dad."

"Give me a break, son. You need more than anything your dad and I can offer. We want you to be happy."

He stood up, crossed the room, and put a hand on her shoulder as he looked her in the eyes. "I'm very happy. I have two loving parents, a great job, more freedom than most people, and a great church."

His mother narrowed her gaze then nodded. "Yes, you do have all those wonderful things, but I happen to know how you feel about Amanda. I can see it in your eyes whenever the two of you are together." She gave him a pitying look. "I can only imagine how much you must miss her."

Jerry paused then shrugged. "It's obviously not meant to be. We live too far apart for anything to come of a relationship. Besides, I'm sure there are plenty of guys in Treasure Island she can pick from."

"I don't think so," she said as she stood, shaking her head. "Look, I need to run while it's still daylight. I hate driving in the dark."

"Be careful and call me when you get home, okay?"

She chuckled on her way out. "Sure, I'll do that. See you soon."

He was more positive than ever that his parents were planning something. And based on history, he wouldn't find out what it was until they were good and ready to tell him.

* * * * *

Harold greeted her at the door the instant she walked in. "Well, did you tell him?"

"No, I couldn't do it."

He chuckled. "I didn't think you could. You always did feel like you had to walk around on eggshells with that boy."

"You have to admit, Harold, he's always been careful with us. I don't know why he thinks we're so fragile."

"Maybe because we are," Harold replied. "Face it, Rosemary, we're a couple of old folks now, and we break easily."

She playfully swatted at him with her magazine. "Speak for yourself."

"I'm just sayin', maybe I better go over there and just let him know we're sick of living here in Atlanta and we want to join the rest of those old folks in God's waiting room down in Florida."

"Don't put it like that."

He grinned and pulled her in for a hug. "Well, it's true."

* * * * *

Jerry stretched and stood up from his small desk in the corner of his den. He'd tried to make an office out of his second bedroom, but he felt secluded all the way at the back of his apartment. He much preferred being in the den, where all his memorabilia from Florida were on display. He'd just polished off a heaping plate of his mother's homemade baked chicken, sweet potato soufflé, and turnip greens, with cornbread on the side. After carrying his plate to the sink, he called his mom.

"Thanks for the food, Mom. It was good."

"I'm glad you liked it. Here, let me hand the phone to your dad. He wants to talk to you."

He heard the sound of a whispered argument, but he couldn't make out what they were saying. Then his dad was on the phone.

"Your mother and I are worried about you, son."

"I know. Mom told me. And I'll tell you the same thing I told her. Don't be worried. I just have a lot of catching up to do. I fell behind on a couple of things while we were in Florida."

"If you ask me, you're falling behind on something much more important than work. When was the last time you spoke to Amanda?"

"Why?"

"Just tell me."

He glanced at the picture of his parents on the side wall. "Dad, I know you mean well, and you're worried about me because you care, but you seriously need to get any notion of Amanda and me being more than friends out of your mind."

"Your mother and I were talking—"

Jerry interrupted him. "You don't need to keep discussing my love life…or lack of it."

"Let me finish. We weren't talking about you." He paused. "We've decided to move."

Jerry felt as though someone had cut a hole into the floor beneath him. "What?" He furrowed his brows. "Where?"

"There's a place in St. Petersburg that we've been looking into. We saw some advertisements on the Internet. I think it'll be much better for us than where we are now."

"But I thought you loved your place. You always said it was convenient because they offer assisted living, and with you and Mom, well, you know…" Jerry couldn't finish his sentence because the mere thought of either of his parents not being independent seemed unfathomable.

"We do like it, but we feel like the weather and beach in Florida are healthier for us. There's a reason people go there when they get old, ya know."

"What about all your friends? Can you just pick up and leave them?" His parents had made a few comments about moving, but they'd always decided to stay put because Atlanta was home—where both of them were born and they had lifelong friends. Jerry didn't want them to uproot for the sake of his love life.

"We won't be the first to move. The Jacksons moved down to Ft. Lauderdale to be near their children, and Harvey Shram is in Macon now."

"But I'm here."

"What's keeping you here besides us? The way you do business, you can go anywhere. And since you sold your condo in Marietta, you don't have to worry about selling property. We think this is the perfect time to make the move—before something serious happens to either your mother or me and while you're still somewhat unencumbered."

"I don't know, Dad." Jerry rubbed the back of his neck. "Since you just sprang this on me, I haven't even thought about it. Give me some time, okay?"

"Don't take too long. We've already given our notice here, and they've contacted the next person on the list to move in. We're ready to put a deposit on a place in St. Petersburg."

"Dad…" He let his voice trail off as he tried to think of a way to ask whose idea it was—his dad's or his mother's.

"We're determined to make this move even if you don't."

Jerry heard the firmness of his dad's voice, reminiscent of the tone he'd used when Jerry was much younger. "I wish you'd discussed this with me first."

"We tried to, but you kept talking to us like we were children."

"I didn't mean—"

"No, I realize you didn't mean to come across that way, but we know when we're being patronized." His dad cleared his throat before continuing. "Your mother and I want to enjoy the time we have left. We want to be happy."

"And moving to Florida would make you happy?"

"Yep."

Jerry let out a breath he just realized he'd been holding. "If you're sure that's what you both want, I'll do everything I can to help you."

"Your mother thinks you might want to move down there with us, but I told her she needs to let you make your own decisions. Quite frankly, I think you should stay here. Having you so close will be a royal pain in the—"

"Harold!"

His mother's shrieking voice in the background made Jerry smile. "I get the picture. Sorry if I've been so intrusive."

"Then stop doing it."

Just like that, huh? "I'll try. So tell me about this place you saw on the Internet."

"Your mother found it. I'll send you a link. Looks pretty nice. They have a swimming pool, a billiards room, and a nice dining hall on the first floor."

"That sounds good. Maybe I should consider moving there."

"You can't. You're not old enough."

"Just kidding, Dad."

"I figured you were, but I'm never sure about these things."

Jerry heard his mother's voice in the background. "What's Mom saying?"

"She wanted me to tell you they even have a beauty shop, a library, and a game room. I'll never see her."

That might be a good thing. "Let me know what I can do to help, okay?"

"You might want to drive us down there. Your mother hates interstate driving."

"Yes, of course."

After he hung up, Jerry sank down in his chair and stared at the wall. He had an odd sensation that his world was shifting and nothing would ever be the same. *This must be what parents feel like when their children leave the nest.*

All sorts of other thoughts swirled through Jerry's mind. His mother was right—he could pick up and move whenever or wherever he wanted. He still had some business interests in Atlanta, but he had minimal contact with them—only two or three times a year. That definitely wasn't an insurmountable obstacle if he wanted to follow his parents to Florida. Then he thought about his dad's reaction—that he was a royal pain. Jerry chuckled. Yeah, when he thought about it, he knew he certainly could be that. He'd caught himself a couple of times…no, make that numerous times, bossing them around during their vacation. His parents were aging, but they were still fully capable of making their own decisions.

Then he thought of Amanda. He had no doubt his mother would jump right into the middle of Amanda's life and stay there unless Amanda told her to leave. And knowing Amanda, she'd never do that— even if she wanted to.

His heart warmed at the very thought of the cute little bicycle shop owner—the one with blond hair, big blue eyes, and an athletic build. She could run circles around most male athletes, but when she smiled, she lit up the room with her feminine charm. And Jerry wasn't immune.

Somewhere along the way, he'd fallen in love with Amanda. Perhaps it was at church, or it could have been when she rushed to his parents' side after the accident. He thought long and hard for a moment. He remembered feeling a little tug at his heart when they'd walked down the street during the festival on the beach.

Another telltale sign was the kick to his gut every time he saw Matthew anywhere near Amanda. He had no reason to believe she was lying about her feelings toward Matthew, but he knew the way men thought. If she gave Matthew the slightest hint of romantic interest, he wouldn't waste a minute before claiming Amanda for his own. As one guy watching another guy, Jerry knew the signs. The way he looked at her, and the way he always seemed to be there when she needed someone, told more than words could ever say.

There was no way Jerry would let that guy continue to be Matthew. Suddenly determined to take control of his love life, Jerry tapped his laptop out of sleep mode and did a search for places to stay in Treasure Island. The condo they'd rented had another family coming a couple of days after he and his parents left, so he knew it wasn't available.

Hopefully there would be something else in the area. Immediately after he got his parents situated and comfortable in their retirement village, he was going to take care of his own love life.

It took him several clicks before something finally popped up. Perfect! This was a three-month rental in a high-rise, and it wasn't too far from Amanda.

He called his parents again, and his mother answered. "When do y'all plan to make this move?"

She chuckled. "By the end of the month."

"So by August first, you'll have a Florida residence?"

"Yes," she replied. "That's the plan. Why?"

"I needed to know so I can help you with the move."

Silence fell over the phone line for a couple of seconds before she finally spoke. "We've already made arrangements to have our stuff moved."

Jerry felt as though someone had stabbed him. "You didn't have to do that."

"I know. We just didn't want to disrupt your life any more than we already have."

"How about your car? I need to drive you down there."

"We've decided to sell the car and try to live without one for a while. Auto insurance is expensive."

"Are you sure about that?" he asked. "How about the times when you need to do grocery shopping?"

"We'll be within walking distance of a grocery store and pharmacy, and the exercise will be good for us. Since we'll eat most of our meals in the dining room downstairs at the village, we won't need much."

The only person truly disrupting Jerry's life was Amanda—and she hadn't asked him for a thing. "I still want to help."

"I understand. I'm sure we can think of something."

Now the only thing he had to decide was whether to let Amanda know he was coming, or surprise her. He pondered both choices and decided it might not be as big of a deal to her as it was to him, so he'd contact her once he was situated in the rental. His lease was up in his current apartment at the end of August, so there was no point in breaking it just to save a few bucks, but he needed to help his parents get settled in.

"Jerry? Are you still there?"

Her voice snapped him back to the moment. "Oh, sorry. I'll rent another condo for a few weeks, so I can be around to help you out."

She laughed. "Your dad said you wouldn't let us do this by ourselves, and he was right."

"Have you told Steven and Jennifer yet?"

"No," she admitted. "We're trying to figure out a way to break it to them."

"Just come out with it." He thought about it for a couple of seconds, and an idea came to him. "Why don't I call and let them know?"

"It might not be pleasant."

All the more reason for him to do it. "I'll call them."

"Okay, if you insist. Just a minute, let me tell your father." She covered the mouth of the phone, but he could still hear part of what they said. His dad started out arguing, but his mother let him know that Jerry had insisted. Finally, she removed her hand. "Go ahead and talk to them."

"Oh, and do me a favor, okay?" he asked. "Don't let Amanda know we're coming." He knew his mother loved surprises.

"This'll be fun!"

"I figured you'd enjoy sneaking up on her."

"We're not exactly sneaking up on her, but I can hardly wait to see her face. I bet she'll be delighted." Suddenly, her voice grew more somber. "When you talk to Steven and Jennifer, don't let them get to you. Have them call your father if they have any questions."

No doubt his dad would set them straight. While his mother had coddled all the kids, his dad had reminded them that they were adults and they needed to start acting like it—which was probably why, when they weren't able to ask for money anymore, they didn't come around as often.

His first call went to his sister. Her reaction was different from what he'd expected.

Chapter Fifteen

....

"I figured they'd eventually do something like that," Jennifer said. "What are you gonna do without them?"

"I just found out, so I haven't had time to work through anything yet."

Jerry avoided a direct answer; he didn't want to admit he'd been thinking about following them to Florida because she'd assume it was to be under their mother's wing. But it wasn't. It was more to be closer to Amanda. He'd never asked for a dime from their parents like his siblings had, but she wouldn't understand that.

"Have you talked to Steven yet?"

"No," he replied. "I called you first."

"Well, brace yourself. He's pretty upset with Dad at the moment."

Alarm bells sounded in Jerry's head. "Why? What happened?"

"Steven's been wanting to break out of the corporate world, so he asked Dad for some start-up money."

Typical. "And Dad turned him down, right?"

"Not outright. He offered a loan with interest."

"That sounds reasonable to me." Jerry didn't understand Steven even thinking about taking money from their dad.

"The way he sees it, they won't be around much longer and they don't need all that money sitting in a bank account. He wants to put it to good use."

Jerry felt his blood pressure rise. "You don't agree with him, do you?"

"Well…if Steven gets any money from them, it's only fair that they give some to you and me."

Before he let her know what he really thought, Jerry decided to end the call. After they hung up, he gave himself a few minutes to cool off. How could his sister and brother be so selfish? Their parents had worked hard to instill good values in them.

He bowed his head in prayer for guidance before talking to Steven. Jerry wanted to give his brother the information without blowing his stack.

When he was certain he could maintain his cool, he called Steven's cell phone. The phone rang twice, so he started thinking of a message to leave.

"You don't have to tell me anything," Steven said without a greeting. "I just talked to Jenn."

Anger instantly rushed through Jerry, but he took a deep breath and slowly let it out. He shouldn't have expected anything else from his sister.

"Did she tell you the details?"

"What details? They're spending our inheritance to live the high life in Florida, right?"

If they'd been talking in person, the only thing that would have stood between Jerry's fist and his brother was Jerry's faith in Christ. However, Jerry couldn't hold his tongue another second. "That is the most selfish thing I've ever heard. How dare you expect anything from two people who gave you everything you needed and almost everything they could afford?"

Steven laughed. "Is that what you think? Maybe that's the way it was when you came along, baby brother, but when Jenn and I were kids, we got most of our clothes from garage sales and secondhand stores. We didn't get anything new until we had our own jobs and could buy them ourselves."

"Why are you holding that against them?" Jerry asked. "They did the best they could."

"They always gave you new stuff." Steven's jealousy came through loud and clear. "I guess that's because they were ashamed of the fact that you were an 'oops' baby and they had to act like they were happy with the little surprise."

Jerry's temples pulsed as he gritted his teeth. Nothing could be further from the truth. Maybe his parents hadn't planned to have him, but in God's world, there were no "oops" babies.

"So what do you plan to do?" Steven asked. "Move down there with them so you can hold their hands all the way to the grave?" He belted out a sinister snort. "That ought to earn you a nice slice of the inheritance."

"You're totally out of line, big brother. Until you get past your pettiness, you won't see that. When you feel like discussing our parents' move, give me a call, but I'm not going to keep talking to you now."

"Fine. Tell them I hope they're happy." *Click.*

Jerry punched the OFF button on his phone, held it out, and stared at it. His brother's behavior was even worse than it had been the last time he'd talked to him. *Just goes to show how bitter people can become without the Lord in their lives.*

He knew he needed to be praying for a change of heart for Steven and Jennifer, but it was difficult watching them hurt his parents. As Jerry bowed his head, he added a request for forgiveness for himself.

The days began to fly by as he made arrangements for the upcoming trip. He secured a three-month lease on a condo in Treasure Island. In addition to getting his personal belongings packed and ready for the move, he had to work ahead to account for the days he'd be out of commission. Then a couple of days before they were due to leave, his parents called and said they wanted to go early. The manager of their apartment building had someone lined up for their place, so he offered to let them stay in the guest unit until they were ready to go. The moving company had already come for their belongings. For once, he had to tell them no.

His mother argued. "We figured you'd be as eager to get this thing over with as we are."

"I can't do it. I still have too much on my plate."

"You always have too much on your plate as long as we're around. I'm serious, Jerry. You don't have to take care of us. We're adults. We can manage."

"I know I don't have to. I want to."

"Your dad already checked on flights, and we can leave tonight."

"Mom."

She sighed. "Okay. We'll wait."

Knowing his parents' urgency lit a fire under Jerry. He quickly tied up all his loose ends and was ready a day ahead of schedule.

All the way to the Florida state line, his mother sat in the backseat and chattered nonstop about all the things they could do once they got settled. His dad kept glancing over at Jerry and grinning. When she finally wound down and closed her eyes for a nap, Jerry turned to his dad.

"Think she's happy about this?"

His dad let out a soft chuckle. "Never seen anything like it. I'm glad she finally gave in and agreed to move."

"She gave in?" Jerry cast a questioning glance in his dad's direction. "What do you mean by that?"

"I've been wanting to do this for years. She kept thinking Steven and Jennifer would come to their senses when I first mentioned it. Then her excuse was staying in Atlanta for you. After you moved your business into your home and sold your condo, I told her all that was a moot point. If you needed us, you could come, too."

Jerry opened his mouth to say he was going more because they might need him than the other way around, but he quickly thought better of it. Let them think what they wanted. He knew he was doing this for them…and Amanda, if he wanted to be truly honest with himself.

"I called the manager of your new place and checked on your furniture," Jerry told his dad. "They said it arrived, and the social worker directed them on where to put it."

"Good. When we talked to them a couple weeks ago, they told us they wanted to welcome us with a turnkey apartment. It'll be nice to be home again."

Jerry thought it was interesting that his dad was already calling his place in Florida "home," even though he'd never been there. What was even more interesting was the fact that he himself had no remorse or desire to turn back, even though this would be the first time other than his four years of college that he'd live anywhere besides the Atlanta area.

When his dad started laughing, Jerry cast a glance toward the passenger seat. "What's so funny?"

"Your mother is more excited over those turtles everyone's so worried about than I've seen her in a long time."

"The loggerheads?"

"Yeah, I think that's what they're called. She's talking about joining some group to help save them. She's been on the Internet looking at pictures and e-mailing some folks. I reckon she'll try to drag me to some meetings to save 'em."

"I'm glad she has a cause," Jerry said. "Mom always did like to look after others."

"Yeah, but turtles?" The elderly man shook his head. "They've been looking after themselves since long before your mother ever came along."

"This will be good for her."

"You're probably right."

Silence fell between them for a few minutes. Jerry glanced at his dad, who seemed deep in thought. Then he started thinking about what all he needed to do. Fortunately the condo was a seasonal rental, so the power and water were already on.

His dad cleared his throat, jolting Jerry from his thoughts. "Thinkin' about Amanda?"

"Not really."

"You need to start. Does she know you're coming?"

"I haven't told her. I figured Mom might, though."

His dad looked straight ahead and shook his head. "Nah, she wouldn't do that to you. She likes surprises too much."

Jerry changed the subject before his dad got the notion to delve too much into his feelings for Amanda. "Are you looking forward to seeing Timmy?"

"Yep." His dad snickered. "That little guy is a pistol. Reminds me of myself when I was his age."

"How so?" Jerry was thrilled he'd hit on a topic his dad obviously enjoyed.

"He always seems to find trouble, even when he's not looking. I figured if I brought him on my treasure hunts, it would give him something to look for, and maybe he'd stay out of trouble."

Jerry cut his gaze over to his dad before refocusing on the road ahead. "Is that why you're always going on treasure hunts?"

The older man lifted one shoulder and let it drop. "Maybe that's one of the reasons. It also gives me something to do."

"So you don't really think you're gonna find one, then?"

"Oh, I'll find one. In fact, I bet I find more than one."

His dad folded his arms and closed his eyes, signaling an end to the conversation. Jerry was grateful for the peace and quiet for a while. He needed a little time in his own head.

The farther south they drove, the lower the sky seemed to be. The hilly ribbon of interstate stretched into a long, flat rope that seemed to go on forever. As they drew closer to Tampa, large billboards dotted the roadside with promises of fun and fabulous food at various resorts and restaurants.

This was home. It seemed strange that after years of going to Florida for vacation, he'd be there year-round.

A startling snore from his dad snapped him from his thoughts. Out of the corner of his eye, he saw his dad wipe the corner of his mouth with his handkerchief.

"Feel better?" Jerry asked.

His dad shook his head. "My neck's stiff. If your mother was awake, I'd say let's stop and stretch. But I don't wanna bother her."

Jerry glanced in the rearview mirror and saw his mother snuggling into the pillow she'd leaned against the door. Her eyes were closed, but she had a smile on her face. It was nice seeing her happy.

"We're almost there anyway," Jerry said. "Another hour, max."

"Good. I'm sick of riding."

It was early evening when they pulled into the driveway of the retirement building that would be his parents' new home. The place was well-maintained and had meticulously manicured grounds. He noticed that the side yard had arbors with swings as well as flower gardens with an assortment of colors and varying heights of foliage for accent. It was peaceful and had an air of tranquillity. The perfect place for someone in their golden years.

"Well?" Jerry asked. "Is this what you expected?"

His dad looked around. "Looks nicer than where we came from."

Jerry agreed. "Let's go inside and see if they're ready for you." He turned around to see his mother stretching, the smile still plastered on her face. "You'll be up all night," he said.

"That's fine." She pulled out her compact and lipstick to freshen up, while Jerry and his dad got out of the car.

"You go on inside, Dad, and let them know you're here. I'll get the suitcases and bring them in."

By the time Jerry had their luggage at the front desk and his mother had walked in, a thirty-something man wearing khaki trousers and a navy golf shirt with DAN on his name tag was in the lobby waiting to greet them. "Welcome home, Mr. and Mrs. Simpson. Your apartment is ready and waiting. One of the maintenance men will be down shortly to take your bags to your apartment."

He led them to the elevator and punched the button. As they rode to the fourth floor, he chatted about all the amenities of the place. "I'm sure you're exhausted, so I asked Margie, the activities director, to wait a couple of days before coming by to see you."

After Dan left the apartment, Jerry took a good look around. He had to admit, he was impressed. Not only was the place bigger than where they lived in Atlanta, it was also much nicer.

"You picked a good one, Mom," Jerry said.

She flopped back on the sofa and surveyed the living room. "It's even better than what they showed on the Internet. I can't believe how spacious it is."

Jerry's dad walked over to the sliding glass door and flipped the lock. He walked outside then came back in grinning. "Nice view."

"I asked for the garden view, if they had one available," Jerry's mother said.

"Come see for yourself." The older man motioned for his wife and son to join him on the balcony.

Jerry scanned the horizon and let out a low whistle. "Not only is this a garden view, you get the magnificent sunset."

A knock sounded at the door, so Jerry answered it. The maintenance man had his parents' luggage on a cart. "Do you need help unpacking?"

"No, thank you," Jerry said as he offered the man a five-dollar bill.

The man smiled and held up his hand. "We have a no-tipping policy, until the Christmas season when the residents get together with staff. But thanks anyway. Let me know if you need anything else."

"How do we find you?" Jerry asked.

"Just pick up the phone and dial zero."

Jerry took the luggage inside and closed the door behind the maintenance man before joining his parents. His dad was opening all the closets and looking inside, while his mother was checking out the kitchen.

"You won't believe what's in here." She peeked around the corner. "Y'all come look in the kitchen."

Jerry and his dad immediately did as they were asked. His mother held the refrigerator door open wide, and Jerry looked inside. It was full!

"Whoa!" Jerry's eyes widened. "Someone did some serious shopping."

"Here's the note they taped to the door." She handed Jerry a yellow slip of paper.

He read it silently and then at his dad's urging, he read it aloud.

"Welcome, Mr. and Mrs. Simpson. We know a move is a major undertaking, so we like to greet all our newcomers with a few essentials to get you started. If you have any questions, please stop anyone in the hallway; hopefully you'll get the answers you need. We're a friendly bunch.

The Tropical Gardens Village Welcome Committee."

"Isn't that sweet?" His mother's cheeks were rosy, and her eyes glistened.

His dad nodded. "They sure do know how to welcome people around here."

When his dad turned and faced his mother with a look of pure bliss, Jerry knew all was right in their world. Now it was time to leave them alone.

"Are you sure your place is ready, son?"

"They told me it would be. All I have to do is stop by the real-estate office and get the key."

His mother glanced at her watch. "It's awfully late."

"Someone will be there until eight, but I'd better get a move on."

As Jerry left St. Petersburg and drove across the bridge leading to Treasure Island, he thought about the drastic move he was making and how risky it appeared to others. However, he didn't see it as a risk. It was more of an adventure—even if nothing happened between him and Amanda. Sure, she was one of the influencing factors in his decision to move, but even without her, he probably would have done this. He liked being close to his parents, but not for the reason his brother accused him. He wanted to be there if they needed him, and after they left Atlanta, there was nothing to hold him there. Besides, he loved Florida.

The woman at the real-estate office smiled as he entered. "You must be Jerry Simpson."

"That's me. I hope I'm not too late."

"When Margaret told me you were coming late, she didn't realize that I only work late on Friday nights to cover the weekend crowd."

"Thank you for staying late. It means a lot to me."

She smiled and handed him an envelope. "I don't mind once in a while. You'll find the key and all the information about the place in the envelope. If you have any questions, call the number tomorrow after nine."

"I'm sure I'll be fine."

Her grin widened. "Oh, I'm sure you will be, too."

Was she flirting with him? Nah, not likely. He backed out the door and waved then turned and hurried to his car. He'd been driving all day, and he was exhausted, close to hallucinating about intentions.

The condo was nice, but the view was nowhere near as breathtaking as the last place he and his parents had rented. He had a small balcony, but it overlooked the next building, and he had to step out onto the balcony and look to his right to see the Gulf of Mexico. It was fine, though. All he needed was a decent place to stay until he figured out where he wanted to live—or if he even wanted to stay there.

Jerry could hardly wait to see Amanda, but he didn't think it would be a good idea to do anything at this hour. Not only was he exhausted from the trip, but he figured she'd be winding down for the day.

He unpacked and settled down in front of the television and found a news station. After he felt sufficiently caught up with what was going on in the world, he got up and got ready for bed. First thing tomorrow, he'd check on his parents and then drop in on Amanda to let her know he was back in town.

* * * * *

"Did you tell Amanda our plans?"

Rosemary shook her head. "I wanted to, but I decided it was time to butt out and let Jerry talk to her first."

Harold's laughter annoyed her, but she didn't comment. Even after sleeping half the trip, she was tired. She'd woken up occasionally during the long drive, but Harold and Jerry were getting along so well that she didn't want to interrupt their father-son time. It was nice to see Harold in such good spirits.

"Did you want to take a shower tonight or in the morning?" she asked.

"I'll take one tonight." He crossed the room and took her hands in his. "But you go first. I want to fix myself a snack."

"If you want me—"

He gently nudged her toward the bathroom. "No, let me take care of myself as long as I can. It won't be too much longer before I won't be able to."

She slowly nodded and had to bite back the tears that stung the backs of her eyes. Harold knew his diagnosis, and after denying it for a few months, he'd finally come to terms with it. She knew that many of his grouchy moments were due to frustration about what they had to look forward to, and she couldn't say that she blamed him a bit.

As soon as she got out of the shower, Harold took his. Then together they cuddled on the sofa and watched a late movie. This was the closest she'd felt to her husband in a very long time.

* * * * *

Each day since Jerry and his parents had left Treasure Island, Amanda had felt sadder than the day before. Rosemary had called a few times, and she'd mentioned that they might take an extra vacation. At least Amanda wouldn't have to wait a whole year to see them again.

Matthew had called the night before and said he was bringing by some new items for her to decide what she wanted to carry in her store. She knew she needed to look at them, but she wasn't in the mood. Maybe he'd let her hang onto them for a few days. Vendors approached him at his events and offered freebies if he'd consider endorsing them. Then he always brought what he liked to her so she had the most up-to-date safety equipment for skateboarding.

In addition to Matthew coming in, she had a group order for a dozen bicycles as well as a couple of vendors dropping by on their regular rounds. She was glad to have a busy day; it kept her from thinking about Jerry so much.

She counted her money and closed the cash drawer. Then she moved to the sales floor to rearrange a few items when she heard the bell.

With a smile, she turned to face her customer. The instant she saw Jerry walk toward her, she felt blood rush to her face. She opened her mouth, but words wouldn't come out.

Chapter Sixteen

....

She continued staring at him as he approached the counter. "What are you doing here?"

Jerry's smile quickly faded as he hesitated. "Should I leave?"

"No." What had she been thinking? She sucked in a breath to compose herself. "I'm just surprised, that's all. I thought…well, I don't know what I thought."

"I take it I surprised you?"

Amanda finally regained her faculties enough to nod. "Yes, that's one way of putting it. How long are you in town?"

"For good." He shoved his hands into his pockets and gave her a look that was disquieting. "Mom and Dad decided to move here, and I didn't want them to come alone."

Amanda cleared her throat. "I've spoken to your mother a few times, and she never said a word about it."

"She wanted to surprise you. To be honest, when they told me they'd already made arrangements to move down here, I was shocked. They'd talked about it before, but I never thought they'd actually follow through."

Amanda wasn't sure why he was in the shop—whether he came to see her or if he was there to pick up a bicycle for his parents. There was one way to find out. "The tandems are out, but one of them should be back tomorrow. I can have it ready the next day, if—"

He held up his hand. "No, I don't think they're ready for bike riding yet. I just wanted to see you before I headed for the store and stocked up on supplies." Jerry started toward the door then stopped and turned back to face her. "What are you doing tonight? Wanna go out somewhere?"

She'd already promised to keep an eye on Timmy while Lacy and Brad went to Pastor Zach for counseling. Amanda tilted her head and slowly shook it. "I'm sorry, but I'm taking care of Timmy tonight."

"Are Brad and Lacy going out?"

Amanda didn't want to say too much about her sister's personal life without Lacy's permission. "Yeah, they have plans. I know it won't be as exciting as what you might have planned, but if you can't find anyone else to do something with, you can come over and hang out with us."

He instantly smiled and nodded. She was thrilled with his reaction, but she tried to backpedal so he wouldn't realize just how much his being here meant. "We're not really doing anything. He wants to look at my bicycle collection, which should be good for at least five minutes. I don't know what I'll do with the other hour and fifty-five minutes he'll be with me."

"Maybe I should bring my dad."

"You can if you want to."

Jerry shook his head no. "Nah, I'll just come alone tonight. After Lacy and Brad get back, you and I can go for a walk or something…that is, if you're up for it."

"Absolutely. I haven't had much time to get fresh air lately, so a walk would be nice."

After they settled on a time, Jerry left. Amanda's heart sang as she went through the rest of the day. She tried calling Rosemary's cell phone a couple of times, but it kept switching over to voice mail. The first time, Amanda left a message, but she hung up each time after that.

* * * * *

"Who is it this time?" Harold asked as they walked toward the dining room on the first floor. Rosemary's phone had been ringing all afternoon.

Rosemary looked at the number in the tiny window of her phone. "Amanda."

"That girl is persistent." Harold chuckled. "You might as well pick up next time."

"I'm not talking to her until I know it's okay with Jerry."

Harold frowned. "You don't have to ask him for permission to talk to anyone."

"I also don't want to lie to Amanda, and I don't know if Jerry's talked to her yet."

"Good point." Harold gently placed his hand on the small of Rosemary's back, and she shivered. His touch never failed to delight her.

She stopped outside the dining room. "Let me try to call him one more time before we eat."

"Maybe he's screening his calls and not answering ours—just like you're doing to Amanda."

Rosemary gave him her standard look. "He wouldn't dare."

"True. Then he'd have to answer to you. He probably just left his phone in another room."

She scrolled through her speed-dial numbers and hit CALL when his number came up. This time he answered right away.

"Where have you been?" she asked without a greeting. "I've been trying to get ahold of you all afternoon."

"Sorry. I had to make some business calls."

"Oh." Now she felt bad. Ever since she and Harold had retired, she rarely thought about work or jobs. Even when Jerry worked on his computer during their vacations, it still didn't seem like work because he could do it anywhere.

"Did you need something?" Jerry asked.

"Have you talked to Amanda yet?"

"I stopped by and saw her today. She's watching Timmy tonight so her sister and Brad can go somewhere, so I'm going to her place."

Rosemary glanced up and winked at Harold, who was watching with interest. "Good. She's been trying to call me, and I've been ignoring her calls."

"Why would you do that?"

"I wouldn't want to ruin anything for you, that's why."

Jerry laughed. "You couldn't mess up anything for me if you tried. Don't worry about it. I'm a grown man."

"Yes, I know, and that's the reason—" She caught herself. "Oh, never mind. Go have fun with Amanda tonight. Your dad and I are about to have dinner."

"Call me tomorrow, okay?"

"You know I will," Rosemary replied. "I'll want a full report."

The sound of Jerry's laughter came through until she flipped her phone shut. She grabbed her husband by the hand, took a deep breath, and tugged.

"Time to meet, greet, and eat," she said. As much as she hated to admit it, even to herself, her nerves were a bit jangled at the newness of everything and meeting so many neighbors at once.

Harold snorted. "I'll have to remember that one. Let's go. I'm starving."

Within minutes, they were surrounded by neighbors welcoming them to their new home. Rosemary watched a couple of men pounce on Harold.

"I'm Marvin," one guy said. "In case you haven't noticed, we're outnumbered by the biddies. We fellas have to stick together."

The woman next to him playfully gave him a light shove. "Don't mind Marvin. He loves it here. I'm Doris, and this is Norma."

Rosemary smiled and said hi to all her new friends. "I'll do my best to remember your names."

"We'll give you a week," Doris said. "By then you'll feel like you've known us forever. Do you play board games?"

"I haven't in a while," Rosemary replied.

"Every Tuesday night we have board games in the recreation room. On Wednesdays, we have church; then afterward we stay in the chapel and watch a movie." Doris turned to Norma. "Help me out here. I can't think of everything."

Norma took over. "Thursday is bowling night. We all go in the Tropical Gardens Village shuttle. On Fridays, the guys get together and shoot pool in the billiards room, so the ladies sometimes get together and decide what we want to do then."

"Don't forget to tell her about charades night," Marvin said. "That's my favorite event."

Doris rolled her eyes. "All the guys like charades because they get to revert to their childhood and act silly."

"It all sounds wonderful." Rosemary turned to Harold, who stood off to the side with his arms folded and a wry grin on his face. "I'm sure we'll take advantage of many activities."

"Trust me." Doris reached out and laid her hand on Rosemary's arm. "After you're here awhile, you won't want to miss a single thing. We're a tight group around here."

Marvin belted out a laugh. "Our kids and grandkids have to call in advance to get on our schedules."

They all sat down at formally set tables in the garden-themed dining room. With no assigned seating, many of them vied for a place with the newcomers, but the largest tables had only eight chairs.

Rosemary and Harold enjoyed a multicourse meal with fruit salad, roast beef, and flan for dessert. After dinner, they were invited to join the others in the evening activity, but Rosemary shook her head.

"I'm sorry, but we still have a few things to do tonight. Perhaps another time."

Norma nodded her understanding. "That's fine. Just holler if you need any help. There's a directory in your apartment with everyone's phone numbers and a book by the elevator on each floor with people's pictures, in case you can't remember names."

After Rosemary and Harold got back to their apartment, Harold flopped down on the sofa. "Those people nearly wore me out."

"But aren't they nice?"

He hesitated then nodded as he smiled. "Very nice. In fact, they're nicer than anyone I've ever met. You did a fine job of picking us out a place to live, Rosie."

Rosemary swallowed hard. She didn't tell Harold that the main reason she'd picked Tropical Gardens Village was the fact that they had an assisted-living wing as well as a nursing home attached. If anything happened to either of them and they needed a higher level of care, they wouldn't have to look elsewhere.

"I don't know about you, but all I want to do tonight is watch a little TV and then turn in." Harold lifted his legs and propped his feet on the coffee table.

"Take off your shoes, Harold."

He snickered as he removed his shoes. "Some things never change."

"That's right, and don't ever forget that."

* * * * *

Brad dropped Timmy off early and left with Lacy to grab a quick bite for dinner before their counseling session. Timmy had his lunch pail in hand, but after his dad left, he turned to Amanda.

"Daddy packed a bologna sandwich and an apple."

"Mmm. That sounds good." Amanda put her hand on Timmy's shoulder and led him to the kitchen.

"I hate bologna. What are you having for supper?"

Amanda pushed back her annoyance toward Brad for arriving early and not giving her any notice. She forced a smile at Timmy. "Macaroni and cheese. Want some?"

His face lit up. "I love macaroni and cheese!"

As Amanda cooked, Timmy chattered nonstop about how he'd started collecting things and his daddy had a train set. Suddenly he stopped talking, which got Amanda's attention.

"What's wrong?" she asked.

"When will Gramps be back?"

Amanda was torn about what to do. She would have loved to be able to make him happy by saying that Gramps now lived in Florida and could come over anytime he felt like it, but she wasn't sure if she should say anything yet. Since Jerry was coming over in a little while, she decided to leave it up to him.

"Why don't you ask Jerry?"

Timmy tilted his head with a puzzled look on his face. "How can I ask Jerry when he's not here?"

Amanda glanced up at the kitchen clock. "He should be here in a little while."

"I thought he went to 'lanta."

"He did, but he missed Florida so much that he came back here."

Timmy grinned. "Is Jerry your boyfriend?"

"No, of course not."

"Daddy said you like Jerry like he likes—"

The doorbell interrupted Timmy. Without waiting for her, he hopped down off the chair, ran full-speed into the living room, and opened the front door. Amanda needed to talk to Brad about that. In today's world, it was dangerous for a little boy to fling open the door without knowing who was behind it.

"Amanda!" Timmy hollered. "Jerry's here."

"Invite him in," Amanda said, before she turned and found both Jerry and Timmy standing in the kitchen. "Oh, hi. Want some macaroni and cheese?"

"If you have enough, sure. It sounds good."

"It's from a box. If we run out, there's more in the pantry. I'm afraid it's one of about three things my sister can cook."

Timmy tugged on Jerry's hand and led him to the table. "Where's Gramps?"

Amanda stilled as she listened to Jerry's answer. "He's at home."

She glanced over her shoulder in time to see Timmy's crestfallen expression. "Oh, I thought he was in Florida with you."

"Gramps lives in Florida now, Timmy." Jerry looked up at Amanda and winked before turning his attention back to the little boy.

Timmy's eyebrows shot up. "He does? Can I see him?"

"I'm afraid that he and my mother are very tired after the long trip from Atlanta. They're resting in their new apartment."

"Can I call him?"

Jerry reached into his pocket and pulled out his cell phone. "Sure. Let me get him on the phone for you, and you can talk to him."

Less than a minute later, Timmy was happily chattering with Harold. Jerry got up and offered to help with the food. She opened the flatware drawer and pointed. By the time they got the food on the table, Timmy was finished talking to Gramps. He put the phone down on the table.

"He's coming to see me tomorrow," Timmy announced proudly. "And we're going treasure hunting."

Jerry laughed. "Why am I not surprised?"

Between bites, Timmy told them all about pirates who stole from the rich people's boats and buried their treasure all over Treasure Island. Amanda made a face.

"I don't like the idea of hunting for stolen treasure."

Timmy held out his hands and shrugged. "Someone's gonna find it. Might as well be us."

Neither Amanda nor Jerry could hold back the laughter at his sincerity. Timmy was so cute at the moment, it was hard to imagine him giving her sister trouble in class.

After they ate, the three of them went for a walk around the block, with Timmy in the middle holding both their hands. Amanda felt way too cozy for comfort as she thought about how they must look like a family.

Timmy was tired, so they made one circle around the block before heading back inside. Amanda wasn't sure what to do next with Timmy. She hadn't been around children much. But she didn't need to worry. Brad and Lacy came home just a few minutes after the three of them got back. After Brad and Timmy left, Jerry asked her to step outside.

Her heart pumped hard as she stepped out onto the sidewalk with Jerry. He took her by the hand and pulled her to his side. "I've really missed you."

She looked up into his eyes and saw the reflection from the moonlight. Her heart seemed to pause. "I missed you, too."

As Jerry lowered his head for a kiss, Amanda felt like nothing could ever go wrong in her life now. The pain Eric had inflicted when he left her at the altar didn't matter anymore, now that Jerry was by her side.

After the kiss, Jerry gently touched her cheek then lifted her chin to face him. "I could easily fall in love with you." He pulled her close once again.

This time the kiss was deeper. More intense. Amanda was in love, and she wasn't about to deny it.

He promised to call the next day before walking to his car. She closed the door and turned to Lacy, who stood behind her rubbing her temples. "Headache?"

Lacy nodded. "It's so intense. Who knew being a Christian was so hard?"

"You just have to trust God, Lacy. Let Him be in charge. Let's go sit down and talk about it." She hadn't planned to be nosy, but Lacy's comment concerned her.

Once she leaned back on the love seat, Lacy stared up at the ceiling as she started talking. "Pastor Zach talked about forgiveness and how God paid the ultimate price with Jesus."

"That's pretty straightforward. What's the difficult part?" Amanda leaned forward so she could hear Amanda.

"That's just it," Lacy said as she turned toward Amanda. "What's the deal with the cross? That was so long ago, I don't get why it matters now."

Frustration took over as Amanda tried to think of a way to remind Lacy of all she'd been taught in Sunday school. Hadn't anything sunk in? She didn't want to make it complicated, but Lacy seemed so overwhelmed that even the simplest concept might be confusing to her at the moment.

"It matters now," Amanda began slowly, "because when Jesus died on the cross, He did it for all people who believed in Him. For the rest of time."

"Yeah," Lacy said, shaking her head, "that just blows me away. Why would He do that?"

"God did it because He loved us. He did it for our salvation."

"You have to admit, that's pretty extreme."

Amanda nodded. "Yes, it certainly is. And that's why I'll always hold my faith in Jesus close to my heart."

Lacy slowly sat up. "I want to be more like you, but right now I'm tired. I'm going to bed."

After Lacy left the room, Amanda bowed her head and prayed for her. That was all she could do now.

She went into the kitchen and was finishing cleaning up when the phone rang. It was Rosemary.

"Harold wants to see Timmy tomorrow, and we wanted to ask if we could meet at your shop before he calls Brad."

"Sure," Amanda said, "that's fine. Timmy really loves Gramps."

"Yes, and Gramps loves Timmy. In fact, before and after dinner tonight, we were surrounded by some of our new neighbors, and we had a hard time getting away. When we got back to our apartment, he said he needed a Timmy fix."

Amanda laughed. "That's cute. Sure, go ahead and call Brad and make arrangements to meet him at the shop."

"One more thing before we hang up." Rosemary's voice cracked.

"What's that?"

"Jerry didn't hesitate to leave Atlanta once he knew we were serious about relocating here."

"That's nice." Amanda knew there was more.

"We think it might have something to do with being near you."

Amanda's heart hammered in her chest. This was what she'd hoped for. "Did he tell you that?"

"Well…no, not in so many words."

Amanda felt crestfallen. "It probably had more to do with the climate and proximity to the beach."

"Maybe just a little, but we really do believe he's falling for you. I hope you don't break his heart."

Amanda began to let out a nervous laugh but caught herself. "Jerry hasn't said how he feels, but I think we're just very good friends." She wasn't about to mention *the kiss*.

Rosemary cleared her throat. "We'll see about that. Would you like for me to call you back and let you know what Brad says about tomorrow?"

"It's not necessary," Amanda replied. "I'll be there all day, and I always welcome friends to the store."

"Very well, then. Hopefully we'll see you tomorrow."

* * * * *

The next morning, Amanda awoke with Jerry on her mind. She hopped out of bed, showered, and dressed in her best work clothes—black athletic pants and a coral tank top. She played with her hair and worked it into a style. She polished her look with a coat of mascara and a light smear of tinted lip gloss. After a quick look in the mirror, she headed for the coffeepot in the kitchen. Lacy stood there staring at the pot as coffee dripped into it.

"You look nice," Lacy mumbled. "Is Jerry coming to see you today?"

Amanda tried to be coy, but she couldn't hide her enthusiasm. "Rosemary called last night and said she thinks Jerry came here partly for me."

Lacy let out a grunt. "Yeah. Anyone with eyes can see the guy has a thing for you. Wake up, Amanda."

"I'm not going to assume anything." She tried to keep the happy lilt out of her voice, but it didn't work. She felt on top of the world about the possibility of seeing Jerry.

Amanda pulled two mugs out of the cupboard and set them in front of the coffeepot. Then she fixed herself a bowl of Cheerios.

After the coffee finished brewing, Lacy poured some for both of them and carried the mugs to the table. "I almost forgot to ask if you'd mind keeping an eye on Timmy for about an hour this morning."

"You know I'm working," Amanda reminded her.

"Yeah, but since you own the place, I figured it would be okay."

"Why? What's going on?"

"Brad wants me to go look at a boat he's thinking about buying." She traced her finger around the rim of her cup then looked Amanda in the eyes. "I'm in love with Brad, and I think he loves me. He said that if I want him to start going to church, he will because he wants me to be happy."

That was all it took for Amanda. "Sure, bring Timmy over. I'll watch him. Rosemary called last night and said Harold wants to see him, anyway."

"Perfect!" Lacy jumped up and carried her mug to the sink. "Timmy loves Gramps."

Amanda grinned. "Happy I can help."

When she arrived at her shop, Amanda did all her opening tasks. A bicycle group came in for goggles and water bottles, but then she found herself alone. Normally during quiet times, Amanda busied herself with ordering and other business matters, but today she felt antsy.

Finally, Brad, Lacy, and Timmy arrived, with Timmy taking the lead. "Where's Gramps?"

"He'll be here soon," she said. "I hear he's excited about seeing his little treasure-hunting buddy."

Timmy beamed. "He told Daddy he has a surprise for me."

"He did?" Amanda had no idea what it was, but she had no doubt it would be perfect.

Lacy stepped up to the counter and got her attention. "We're leaving now, okay?"

"When will you be back?" Amanda asked.

Lacy turned to Brad, who shrugged. "An hour or so? We'll call if we're any later."

Amanda thought for a moment then offered a nod. "We'll be fine, won't we, Timmy?"

Rather than answer her question, Timmy pointed to a skateboard display. "I want one of those." He turned to his dad. "Will you buy me a dark blue skateboard?"

Brad tilted his head forward and gave Amanda a look of pure exasperation; then he turned back to Timmy. "When you're a little older."

Timmy scowled at his dad, so Amanda took charge. "That's something you can look forward to, Timmy! I have a friend who can teach you all the tricks, when you're…" She glanced up at Brad and mouthed the word "*seven*."

Brad nodded. "Seven," he said.

With his forehead furrowed and his lips pursed, Timmy thought it over for a moment. "That's a long time."

Amanda grinned at him and leaned forward. "It seems like a long time now, but time will go by faster than you can say *boo*."

Lacy headed for the door. "C'mon, Brad, let's go."

He followed her as he waved to his son. "We'll be back soon. Have fun!"

After they left, Amanda tried to think of something to entertain Timmy and was relieved when she spotted Jerry's SUV pull around the corner. "Hey, Timmy, I think Gramps is due to arrive any minute."

Chapter Seventeen

Jerry and his parents walked into the shop, all of them smiling. Timmy ran straight to Harold and flung himself full-throttle into the elderly man's arms. Jerry reached out to stop him, but Harold managed to sidestep him and catch Timmy at the same time. Amanda was impressed by his strength.

"Gramps!" Timmy hugged him tight. "I missed you so much!"

Amanda saw the misty look in Harold's eyes. "I missed you, too, little guy. Are you having a fun summer?"

Timmy leaned back and frowned. "Summer's almost over. I have to go back to school soon."

"Yes," Harold acknowledged, "but you'll be a first-grader, not a kindergartner anymore."

Timmy's frown quickly turned into a smile. "I'll be one of the big kids at school."

Rosemary lifted her finger, and Amanda turned to her. "I need Jerry to take me somewhere. Do you mind if I leave Harold here?"

"Of course not." Amanda felt that all was right in her world now, so anything was fine. "I'd love for him to hang out here with Timmy and me."

Jerry winked. "We won't be gone long. Mom and Dad sold their car before the move, so I'll be their main mode of transportation for a while—at least until they figure out how to coordinate their errands with the Tropical Gardens Village shuttle."

"Take your time." Amanda looked over at Timmy, who was already deep in conversation with Harold. "We'll be just fine."

When Jerry and Rosemary slipped out, the only person who noticed was Amanda. Harold turned around. "Where's my wife?"

"She and Jerry left for a little while."

He made a face. "I wish they'd told me they were leaving." Then he turned to Timmy and exaggerated his face even more.

Timmy laughed. "Gramps, you're so funny!"

Harold made another face, which sent both of them into a fit of laughter. Amanda loved the joy that flooded her shop.

They both made faces at each other for a few minutes and then started up a new conversation, when Harold reminded Timmy about Babe Ruth's bungalow. Timmy told him his dad had driven him by it and it wasn't any big deal.

For the next hour, Harold managed to keep Timmy occupied, but eventually lunchtime approached. "I'm starving," the little boy said. "I want a hamburger."

"Your daddy said they'd only be gone a little while. I'm sure he'll be back any minute."

After another half hour passed and still no Brad, Amanda tried calling Lacy on her cell phone, but there was no answer.

"Call Jerry or Rosemary," Harold said. "Maybe they'll bring us something to eat."

"Let's wait just a little bit longer before I call them." Amanda didn't want to interrupt whatever Jerry and Rosemary were doing. Brad and Lacy lost track of time when they were together, but that wasn't typical of Jerry. One of the many things she loved about him was that he was responsible.

Another half hour passed. Amanda was annoyed with her sister and Brad because it was their responsibility to contact her, since she was watching Timmy. Timmy had resorted to whining, so Amanda knew she had to do something.

"Want me to call and order a pizza?" she asked.

Timmy frowned. "I already told you I want a hamburger."

"Want me to go out for some burgers?" Harold offered.

She wasn't going to take a chance and have Harold go off looking for hamburgers. She didn't know how well he was acquainted with the area. However, she had no doubt he could look after Timmy for a few minutes—if she didn't stay gone too long.

Amanda looked at the clock. "It's lunchtime, and the hamburger place will be packed. Want me to run home and whip up something really quick?"

Harold's eyes lit up. "Got any peanut butter?"

"I'm pretty sure I do." She turned to Timmy. "How does peanut butter sound?"

Timmy looked at Harold, who nodded. "I'm pretty sure that's what the pirates ate," the older man said.

"I want peanut butter!" Timmy clapped his hands. "We'll eat pirate food!"

Amanda smiled. Harold definitely had a way with Timmy, which confirmed her instinct to let them stay in the shop while she ran out.

"What do you want me to do if a customer comes in?" Harold asked. "I'm a pretty decent salesman."

"I can see that. If someone wants to buy something, tell them I'll be right back. And if the phone rings, you can either let it go to voice mail, or you can just answer it with the name of the shop and take a message."

Harold offered a clipped nod. "Sounds easy enough."

Amanda grabbed her handbag and headed for the door, with only a slight hesitation. She'd been put in an awkward situation, and this was the only thing she could think to do.

She ran most of the way home, headed straight for the kitchen, made a half dozen peanut butter sandwiches, grabbed a bag of chips, and tossed them all into a canvas bag. Then she went back to the shop as quickly as she could.

As soon as she opened the door, her heart skipped a beat. Harold and Timmy were nowhere in sight. She dropped the bag on the floor, ran back to the storage area, and knocked on the restroom door. Still no sign of either of them.

Panic quickly gripped her. What had happened? Harold seemed to understand his responsibility with Timmy. Maybe something worse…

She shuddered then closed her eyes to pray about what to do. She picked up the phone and speed-dialed her sister. Lacy didn't answer, so she left a message to call her ASAP. Then she called Jerry. "Your dad… Timmy…they're gone."

"What?"

Amanda took a deep breath and started over. "Lacy and Brad still haven't come back, and Timmy got hungry, and your dad was here entertaining him, and they didn't want pizza, and I didn't know what else to do—"

"Whoa, slow down," Jerry said. "Start over. What happened?"

"That's just it." Her voice was tight and high-pitched. "I don't know. I ran home to get some food, and when I came back, they were gone."

"Who was gone?"

"Your dad and Timmy."

"You left my dad and Timmy in the shop while you went home?" Jerry's voice had a harder edge now, which only made her feel worse.

Panic swelled in her throat. "Yes. And my sister isn't answering her cell phone."

"We'll be right there." Then the phone went dead.

Amanda called the businesses located on both sides of her shop, but none of them had seen an elderly man and a little boy. She put down the phone, inhaled deeply, and said a prayer for Harold and Timmy to be found safe.

Jerry and his mother made it back to the store within fifteen minutes. She noticed the angry scowl on Jerry's face and the terror on Rosemary's. And she couldn't blame them a bit.

"Why did you leave them alone?" he demanded.

She'd asked herself the same question. "I shouldn't have. They told me they'd be okay for the few minutes it took me to run home and get food."

Jerry set his jaw and shook his head. "You know my father's condition. How could you put him in charge of a little boy? What if—"

Rosemary reached out and squeezed Jerry's arm. "Stop. It's too late for blame. We just need to find them and deal with this later."

"I'll take one of the bicycles and look for them," Amanda said.

"No," Jerry replied. "You've done enough damage already. You can stay here while I go looking." He turned to his mother. "Stay here with Amanda."

Rosemary tilted her head and lifted a brow. "I'll stay here so Amanda can help you look." Her voice had a commanding tone.

Jerry opened his mouth to argue, but he narrowed his eyes and nodded. "Fine. I'll take the car. Amanda can go on a bike."

Amanda went to the back, grabbed one of the rental bicycles, and started for the door when Brad and Lacy came walking in with dreamy smiles on their faces. All it took was a couple of seconds before they realized that something wasn't right.

"Where's my son?" Brad asked.

"Timmy and my dad are missing," Jerry blurted.

All the color drained from Brad's face, and Lacy gasped. Amanda had no doubt her sister was genuinely concerned.

Brad turned to Amanda. "How did that happen?"

Rosemary came to her rescue. "Let's talk about what happened later. Right now, all of you need to go find my husband and Timmy."

Everyone exchanged cell phone numbers and set off looking for the missing guys. Amanda headed toward one of the neighborhoods behind the shop. She had a hunch—even though it was a long shot.

She slowly rode up and down the grid of streets flanked by tiny older Florida-style houses. Right when she'd decided to go one more street before turning back, she caught sight of a gray-haired man and a little boy walking hand-in-hand. Her heart flipped as she pedaled faster toward them. When she got within twenty feet of them, they turned to face her, and she realized it was someone else.

"Hi," the little boy said. "My grandpa and grandma came to see me."

Amanda felt sick inside. "That's nice." She asked if they'd seen another man and little boy. They said they hadn't, but that if they did, they'd let them know someone wanted to see them.

They waved as she took off to look some more. After a half hour of searching in vain, she gave up and headed back to the shop.

When everyone came back, Jerry pulled out his phone. "I'm calling the cops before it's too dark to see."

Rosemary walked over to the window then turned around. "They're here."

"What?" Jerry ran to the window and looked out. "They're coming up the street on one of your tandem bikes."

Brad ran outside and started yelling at Timmy and Harold. Amanda wanted to crawl into a hole and hide for the rest of her life.

"Timothy Charles Deavers, where have you been?" Brad hollered at Timmy. "We've been looking all over Treasure Island for you."

Timmy's chin quivered. "I wanted to show him where Babe Ruth used to live, but I can't find it."

Harold squinted. "So we went on a little treasure hunt. I think we finally found what we were looking for."

Brad unsnapped the chin strap on Timmy's helmet and removed it from the boy's head. Timmy couldn't fight back the tears any longer.

Lacy was right behind Brad, with tears streaming down her cheeks. Timmy was obviously shocked at his dad's anger. Lacy didn't waste another minute before she threw her arms around Timmy.

"We both wore our helmets," Harold said. "You should at least be proud of us for that."

Everyone glared at him, so he hung his head. Rosemary linked her arm in his and patted him on the shoulder. It obviously didn't make him feel any better.

Amanda stood and watched in amazement as Lacy gently rubbed the little boy's arm and uttered soothing words until he stopped sobbing. Then Lacy turned to Brad. "Let's go now. He's okay."

She helped him into the backseat before she turned to Amanda. "We'll discuss this later." Then she lowered herself into the front seat of Brad's car, and they took off.

When Amanda turned around and saw the look of despair on Harold's face, she felt sorry for the man. "Are you okay?" she asked.

He shook his head then looked down at his feet. She knew he felt shame over what had happened, and it took every ounce of self-restraint not to run to him like Lacy had with Timmy. She didn't want to humiliate him any further.

When she dared a glance in Jerry's direction, she saw his balled fists at his side. This wasn't a good time to try to talk to him.

Amanda thanked the Lord for finding Timmy and Harold safe, and then she asked for forgiveness. She never should have left them alone—not even for a minute.

"This isn't your fault, Amanda," Rosemary whispered. "My husband knew better than to leave."

Harold looked up at her with glistening eyes. "I don't know what I was thinking. Timmy and I were talking about Babe Ruth's house. One thing led to another, and the next thing I knew, we were out looking for his house. He said it was right around the corner, and he made it sound like we'd only be gone five minutes. I figured we could get back before you, but when we couldn't find it, Timmy was so disappointed that I said we could look for treasure instead. We sort of forgot and lost track of time." He paused and visibly swallowed hard. "I hope you didn't lose any business because of me."

"Don't worry about business," Amanda said as she tried hard not to notice Jerry's glowering face. "I'm just glad you and Timmy are okay." She remembered the food she'd brought back. "I have some peanut butter sandwiches."

"I'm not hungry. Timmy and I…well, we stopped off and got burgers. I'm really very sorry."

Jerry stepped in front of his dad. "I need to get my folks back home." He escorted his parents out the door and left without saying good-bye.

Amanda stood there staring after him, feeling as though the world had ceased spinning. The man she loved had just walked out the door of her shop—and probably her life. She doubted she would ever see him again.

It was late, so she flipped the CLOSED sign and left. When she got home, she was surprised to see Lacy there.

"You really messed up big-time," Lacy said. "How could you have been so irresponsible as to leave a five-year-old boy in the care of a senile old man?"

That did it. Something inside of Amanda snapped. She turned and glared directly at her sister.

"How can you say such a thing after leaving Timmy for what was supposed to be an hour that turned into three?"

"We said an hour and a half or so."

"You said an hour. And the least you and Brad could have done was bring Timmy some lunch or at least made arrangements for me to feed him. It was almost two o'clock and the poor kid was starving, so I did what I thought was best and went to get him something to eat. I couldn't get ahold of you." Amanda knew her voice was a few decibels higher than normal, but she didn't care. Lacy had pushed her too far this time.

"He wouldn't have—"

"Don't try to make me fully responsible for what happened, Lacy. Yeah, I made a mistake, but if you and Brad hadn't been so selfish—" Amanda stopped herself and hung her head. "I didn't mean that."

"I hope not." Lacy chewed her lip before gesturing toward the other room. "Let's go sit down. I have some news."

Amanda followed Lacy into the living room, where they sat across from each other. "Okay, so what's the news?"

"Brad and I are getting married. He proposed, so we went to look at rings. That's why we were so late." She held out her left hand to show the glittering diamond.

Amanda stared at the ring then looked Lacy in the eyes. "Why didn't you at least call and tell me you were running late?"

Lacy shrugged. "I forgot."

"You forgot," Amanda repeated, as she stood on shaky legs. "Then don't call me irresponsible. I might have messed up, but at least I didn't forget about Timmy." She started for her room before she stopped and turned around. "Another thing, Lacy. Harold isn't a senile old man. He's a wonderful person who loves Timmy enough to entertain him while I worked."

Lacy didn't say a word. She just splayed her hand in front of her face and stared down at the diamond ring.

* * * * *

The next day, Amanda went to work with a heavy heart. Fortunately, she had an early rush of customers, so she didn't have much time to think about what had happened until after lunch when it suddenly got quiet.

As she stood behind the counter, trying to concentrate on her next order, her mind drifted to the events leading up to lunch the day before. The more she thought about it, the more convinced she was that she could have prevented it. Finally, by the time she closed the shop, there was no doubt in her mind that the whole thing was her fault. She didn't have Jerry's new address, or she would have sent a written apology. So she did the next best thing. She called.

He answered abruptly, letting her know he'd checked caller ID. After she apologized, he said, "Fine. I understand," in a very clipped tone dripping with icicles.

After they hung up, she felt worse than before she'd called. Over the next several days, she continued to fret over the incident. However, Lacy seemed to have forgotten all about it. All she was interested in was planning her wedding.

"Timmy said he's happy to have a teacher become his mommy." Lacy giggled. "He seems to think I have some inside information on school or something."

"I'm glad you worked through your issues with him. He really is a sweet little boy."

Lacy looked at her, a puzzled frown furrowing her brow. "Issues? What are you talking about, Amanda?"

"You know. You had problems with Timmy in class."

Lacy shrugged. "It really wasn't all that bad. He's just an active little boy." She gave Amanda a look of annoyance. "Why do you always dwell on the negative?"

Amanda retreated. Was she negative? She never saw herself that way.

On Sunday she went to church and found Matthew sitting near the side door. He motioned for her to join him, so she did. She was surprised when she turned around and spotted Jerry walking in with his parents. He glanced over at her, did a slight double-take, then turned all his attention on his dad. His mother smiled and waved. Amanda waved back.

After church she followed Matthew to the fellowship hall. Without making any effort to be social, Jerry ushered his parents out the church door. Her heart sank. Seeing him in church gave her some hope that perhaps he'd be willing to at least talk.

"Why so glum?" Matthew asked.

Amanda told him what had happened, and he just stood there without saying anything. When she realized he wasn't responding, she asked his opinion.

"Do you really wanna know?" he asked.

She nodded. "Yes, of course, or I wouldn't have asked."

He closed his eyes then opened them and looked her in the eyes. "I'm glad he's mad at you."

"What?"

"This isn't easy for me to say, but I might as well come out with it. I've wanted to have more than a platonic relationship with you since we first met, but you were so intent on just staying friends, I held back and waited for the right time to say something."

Amanda's mouth instantly became dry. She squeezed her eyes shut then offered him an apologetic grin. "I'm sorry, Matthew."

He nodded with a matching smile. "Yeah, me, too." He took her hand and held it between his as he captured her gaze. "Now for some advice about Jerry. If you really care for him as much as I think you do, don't just stand here talking to me. Go after him."

"You know I can't do that, Matthew."

"Why?" he asked. "Are you too proud?"

* * * * *

"Stop being so foolish, Jerry." Rosemary was exasperated with her son. She was tired of him taking out his own frustration on Amanda. "Everything is fine."

"This could have turned out much worse."

"But it didn't," she argued. "You and Amanda have something special. I don't want to see you let it slip away."

"Maybe it's not as special as you think. Did you see her sitting next to that Matthew guy in church?"

Rosemary looked up at the ceiling and silently counted to ten before leveling her gaze on her very stubborn son. "Yes, of course I saw her sitting with him, and that's all the more reason you shouldn't hold a grudge for so long. Amanda is a very attractive, sweet, smart young woman who isn't going to stay single all her life."

"Good for her."

Rosemary wanted to shake Jerry, but it wouldn't do any good. He'd always been stubborn, and it took him days to work things out in his own mind. She needed to get him started, though, so she decided to go for the jugular.

"Don't forget the time he took off when you were supposed to be with him and we had to call the police."

Jerry's face turned a bright shade of crimson. "That was different. We didn't know he had Alzheimer's."

"We knew something was wrong, or I wouldn't have asked you to stay with him while I went to my hair appointment."

"Yeah, well…"

"Then there was that other time when we all went to the mall together. You turned your back for less than a minute, and when you turned around, he was gone."

He tightened his jaw and stared straight ahead. Finally, he stood up from the chair in his parents' apartment. "I'm going home."

Before he got to the door, he hesitated long enough for Rosemary to say one more thought. "Just don't miss out on this chance to work things out with Amanda. No one is perfect, you know."

* * * * *

All the way home, Jerry pondered everything his mother had said. As usual, she was right. Now that some time had passed, he knew this wasn't Amanda's fault. Sure, she was aware that his dad had Alzheimer's, but she didn't realize he had a tendency to wander off. Jerry knew he should have said something.

Jerry also knew that part of his reaction was based on his feelings for Amanda. He had never intended to fall in love, but he did it anyway. Every nerve in his body was sensitive when she was around. It didn't take much to set him off.

When he saw her in church with Matthew, he almost went out of his mind. She'd told him she and the skateboarder were just friends, and he didn't doubt her sincerity in the least. However, he saw the way Matthew looked at Amanda, and it wasn't like he was looking at a friend. The guy was head over heels.

As all his mother's warnings ran through his mind, he knew she'd given him good advice. If he continued being stubborn, he risked losing out on being with the only woman who'd ever given him sunshine on cloudy days merely by being in the same room with him. Her smile sent a signal to his heart that all was right in his world.

He picked up some of his clutter then pulled out the papers he'd need for work the following week. Then he sat down in front of the television and channel-surfed until he felt like he'd go out of his mind. Finally, he picked up the phone and called his mom.

"You were right."

"Is this Jerry?"

"Yes. Did you hear what I said?"

"Of course I did. I know I was right, but I didn't expect you to come to this conclusion so soon. You generally have to stew over things for at least a few days."

"I feel like a class-A jerk."

His mother laughed. "No, sweetheart, you're not a jerk—just a lovesick man who can't handle the emotions."

Jerry wasn't sure what to say to that, so he expelled the air in his lungs. "I have to do something, but I have no idea what."

"Start by telling her how you feel."

"I don't want to scare her away."

"Trust me, Jerry, you won't scare her away. Just go see her and talk to her."

"Let me think about it some more." The mere thought of going into her shop, having no idea if she'd listen or kick him out, made him dizzy. What was worse, however, was the possibility of Matthew stepping in and riding off into the sunset with the girl.

"Your father wants to talk to you."

"Put him on." Jerry drummed his fingers on the table while he waited and listened to his parents whispering.

Finally, his dad came on. "I want to apologize for causing all this trouble."

"Thanks, Dad."

"If there's anything I can do, you know I will."

"Yes, I know."

"Well, if you don't have anything else to say, I'll give the phone back to your mother so she can finish talking some sense into you."

Jerry talked to his mother for a few more seconds. She asked him to take her to the beach later in the week, and he said he would. There wasn't anything else he could do at this hour, so he kicked back and watched more TV until bedtime.

* * * * *

Amanda had played through the scenario over and over in her mind. Jerry had been right. Matthew did see their relationship as being more than friends—or at least wish that they would be—and she hadn't seen it coming. She didn't think she'd done anything to encourage it, but obviously she had—and it bugged her.

Monday and Tuesday were normally slow days, but some schools still hadn't gone back in session, which meant kids and their families were taking last-of-the-season vacations. Lacy was so busy with her own life, between wedding preparations and teaching, that she wasn't around the house much. Amanda was glad to have the house to herself most evenings because she didn't feel like making small talk.

Business finally slowed down by Thursday, so she took advantage of the lull to rearrange the stock. She'd taken a retail crash course where she learned to constantly move things around to increase sales. She'd just finished moving one of her skateboard displays to the opposite side of the showroom when she heard the bell on the door.

Chapter Eighteen

....

Rosemary smiled as she walked toward Amanda. "Hi there."

Amanda smiled and clasped her hands together to keep them from shaking. The only time she'd seen Rosemary since the incident had been in church, when it was apparent that none of the Simpson family wanted anything to do with her.

"How are you, Rosemary? Did you need a bicycle?"

"Not today, dear. I just need your listening ears." She glanced around. "Are you busy?"

Amanda shook her head. "No, it's been pretty slow today. What's up?"

"Jerry feels terrible about how he reacted."

"Does he know you're here?"

Rosemary's nose crinkled as she smiled. "What do you think?"

Amanda leaned over and looked outside. "How did you get here, then? Did you get a car?"

"No. I had a friend drop me off. She's coming back for me in a half hour, so I need to get this off my chest pretty quickly."

"Okay. So why do you think Jerry feels bad?"

Rosemary told her about how they'd learned of Harold's Alzheimer's—after he'd pulled his disappearing act several times with both Jerry and Rosemary. "So you see, this isn't the first time he's taken off like that. Jerry and I should have told you that we have to keep a close watch on him."

"Where is Harold now?"

"He and a bunch of his friends are shooting pool back at Tropical Gardens. I don't think he even knows I left the building."

Amanda smiled. "I'm glad he's enjoying himself."

"Oh, he's having the time of his life, and part of it's due to Timmy. I haven't seen him this happy in years."

"Timmy obviously adores Harold, as well. He's a sweet little boy who just needs some attention, and now he's getting it."

"Jerry enjoys being around you."

Amanda rubbed her neck. "I like him, too. How much longer do you think he'll be in Treasure Island?"

Rosemary frowned. "What do you mean?"

"He told me he has a short-term lease. I wondered what he'd do when it was up."

The sound of a horn honking outside caught their attention. Rosemary waved then turned back to Amanda. "My ride's here. Just remember what I said. Nothing that happened was your fault." She stepped up to Amanda and pulled her in for a hug. "Give my son another chance."

Amanda smiled. "Take care, Rosemary, and tell Harold I said hi."

"I'm not telling him I came here. He thinks I interfere too much already."

After she left, Amanda thought about what Rosemary had said. Only now, she found herself angry with Jerry for blaming her for Harold and Timmy's disappearance. Her emotional roller coaster over the past week, with all the highs and lows, was almost too much to handle. Her stomach churned, and she felt achy all over.

Friday and Saturday were busy days, and she went home exhausted. When she awoke on Sunday morning, her skin felt as though it had been scraped by sandpaper. Lacy came out of the bathroom, took one look at her, and took a step back.

"Whoa, you look awful."

Amanda went into the bathroom and looked at her reflection in the mirror. "Where's the thermometer?"

"In the kitchen," Lacy replied. "I'll go get it."

With a temperature of 101, Amanda couldn't very well go to church and risk exposing others to something if she was contagious. Lacy told her to go back to bed, and she'd bring her some tea and toast. Amanda did as she was told.

Lacy didn't waste any time. Less than ten minutes later, she brought a tray into Amanda's room. "Brad and Timmy will be here in a few minutes. We're going out to lunch after church and then taking Timmy to a skating rink for a classmate's birthday party."

Amanda's lips were parched as she sipped the tea. "Don't worry about me."

"Call if you need me." Lacy hovered by the door. "I'll check my cell phone messages after church."

By midafternoon, Amanda knew she wasn't going to be well enough to go to the shop the next day. Tiffany was back in school, so she wouldn't be able to work until after two thirty or three. The only option she had to open her store was Matthew. After only a slight hesitation, she called him.

"I'll be glad to work tomorrow," he said. "I'm taking a break from the tour until next month when we gear up for the holiday season."

"Thanks, Matthew. I need to go back to bed now."

"Let me know if you need anything, Amanda. I'm sorry you're sick."

"I'll be fine in a day or two," she said.

"I can work all week if you need me."

* * * * *

Jerry couldn't get Amanda out of his mind. He'd looked for her in church, hoping to have a quick chat with her to try to make amends. But he didn't see her. His mother seemed nervous as she glanced around, too.

After the service, he drove his parents back to Tropical Gardens Village and hung out for a little while before heading back home. He'd never felt so lonely in his life as he had since that fateful day of his dad taking off with Timmy. All he wanted was to be with Amanda, and now he wasn't sure that was possible.

Monday morning, he got up early and did as much work as possible. The Asian market was ending their day when he began, so he had dozens of e-mails to deal with the second he signed on.

As soon as he caught up, he decided to run by Amanda's shop to see if she had a minute to chat. The second he opened the door and saw Matthew standing behind the counter flipping through a magazine, his blood boiled.

Matthew looked up and waved. "Hey, Jerry. Need something?"

Jerry needed Amanda, but he wasn't about to tell Matthew that. He looked around for something to buy and spotted a sports bottle. "I need one of those."

"Is that all?" Matthew said as he rang it up. "You look like you have something on your mind. Wanna talk about it?"

"No." Jerry couldn't help his abruptness. "Where's Amanda?"

"Home." Matthew lifted a soft drink cup and sipped through the straw. "I'm filling in for her today and maybe tomorrow. Want me to give her a message?"

"I don't think so. See ya around." He knew his tone was terse, but it reflected his feelings.

The second Jerry left the store, he wanted to go back in and find out what Matthew was doing working in Jerry's girl's store. But she wasn't Jerry's girl. She obviously had more confidence in Matthew than she did him.

He headed straight to his parents' place. On his way there, he called his mother and asked if she could go for a ride. The concern in her voice made him feel bad, but he needed to talk to someone who understood him.

As he pulled up to the front door, his mother came right to the car and got in. "What happened?" she asked, worry lines etching her face.

Jerry told her about Matthew working at the store. "I'm afraid I might have blown any chance with Amanda by the way I acted a little while ago."

"Maybe not," she said. "How do you like living in Treasure Island? Do you think you'd like to stay there?"

He stopped at a light and looked at her. "What does that have to do with anything?"

"I don't want you to stay in a place you don't like just because of your feelings for Amanda."

"You know I love Treasure Island." He paused and thought about making it his permanent home. "I'd love to stay."

"And how about Amanda? Are you sure you can handle a relationship?"

He nodded. "Absolutely. In fact, that's all I want right now."

"Then you need to show her how you feel. I have an idea." She pointed to a coffee shop. "Let's go in there and talk."

By the time Jerry took his mother home, he had a plan. Maybe it would make a difference with Amanda, and maybe it wouldn't. But at least he was taking action to do something productive for his future.

* * * * *

Amanda felt better on Tuesday but still not well enough to work all day. Matthew opened the store, and she worked late morning to midafternoon, when Tiffany came in after school. It gave Amanda a chance to ease back into her normal activity.

Each day for the rest of the week she felt a little better. She was able to attend church. She sat with Suzanne, whom she hadn't seen in several weeks.

"How was your trip to Europe?" she asked.

Suzanne shrugged. "It was okay at first, but I missed home."

"Glad you're back."

Every once in a while, like when they stood up to sing, Amanda glanced behind her, hoping to catch a glimpse of Jerry and his parents. But she never saw them. He wasn't at the Bible study, either.

On the way to the parking lot, Suzanne stopped her. "Why are you acting so strange?"

Amanda was tempted to brush off the question, but she really needed to talk. "Do you have about an hour?"

Suzanne nodded. "Let's go to my place, and you can tell me over a salad." She patted her belly. "All that rich food in Europe..."

After telling the details and pouring out her feelings, Amanda saw a smile form on Suzanne's lips. "Looks like you might be in love...this time for real."

Amanda nodded. "Yes, I'm afraid so. But I also think I blew it."

"Maybe not. Why don't you talk to Jerry?"

"He's so mad at me he's not talking."

"Then give him some time," Suzanne advised. "Why don't you call him later this coming week and see if he's open to discussion?"

"I can do that."

On Monday and Tuesday, Amanda reached for the phone to call Jerry, but she chickened out. Finally, on Wednesday morning, shortly after she opened the store, she followed through. When he answered, he didn't sound the least bit upset.

"I've been wanting to call you, too," he said. "Mind if I stop by for a few minutes later this afternoon?"

Her heart leaped. "That would be great!" She was past the point of being coy or hiding her feelings from Jerry.

After lunch she kept watching the door, hoping to see Jerry walk through. Her nerves stood on end each time the bell jangled.

When Jerry arrived, she was finishing up with a customer who'd bought a bicycle and an entire set of safety gear. Jerry stood off to the side, hands in his pockets, patiently waiting. After the customer left, he approached the counter.

"Customers like that'll keep you in business awhile."

Amanda smiled as she came around from behind the counter. "True." Suddenly a wave of shyness washed over her. She glanced down then looked back up into his eyes. "Thank you for stopping by. How have you been?"

"Miserable." He cleared his throat. "I want to apologize for being such a jerk. I overreacted."

"I'm sorry, too. I never should have left them here alone. I had no idea—"

"I should have told you that might happen," Jerry said, interrupting her. "It was my fault, not yours."

Amanda lifted a shoulder then let it drop. "You trusted me, and I let you down."

After a few minutes of self-blaming, they both laughed. "I think we've beaten ourselves up enough," Jerry said. "Let's learn from our mistakes and move forward."

A lump formed in Amanda's throat; since she couldn't speak, she nodded. The warmth in Jerry's expression melted her heart. She wanted to reach for him—to hold on and never let go. But she didn't. She just stood there wondering what would come next.

"I've never felt this way about a woman before," Jerry said softly.

She blinked. Had she heard right? "You haven't?" Her voice came out in a squeak.

He chuckled. "This really isn't the place to talk about how I feel... how we feel. I just wanted to see you again."

"I wanted to see you, too."

The look on Jerry's face was one of pure joy. He took a step toward her, hesitated only for a second, then pulled her into his arms. "We'll talk later, okay?"

After he left, Amanda found herself sighing a lot. In the short time he was in her store, something had changed between them.

Amanda expected to hear from Jerry by the end of the week, so when she didn't, disappointment clouded her day on Saturday. She knew she hadn't dreamed Jerry's visit, but perhaps she'd misread his intentions.

On Sunday Jerry was in church without his parents. She paused before approaching him, but when he smiled and headed toward her, she met him halfway. "Would you like to sit with me?" he asked. "My folks decided to go to chapel at Tropical Gardens Village. That's where all their friends go."

"I'm glad they're adjusting so well."

"Yeah, me—"

"Amanda!"

The sound of her name caught her attention. She turned and saw Suzanne waving her over.

Amanda turned back to Jerry. "I already told Suzanne I'd sit with her. Would you like to join us?"

He started to shake his head then obviously changed his mind. "Sure, if there's room."

"There's always room."

Suzanne seemed genuinely happy for Amanda as they chatted before the service began. After church, Jerry said he'd promised his parents he'd come by, so he was skipping the Bible study. "I'll call you sometime next week, okay?"

After he left, Amanda told Suzanne what was happening. Suzanne gave her a hug. "I think he's the one."

The next day, business was slow—typical of most Mondays. Amanda kept expecting to hear from Jerry, but she didn't.

On Tuesday she'd been at work only about an hour when Rosemary walked in and announced that she needed a tandem bicycle ASAP. "I hope you have one available. I figured you might since most vacationers have gone back home."

"Sure, I have one. When do you need it?"

"Right now." Rosemary cast a nervous glance over her shoulder. "I don't have long."

Amanda thought the woman's behavior was strange, but she agreed to get the bicycle. "Wait right here. It's in the back." She thought about Rosemary's sense of urgency and then remembered that Jerry's parents had sold their car. She wheeled the bicycle out on the sales floor. "How did you get here?"

Rosemary shrugged. "I have ways of getting around."

Amanda got the paperwork started, and Rosemary quickly signed everything. She kept looking over her shoulder and acting nervous.

"Would you like for me to help you get it to the car?" Amanda leaned forward to see if anyone was outside waiting, until Rosemary broke into a fit of coughing. "Let me run and get you some water."

Rosemary stopped coughing and held up her hand. "No, I'm fine."

"I'll help you." Amanda started to wheel the bike toward the door, but Rosemary grabbed the handlebars and yanked the bicycle away. Something strange was happening.

Suddenly the phone rang. "Why don't you get the phone, Amanda?"

"Okay, wait right there a sec."

She heard the bell on the door as Rosemary struggled with getting the bike out. She felt torn, but after Rosemary's insistence on her answering the phone, she figured the woman wanted her to leave her alone.

After she said, "Treasure Island Bicycle and Skate Shop, may I help you?" she heard a click on the other end of the line. That was strange. She quickly put down the phone and ran out of the store to help Rosemary and see what the woman was so nervous about. To her dismay, there was no sign of Rosemary or the bicycle.

Later that day, Jerry called. "Can you stop by my place later, after work?"

"Sure," she replied. "I wanted to talk to you about your mother's strange behavior this morning."

He chuckled. "Okay, you can tell me all about it when I see you."

After she hung up, she leaned back and thought about Jerry's reaction, which was rather odd itself. He didn't even seem curious after she mentioned his mother's odd behavior.

The rest of the afternoon dragged by, but finally it was time to flip the CLOSED sign. She quickly went home to change into something a little nicer then called Jerry to let him know she was on her way.

"I'll be waiting outside," he said.

All the way to Jerry's, she thought about how weird the whole day seemed. She said a prayer for Jerry, his parents, her sister, Brad, and Timmy. By the time she got to the condo parking lot, an extraordinary sense of peace surrounded her.

She parked her car then headed toward the main entrance of the high-rise. Then all of a sudden out of the corner of her eye, she spotted someone coming toward her, wheeling a bicycle. She turned and spotted Jerry beside the bicycle-built-for-two—the one his mother had rented that morning.

"What—?"

Jerry laughed. "My mother and I came up with a plan. Wanna go for a ride?"

She tilted her head then smiled back at him. "Sure."

He offered her a helmet, and after they had them securely on their heads, they took off toward the beach. Jerry seemed to know where he was going, so she just settled back and helped with the pedaling.

When they finally got to one of the secluded spots on the beach, he steered toward a place to secure the bicycle. Then he reached for her hand and led her to a lone palm tree.

"This is nice," he said. "I've been wanting to be alone with you for a long time."

"It's very nice," she agreed. "But I don't understand what's going on. Why did your mother come into the shop and rent the bicycle instead of you?"

Jerry laughed. "When I told her my plan, she insisted on doing something to help."

"Your plan?"

He shuffled his feet for a few seconds then took her hands and looked into her eyes. "My mother pointed out that you might not believe me when I say I'm here to stay."

"Well, that thought has crossed my mind."

"That's why I've been out looking at places to buy."

Her heart hammered in her chest. "So you bought one?"

He shook his head. "I started to, but I decided to let you help me pick it out."

"Why would I—"

Jerry stopped her by gently placing a finger over her lips. Once she quit talking, he gently caressed her hair then traced her face with his fingertips. The slightest touch sent her senses reeling.

Then he stopped and took a step back. "What's wrong?" she asked.

"I have a question for you…sort of a preliminary question, that is."

"Huh?"

He took a deep breath then blew it out. "Okay, here goes." Jerry looked down at his feet then looked her in the eyes. "Do you think it's too early for us to talk about a future together?"

"Like, what do you mean a future together?" She didn't dare assume anything at this point, but she was hoping…

He took her hand in his as he dropped to one knee. "Amanda Burns, I love you with all my heart, and nothing would make me happier than if you'd agree to be my wife."

Amanda opened her mouth, but nothing would come out. This was the last thing she'd expected when Jerry asked her to come over. She looked down at him as he waited, and she felt joy as it began in her heart and spread throughout her entire being.

As tears formed in her eyes, she nodded. Jerry jumped to his feet and pulled her to his chest.

"I have a ring that was my grandmother's." He let go of her with one hand and fumbled around in his pocket before pulling it out. "We can go shopping for another one you like, but until we find the perfect ring, I'd like for you to wear this one."

She held out her hand, and he slipped it on her finger. It was a perfect fit!

"I love it!"

After a long, tender kiss, he stepped back and suddenly started laughing. What was he up to now?

"What's so funny?"

He shook his head. "My dad was right all this time. He said there was treasure on this island."

"What kind of treasure?"

"Unconditional love—and we both found it. My dad and Timmy have a relationship that my dad's always wanted with his grandkids but hasn't gotten. And now I have you. My mother is thrilled that he and I have both finally found what we're looking for."

Want a peek into local American life—past and present?
The *Love Finds You*™ series published by Summerside Press
features real towns and combines travel, romance,
and faith in one irresistible package!

The novels in the series—uniquely titled after American towns with unusual but intriguing names—inspire romance and fun. Each fictional story draws on the compelling history or the unique character of a real place. Stories center on romances kindled in small towns, old loves lost and found again on the high plains, and new loves discovered at exciting vacation getaways. Summerside Press plans to publish at least one novel set in each of the 50 states. Be sure to catch them all!

COMING SOON

Love Finds You in Revenge, Ohio by Lisa Harris
ISBN: 978-1-934770-81-8

Love Finds You in Poetry, Texas by Janice Hanna
ISBN: 978-1-935416-16-6

Love Finds You in Sisters, Oregon by Melody Carlson
ISBN: 978-1-935416-18-0

Love Finds You in Charm, Ohio by Birdie Etchison
ISBN: 978-1-935416-17-3

Love Finds You in Bethlehem, New Hampshire by Lauralee Bliss
ISBN: 978-1-935416-20-3

Love Finds You in North Pole, Alaska by Loree Lough
ISBN: 978-1-935416-19-7

summerside
PRESS

FALL IN LOVE WITH SUMMERSIDE